BRING DEEPS

BRING DEEPS

Elizabeth Arthur

BLOOMSBURY

First published 2003
This paperback edition published 2004

Copyright © 2003 by Elizabeth Arthur

The moral right of the author has been asserted

Bloomsbury Publishing plc, 38 Soho Square, London W1D 3HB

A CIP catalogue record for this book
is available from the British Library

ISBN 0 7475 6804 9

10 9 8 7 6 5 4 3 2 1

All papers used by Bloomsbury Publishing are natural,
recyclable products made from wood grown in well-managed forests.
The manufacturing processes conform to the
environmental regulations of the country of origin.

Printed by Clays Ltd, St Ives plc

www.bloomsbury.com/elizabetharthur

www.elizabetharthur.org

For Steven

1

EACH TIME SEBASTIAN COMES to me the Orkneys come as well, although I loved him far more than I loved the islands. But in my mind there is no other place to find the man I loved save in that landscape where my body loved him. Indeed, if I, as memory, am like Sebastian's weft, the islands are his warp, since they still hold him, and time itself – immortal time – now seems to me the loom on which Sebastian must be woven. I look into the past, and see him there, right now, in the dark cunning entrance to the tomb on Long Holm. I see him looking out to see me looking in – his sight a part of what I saw in him. His sight was not the kind of sight in Scotland known as *fey*. It was the sight of someone witnessing a treeless landscape. He tried to see the prehistoric people who had known the past as now – had lived within the thing we call *the past* as present. And I believe he guessed correctly what those people's story was; he read a tale within their stones as if they were this page I write on. But his own tale was something else again, and only at the end – too late – could I draw forth, out of the silence he wrapped around him like a shroud, the words that let me know him.

And yet I knew him right away. It was in London that we met, where all paths cross, and our paths crossed for just an hour; it was, however, an hour which stretched so wide, so deep, so high, I knew at once that time would never after seem the same to me. And as I start to write, I see again, as I have seen before – back in the fog that was my life before Sebastian – that one short word, if it is *time* or *love* or *sight* can be a cargo ship which holds a lot of freight in it. Or maybe they are doors, those words like *time* and *love* which can blow open on many rooms, each different, and Sebastian was a place that I was blown to by the winds of time and sight when I walked out the door of my hotel room. I saw him first. He walked out of the lift, then stopped, and glanced from left to right – a hunter seeking prey, or something he had lost, perhaps. His eyes went past me, then returned, and in the time before they did, I felt a shock of recognition I have no words for. No words except that word. It was a *re-cognition*, when all things I had known before unframed and then reframed themselves. In fact, it seemed to me that it was I who had misplaced – or lost – a thing that now I'd found again. I thought: *I've found a man. And not just any man. My man. How could I have forgotten him?*

So that was the beginning. He later told me that he felt the same – not quite the same, but close enough for measuring. That, as he saw me seeing him, he thought that he remembered I had looked at him this way before. Where? Somewhere. Anywhere. At first, he did not know that I – the woman whom he saw – was Emrys Havers, the woman whom he'd come to meet that day. And so he searched within the spreading circles of his mind to find the place in which he'd known me, and while he did, I started

2

walking toward him. He saw my walk – my gait – and this gait shook him, made him know more strongly that, somewhere, he'd known me. I was, he later said, like some remembered bone he'd found, some henge he'd walked through once, an artefact he'd studied. And while I kept on walking – arm outstretched to take his hand – he still believed he must have known me somewhere. But there his mind let go and looked no farther for the truth. *She was and she was not. Now here she is,* he thought.

And there I was. I was in London, on my way back from the Middle East. It was July, and in mid-May, just as my teaching for the spring came to an end, Sebastian had written me about my new translation of the lay of Gilgamesh, which had been published in the year before, and been ignored by many readers. However, I myself had loved the work, because I'd spent a long, long time discovering its deepest form, then placing it on paper. When I'd first started my translation, I had thought that I would do what scholars did, set numbers for the lines and columns. This makes it easy for a reader who knows cuneiform to check one text against the other. Of course, who knows cuneiform except for other scholars? I'd let that plan of action go quite quickly. I'd thought for longer, though, that I – as others had before – would leave blank spaces where clay tablets had been broken.

But then, as the years passed – it took me seven years before the end – I seemed to sink into the clay like something buried in it. And more than that, I seemed – on looking up from where I lay beneath that clay – to see, as palimpsests, the words that had gone missing. I saw them very clearly; I also heard them in my head, as if a voice were really speaking them. And it seemed strange to me, as I went on and found my work was now a poem – no lines, no numbers, things made new again – that others who had done this work had not seen these same scenes, heard these same voices, and surrendered to them. The story starts: *The one who gazed into the great Abyss I will make known to all the lands he left behind him*. Or, if you read another version: *I will make known to all the lands the one who has seen everything*.

My own translation runs: *He saw the great Abyss – King Gilgamesh, born of a human father, goddess mother*. It then goes on: *And I will tell the tale of what he saw when he saw all – the tale of all the lands that his feet walked upon. He saw within his mind the great Abyss, and then he found it and he crossed it, though the way was dangerous. He brought back to his people word of what he knew so that they, too, could know the world as it had been before the Flood had taken it*. And though I filled in what was missing, the story that I told was nonetheless the story told by all who'd come before me. Though parts seemed new, the vessel that contained them was still the same old ship that it had been for five millennia. In it, Gilgamesh first encountered Enkidu, his best friend – a man created by the gods to be a match for him, his double – and then when they, together, had laid waste to many things, lost him to death, because the gods would punish them.

This, he could not accept. He went half-mad with grief, and in his grief, set out to find eternal life for him and his lost lover. Of course, he did not find it, though he poled across the Waters of Death and found a seer on the far side of them. Before he did, however, he broke stone things in the boat, and I thought maybe that these stones were megaliths – Great Stones, in Greek – because the ferryman

4

told him what he had done, after he'd done it. *By your own hand, Gilgamesh, you have done this, have broken all the stone things which you need to cross the Waters of Death, have pulled out all the ropes which would have pulled you to the life you longed to find again.* He managed to get across, in any case, but when he had, not even Utanapishtim could inform him why the gods had made the Flood which had destroyed the earth once, or whether, in the days before the Flood had come, there had been such a thing as life eternal.

So, although Gilgamesh had gone on a hard journey to attempt to find a different world, he'd found what most who quest will – the others finding God – that he had lost Enkidu for all time, and that, in his turn, he would die someday. His works must be his immortality, and he had two that he might leave, the first of which was Uruk, the Sheep-Fold. This city he had tried – at times, at least – to shepherd well. He thought its fine brick walls, kiln-fired, would last forever. What lasted longer than the walls, however, was the other work he left – the tale he carved on clay about his journey to the hidden places. So I, too, as I worked, saw that the tale was what might reach beyond my death, and that I must attempt to make this work quite perfect. I strove to make it something which would last upon the earth as long as any book which spoke a universal language.

The striving was not hard. Indeed, when I looked out upon the scenes I saw, heard words within my head as if real voices spoke there, it seemed I would be casting forth into a storm a man I loved, not to embrace the scenes, the words, which came to me. So, though the walls of Uruk had long since crumbled into sand, the tablets broken with years' passing, I felt as fortunate as Gilgamesh had felt, before he lost his friend, that I could cross the gaps, the words that were not seen, and see the thing that stood behind them. When I was finished with my work, I was convinced that I had done it well, had made it whole as I could make it. Really I felt that it – the book itself – had written *me*, had come to me as if it were my lover. At first, it had just stood there, right on the edge of sight, and then had moved to hold me tight against it. Then, when it left me, and went forth into the world, I felt that I had lost a fundamental part of me.

This I did not expect. That to let go of what I'd made would be so hard – that it would leave me feeling naked; as if I were now missing not just clothes, but skin, as if the thing I'd made had been both in and also wrapped around me. I wished I'd never let it go. I wanted to get back what I had lost. I wanted Gilgamesh to be, with Enkidu, inside me. I was just forty then, and while I felt that turning forty was a triumph, I also felt as if the poem I'd made had been a world whose walls I'd built to dwell inside, and now the walls had crumbled. The work so long had been my world that I felt stranded by a vessel I myself had made, which then had sailed without me. And then there was my partner. He was a lawyer who had planned to practice law, but then had come to teach it. When we first met, he was about to lose, to death, a sister whom he loved, and I'd just parted with another lover.

And so we'd come together, and had stayed for seven years – the same years I had started, worked on, finished *Gilgamesh and Enkidu*. My partner was a good man, truly good, and while I owned my tale, I'd never felt a lack in what he furnished. But though I'd met him at a time when he was feeling hot dark grief for someone who would die from trusting – far too much – a man she'd slept with, he loved me with a calm, unruffled love that did not seem to come from a beginning such as ours had been. His only sister, and she died at thirty-one – a hard, hard death, and one which I had only glimpsed the end of. Yet I had seen enough to know that this disease was just as cruel as if it had been meted out by gods as punishment. Perhaps, in fact, my brief exposure to that all-too-vicious death was what had drawn me fully into *Gilgamesh* – since only something vast and dark that comes, at times, from love, might make you take, as true, the story.

Because, when Gilgamesh first lost his lover, he sat beside his lifeless form for seven days – refused to put him in his tomb, refused to let death rob him – and now I saw that grief might truly drive you mad like that. It had not done this to my partner. But he had put into my world – my work and also me – all of the hope that now remained to him. The day I finished *Gilgamesh and Enkidu*, I came home late at night to find him waiting in the kitchen. 'You've finished it at last,' he said. 'You've wed the word to world. Congratulations, Emrys. On to other weddings.' And with these words, he slipped a golden ring – so thin it almost was a wire – upon my finger, and there it stayed, although now that I'd lost my crazy king – half-god, half-man – I knew that other weddings would not follow. I felt half-mad myself, half-dead or half-unhinged – just halved in every way a person could be. I'd almost drowned when I was five, and I had lost my parents young, but I had never felt a thing like this before.

I woke, I walked the streets, I slept, and all the time I felt as if I were now missing all enclosure. I could not make love with my partner. I could not do good work. My life seemed like a fog I sailed in. And it was in this state that I received a letter from an archeologist who lived in Orkney, Sebastian Ferry. He wrote to say he'd found my book light in a place which had been dark to him, to say he'd loved the fact that I had seen that Gilgamesh and Enkidu were lovers. He also said that he had waited for a tale like mine, which told the truth about an age now lost to us. He said his own work had revealed that this lost age had known desire more intense than what the world had known after the word had ceased to be an incantation. He asked if I would meet with him to talk of this and other things – like ancient words – if I should ever come to London. I planned to be there soon, *en route* to home, once I had done, or tried to do, some work that took me to what used to be the city of Nineveh. I was so pleased to hear from someone who had truly liked my book, I wrote to say I'd be delighted to meet him. I set a date and time which corresponded with some dates and times which he had said were possible for him.

Time passed, then. Normal time. The world's time. I parted with my partner, went to Nineveh, saw nothing there, and then I was in London, on my way back home again. By then, Sebastian had confirmed that he would come to my hotel at three o'clock that day. He called me from the lobby, and when I heard his voice, a deep, rich, life-filled voice – so deep and rich it seemed to slide inside me – I told him he should come up to my suite, where we could talk without the noises of the public spaces. And I believed this, too – this thing I told myself – until I saw Sebastian come into the passage where I waited. Then, when I saw him pause, and turn first one way, then the next, as if he searched for something he had lost there, I knew that that deep voice had started an awakening of all my senses. I'd been, I'd thought, half-dead, but now it seemed that I'd been merely half-asleep, and now had woken up to find Sebastian. Yes, there he was, and I, on seeing him, thought: *There is the thing I lost an age and more ago. There is the reason why I wrote Gilgamesh and Enkidu. It needs no other reason now. It makes no sense, but there he is. A man. A man at last. And not just any man. My man, long lost to me.*

I took a step. He turned and saw me. Yes, Sebastian Ferry, Emrys Havers. We shook each other's hands. His hands were wet; it rained that day. He wore a long oiled coat, and as he moved, the wedge-shaped pieces of its fabric made a sail about his body. This sail fell stiffly out around him, so that the movements that took place within the sail were almost hidden, and yet it seemed that I could sense the gestures of his legs as he strode next to me along the corridor. We reached my room, and when the door had closed behind us on the hall, I asked him for his coat. He shrugged it off and let me hang it up for him. And then I saw his clothes, a pair of blue jeans, old and soft, a soft deep red-brown shirt, the shade of rich, exotic, foreign soil. This shirt had snaps, not buttons, and when I noticed this, I thought at once that snaps would make it easier to take off him. He wore a belt as well, a dark-brown webbing belt tied with two gold metal circles.

Then, on his feet, were canvas shoes with blunt round toes which had, upon their tops, a semi-circle of rubber. I saw that he had drawn the leather laces of his shoes over and down through rivets punched in the canvas, rather than in the common manner, up and through them. This made me think of his two feet as gifts – the shoes the wrapping and the laces ribbons. We walked toward couch and chair.

We sat. Sebastian chose the damask fabric of the chair to seat himself upon. I sat upon the couch, and asked him if he'd like some tea, and when he said he would, picked up the telephone. And now began an hour in which I fell in love so hard, so deep, that I would never climb back from the place I'd fallen to. And when I try to disattach the man I met that day from the Sebastian I later knew, I cannot do it. Indeed, I see him, now, not only as he was that day, but as he was for all the time that carried *time* upon its back, and also *love* and *sight* and *knowing*.

What did Sebastian look like? Well, I'm five eight, and he was five eleven, so he looked like the right height for a man to me. When we stood face to face, or walked at one another's sides, I could look easily into his eyes, while his eyes held me. And he was slim, no extra body fat at all, just lean, good muscle, just arms that fit, in length, the height of him. He had blunt hands, blunt fingers, broad, and with the fingers shorter, maybe, than you'd suppose of fingers with such knowledge in them. But it was not the shape that mattered, with his hands, it was the way in which those hands helped him to find expression. He used them to gesture, always, holding them up, their palms away from him, his wrists cocked slightly backwards. *How blind they are*, he'd say, of archeologists who could not see the things he could – his hands thrown up, resigned to this. Or, of the age he loved, he'd say – his hands delighted by the thought – *in neolithic times, of course, all things were circles*.

In that age, he would say, to find, to feel, to show the oneness between self and other, lover and loved, was the sole purpose of a life. It was a kind of dance, he'd say, that led the people who had lived straight to the circle as the form that spoke to them. And when he said this, his hands

10

spoke as well – not as arresting shields, but in a way that reached to hold the purity of circles. He used his hands quite differently when he was truly angry, and he was angry frequently with me. Then, he would take one hand and place the tips of thumb and fingers all together, letting his hand move back and forth upon the fulcrum of his wrist as if to demonstrate the way you'd break the neck of something. And it was not just hands Sebastian used this way, but his entire body – and not just when he knew that he was angry.

In any case, the gestures that his hands made – kind or unkind – were small fragments broken off from the whole being that was Bastian. Our strides were similar, indeed, as I had seen, but his was quicker than mine was. He moved into the world like someone racing to catch up with time, a man who asked no clocks to tell him yesterday had passed and would not come again, now. But he could be as motionless as he was quick and brisk, his body holding stillness deep within it. That day in London, when he crossed his legs, he took one canvas shoe from where it had been set, quite flat, upon the floor, and with one solid movement, placed ankle on his thigh, and left it there for many minutes.

Above this still, crossed leg, he looked at me with eyes that were not kind, and did not try to be. Indeed, about his face, it was his eyes which mattered most. I have been told that I, too, have these eyes, though mine are larger than were Bastian's. His eyes were wide apart, and at that width, were small. I did not notice, that first day, if they were blue or brown. But I did notice that Sebastian did not blink as much as most men I had known, and did not shift his eyes as frequently. As with his body, when he moved his eyes, they changed direction fully, but when he looked at me, he stared at me, that questioning, unwinking gaze a challenge I found more challenging than all the broken clay on earth. His eyes said, almost always, *OK, prove it.*

His lips, though, never said that. He had a beard, cropped short, and this beard framed his lips, forcing attention to them. His lips were sensuous, and red, but not too red, and not too full, although they had a softness to them. A waiter knocked and set a tray of t̶e̶a̶ ̶a̶n̶d̶ ̶b̶i̶s̶c̶u̶i̶ts on the table, then left the room again. I set the two cups out, then lifted up the pot, and hoped I wouldn't spill the tea from trembling. The cup I handed him was white, its thin rim ringed with gold, and when I saw Sebastian's hand upon the cup, I thought that, while they didn't match, they seemed to complement each other. As Bastian raised the cup, and held it to his lips, I saw the archeologist he was – the man who interacted with all manner of made things – and also saw the man I longed to kiss now.

Sebastian sipped his tea. He said, 'This is so kind of you. I've always loved the lay of Gilgamesh. I do love words, especially obsolete ones. It seems to me that each is like a secret waiting to be learned, a passage waiting to be dug so you can find the thing that lies beyond it.'

'I feel that, too,' I said.

'And in your version of the tale, I thought you brought into the light the way the *stone things* of Uruk are broken memories of a worshipped Goddess. *By your own hand, Gilgamesh, you have done this.*'

'You know that line by heart?' I said.

'I know a lot by heart. The time of the Great Stones was everywhere the same, I think.'

'Where were you born? In Orkney?'

12

'Not far from London,' he replied. 'Near Silbury.' And when he saw that this meant little to me, he told me something of it. Told me that, as a boy, he'd gone for walks to the great hill, had studied it, had climbed it, had rolled down it. He'd celebrated harvests by walking to the hill; he'd celebrated plantings by watching how the rains would gather deeply in the trenches all around it. And then he said that this was what had brought him to the study of what he had, all his adult life, studied. For centuries the archeologists who'd lived before *we* had had thought that Silbury was a Bronze Age barrow. But he had watched the final, futile excavation there, by men who – even in his youth – had been convinced the hill must hold great treasure. What treasure? A stupid golden horse, perhaps, or other metal things must lie, they thought, beneath that perfect soil.

Of course, these were the same men who had thought, he pointed out, that for the henges to be built, some autocrat would need to be in charge of them – who'd thought that Stonehenge must be, more than anything it was, an evidence for the concentration of power. No wonder, then, that they had also thought a tribe would build a hill as high and round as Silbury just to thrust golden treasures in. But he, Sebastian, had been there when they'd found the hill held nothing and never had, the hill was all there was – a mound that had been built to make the earth round. Then, they'd at last admitted it was the greatest of the harvest hills that had been built – for reasons they could simply not imagine – by the neolithic peoples.

'You've studied megaliths?' he asked.

'A little, yes, I have. But mostly the creation myths which might have made them.' And then I talked some more of

13

this, and of my book, since Bastian turned the talk around again, from Silbury to the tale of Gilgamesh. He asked me how I'd gone to it – yes, gone, as if it were a place – and I said I had gone to it because of language. Because it seemed to me miraculous that with cuneiform, something quite new had come into the world, a written language. I said I still remembered what it had been like for me when I had learned to read, as a small child – how I had seen, all of a sudden, that symbols placed upon a page were more than marks there. When I had seen this, I'd seen, too, that I was needed, that – without the me who walked beneath the gate that was each letter – each gate would stay shut tight. I had so liked this – being needed – that it had made my life for me, and made it in the old sense. Formed it, shaped it, wrought it.

'From there to the first writing it was only a small step for me,' I said.

'I know about those small steps. *Here*, and *there*, and *there*,' Sebastian said, and nodded.

And when he nodded, he regarded me so intently that I might have been a pot sherd he'd unearthed and now he studied. And for the first time I admitted how I felt beneath that look – happy to be a henge which might be walked through. I had had words, and had loved words, but this was more than words – it was a force I'd never felt before I felt it with Sebastian. What I had felt before had been a shadow of the thing; this was the thing itself, a beaker giving shape to all that lay inside it. And it was pure desire, the thing that had been forged out of the stuff which also made the earth once. Gold treasure, harvest hills, and writing, open gates, were all as potent as they were because they were created by this potency. It was as if, when Bastian

14

walked out of the lift, the fabric of the world that I had always known was torn, and for the first time in my life I saw what truly lay beyond it.

And it was this. Just this. A hunger that could kill, a hunger that I felt down to the bone of me. It was just this, pure want – raw want – quite unadorned by any of the things with which our kind has clothed the world to try and make it safer. The world was stripped, in fact, and all I wished was to be stripped as well – or maybe, first, to strip Sebastian. I saw, in my mind's eye, the scene in which I would undress him. I first would set my cup upon the table, then I would stand, move forward, kneel before his legs, and hold his knees, quite lightly, for a moment. Then I would push them to the sides, and run my hands along the lines which were the inseams of Sebastian's blue jeans. When my hands reached the end of those two inseams, I would slide them to the place where golden circles held the belt, and tug, until they could not hold it any longer.

'Oh, yes,' I said. 'Well, maybe what was hardest to decide was whether to include the final tablet, which hadn't been inscribed when all the rest had. In it, Enkidu comes to life again. I left it out.' I smiled. We both smiled. We saw this was absurd, and as we did, I pulled his belt out in my mind, and heard the noise it made, a kind of shushing sound. I kneeled between his legs, and then, with one quick twist, took out the button from the hole that held it, unzipped the zip which lay below it, and then unsnapped the snaps to take his shirt off. Sebastian just stayed seated in his chair, while I untied his shoes, pulled down his pants, and with my hands, took inventory of all that I'd discovered. He just stayed seated in his chair and watched me with those eyes which said, *Well, OK, Emrys, prove it.*

But when I had – when I had proved that touching Bastian Ferry's body was, in fact, the thing my hands were made for – he touched me, also. He put blunt fingers on my skin; he made his hands like cups to hold my breasts while I just kneeled there. And then we rose – in my mind's eye – and Bastian took me by the hips, and pulled me to him, freed me from my clothing, and took me to the bed, and there he let our bodies be the single body they were meant to be. I thought: *Oh, god, please take me*. But from my mouth quite other words emerged, about the love of Gilgamesh for Enkidu. Sebastian later told me that he felt this also. He said that he had sat within the circling damask of the chair, and had so urgently desired to place a single finger to his lips, and say, 'All this can wait,' that he had almost done it.

He said that when he had been speaking of the harvest hill – had heard his voice explaining that they'd found fine radiating spokes of twisted string beneath the soil there, and that this string was used to separate the layers of chalk and gravel, soil and clay and turf – that he had wished, instead, to hear his own voice say: 'Enough of this. Shall I take you to bed now, Emrys?'

And while I knew from everything about him – his eyes, his hands, his voice, the way he lifted one quick leg and crossed it on the other – what it would be if he should rise and take me, Sebastian said he knew from just my hands as those hands poured the tea for both of us. He said that he had watched, with thirst he couldn't quite explain, the way I lifted up the gold-rimmed teapot, then tilted it above first one and then the other of the two cups beneath it. He said these seemed, as he surveyed them, quite suddenly like chalices. I talked, he said, and listened, sipped, regarding him, and simultaneously engaging in an ancient ritual of containment.

'You couldn't fool me, then,' he said. 'I knew. You could wear all the clothes you liked, bulky, concealing clothes, good grief, you looked like you were wearing twenty vests. I knew, though, when I watched your hands, what it would be to take you. You should have worn gloves, if you wished to hide from me.'

'I didn't want to hide from you,' I said. 'I wanted you to hold my breasts. I wanted you inside me.'

'Well, now that's where I am,' he said. 'You lucky woman. Do you always get the things you want?'

'Oh, very rarely. Never.'

'Well, now you have,' he said. And then, as we lay in bed together for the first time – in that same room where we had met, but three weeks later – he told me he had thought, three weeks before, of telling me about the Kennet River, as we discussed the harvest hill of Silbury. He'd thought of telling me that in the region around Avebury, the peasants, until three hundred years before this, had called the Kennet *Cunnit*, the Swallowhead the *Cunt*, and that it took so little sight to see – those words to guide you – that the hill of Silbury was one vast Goddess mother, the hill her pregnant belly, the Cunnit River the passage to her womb.

'The Swallowhead, as well,' he said. 'I liked that. The chalky water that issued from it was quite white. How "cunt" could ever have become obscene, I can't imagine. The medieval clerics' Mouth of Hell. But in the Latin, *cunnus*, and in Middle English, *cunte*. In Old Norse it was *kunta*; there's Kunta Cave in Orkney.'

'You almost told me *that*?'

'Almost. But I didn't. Your hands were not quite bare

17

that day,' he added, but with a laughing edge to it, because he had – he thought – already won that first great victory.

And it was true that, then – three weeks after we met – my hands were bare, quite bare, like all the rest of me. The ring my partner had presented as a gift the night my book was done had been left behind me. The day we met, Sebastian had seen it on my finger, and read its meaning wrong. It was the ring, he said, which kept him from the thing he wished to do – the ring which held him as in bondage. He stayed within the bonds, and merely watched me pour the tea, thinking – he said – I was already taken. He did more than just think. He tested me, that day. He asked if I were married to another scholar in my field. And I, in looking back upon this moment, cannot think why I did not know better than to lie in it. Because, of course, I wasn't merely not the wife of anyone that day, it had been seven months since I had made love with my partner.

But somehow, I felt then that if I told Sebastian I wasn't wed, he'd think I'd lied already with the ring I wore; he'd think I was a woman who so needed to be owned by some man – any man – that I would lie about it, with symbols. So I said no, he was a lawyer who taught that theories of retributive justice were wrong, and had the facts to back this up, as well as myth and poetry.

'Retributive justice,' Bastian murmured. 'He doesn't think that people should be punished. What, not at all?'

'No, not at all,' I said, and noticed even then a hooding of Sebastian's eyes, a bright blank look, as if he sought for something that was missing. He seemed, I thought, to look back through the circles in his mind, to find the single time and place he looked for.

'He sounds like a good man,' Sebastian said.

'He is a good man. Deeply good.'

'And you? Do you believe that, too? That no one should be punished?'

'I think that life is punishment enough,' I said. 'But then I've never felt I quite belonged to now – this time, this world, I mean.'

'I feel that, too, of course,' said Bastian. 'Thus my work. But Orkney, where I live now, is different. Time slips there. There are lines of power.'

'What are you doing there?' I asked.

'I've found a chambered tomb. I live below the tomb, on Long Holm. I'm excavating it. I'm finding dogs' skulls, as they found at Cuween Hill.'

'Some hunting ritual?'

'Perhaps. Or maybe they just loved their dogs,' Sebastian said. 'I love mine.'

'You live alone?' I asked.

'Well, with my dog,' he said. 'Some seals, at times, for company. There are lots of legends about seals. You know them? Silkies?'

'I've heard of silkies, yes,' I said, but did not think of them. I thought: *He lives alone. He lives alone. He can be mine, then.* But just as I almost said, 'You know, the man I live with; we're not married,' Sebastian rose to go, the hour we'd agreed upon already over. He went to get his coat from where I'd thrust it out of sight and when he'd shrugged it on, I could not stop myself from walking with him to the lift or then from riding down with him. If we had been alone, perhaps I would have had the courage to speak to him of what I really wanted. But there were others with us, leaning against the mirrored walls – in which I tried hard not to look, to find myself.

So we rode down together in silence, and at the door to the hotel he shook my hand again. He thanked me for my time, and for my book, which might, he said, help him with megaliths in ways he couldn't see yet. Then he was moving through the door into the rain beyond, and as he turned his back to walk away, I almost ran right after him. I told him this, those three weeks later, in that same hotel, to which he said, 'You shameless woman,' smiling. Then – that first occasion – he smiled, too, before he turned and left me, while I thought: *Oh please, don't leave me here, Sebastian*. But he was gone, regardless, taking with him all his parts, already loved, already needed – taking with him his rich voice, his asking eyes, and all the gestures that had made the world I knew unravel and then knit back together again.

And as for me, I did not know that, in a sense quite different from the way in which I'd longed for it to happen, Sebastian had already taken me. He'd been a wind which blew into my life, and took me from the place where I'd been stranded, half-alive, half-dead, to a new place I could not fully see yet. But I could see that the great city where I'd spent my life – which I had called *Uruk*, though it had other names as well – that city was now gone, its fine brick walls in ruins. The House of Ashes I had known, quite recently, as all there was of life, was blown away, a part of history. And as for those great waters which were the Waters of Death that Gilgamesh had crossed, they had become the waters of life to me. All that Sebastian need now do was reach his hand out and unlock the locks that locked the past in place, by taking me.

2

HE LEFT, THOUGH. HE was gone. And I was gone, as well. I now discovered what that was – *to be quite gone*. I went back up the lift, and to the room, and shed my clothes to find that I was thoroughly aroused – as wet, it seemed, as I had ever been before. And I was simultaneously dismayed by this, and quite transported, since to feel alive again, if even for an hour, seemed worth whatever sacrifice it might require. But he had left; Sebastian had left. He'd walked off in the rain, his oiled slicker snickering from side to side, a sail again. What if he'd left forever? I didn't know, I couldn't guess. Whatever was to come, before he'd left, he'd made me wet like this. Perhaps it was no accident that he'd spoken, before he left, of silkies, since such a transformation was, as well, a thing you had no choice about. When some grey seal, with fur as soft as silk, took off his coat, and walked on land, it was foregone that he'd bewitch a human woman. And when he had bewitched her, he would plant in her a child who would be moored until she died halfway between the world of land and sea, halfway between the worlds of seal and human.

So I, too, was bewitched now, caught within the net

which had been cast out by Sebastian Ferry. I was transported and dismayed, at the same time, because I'd thought that life was somehow under my dominion. Not all of it, of course, just some of it – the part that was myself, my words, my body. I'd thought that just as I could choose my words, I could select the path I took, and even where that path might take me. I'd cherished choice, in fact; each word I chose to use for words that had been lost had been a kind of victory. I had said, to the words I'd borne, 'You *here*. You *there*. You *there*,' and they, though sometimes struggling, had let me rule them. But now, I was the ruled. I was so wet, it was as if I held the waters of earth within me. And though I knew myself, from this, to be once more alive, I also knew the authorship was Sebastian's. Yes, authorship it was. His hand, reaching through space. His voice, his eyes, the gestures of his arms as he went wide with them, then drew them in. They were a pen which wrote upon my flesh just what they would, and left me with no say in what my body said.

And though this made me feel – and for the first time in my life – as if I really were alive, it also made me fearful. What if he did not feel as I did? What if he would not take me? Perhaps, like any silkie, Sebastian had shed his coat, and then had seeded me, not with a child, but with a dream that would be mine to bear alone now. What if this dream was doomed to die, as all are doomed who cross the line from what is known to what is unknown? Enkidu, too, had been transformed – and by desire – from what he'd been to something else entirely, and he had died for it. For when the temple priestess spread her robe upon the ground, and let him lie upon her for six days and seven nights continuously, this time he'd spent in love had changed him so that he would be a match for Gilgamesh. This killed him, in the end. The gods were fickle, just as they'd been fickle when, long before, they'd sent the Flood that took the earth they once had loved, and almost drowned it.

Sebastian, though, had sent no temple priest. He'd come himself, and then he'd gone. And this half made me afraid, half made me angry. I called the desk, picked up my bags, then rode to Heathrow in the rain, so I could catch my flight to Kennedy. But all the while inside my head – and then, when I was airborne, on the page – I wrote the letter I'd send when I got home again, if I still thought, then, of Sebastian. If I did not, I would not send it. It would be my choice what to do. Meanwhile, there was no danger in just writing. But it was not so easy. I drafted something once, and then again – each time I wrote removing more of it. At first, I poured my heart out, then – half-angry, half-afraid – I grew more cautious, wrote much less, engaging in the opposite of what *Gilgamesh and Enkidu* had taught me. This time I'd do it differently. I would say less than I could see. I would, I thought, say almost nothing. I'd break the words so they were half-words, leaving the whole half-formed. That way, if Bastian did not feel the way I did, I would not make myself into a fool for him, or love, or anything.

Yes, let him come to me, I thought. I'd let him come to me. I half believed, for half a day, that I could do this. But I found out, and almost right away, that I was wrong – that if he did not come to me, I'd beg him, anyway, to take me. Because, when I got off the plane, and found my partner waiting, I felt I had already betrayed him. We hugged and kissed, and claimed my bags, and then went home, and went to bed – where I attempted, one last time, to love him.

23

But though I was still wet – as wet as seals, as wet as seas – I couldn't let him touch me. And when I realized this, I sobbed and sobbed within his arms, although I could not bring myself to tell him. And so I wrote my letter. I had no choice. I wrote and spoke of new horizons – new lands, I think I said, that I desired to walk on – spoke of new work, of megaliths, of Orkney, how it lured me. I said that it was rare that I met someone – anyone – whose company I preferred to solitude.

I had gone back to work – or tried to – so I wrote the letter in my office, and though I was not teaching, students sometimes found me. When one came by, and knocked upon my door, I hid the thing I wrote by covering it up with paper. It was as if the words, even half-glimpsed, by anyone but him, would strip the flesh right off my bones, and leave me with nothing in which to clothe myself. My letter, one page long – hand-scrawled, blue ink upon a cotton page – took three long days from start to finish. I put things in, then took them out, then put them in again, and copied the letter endlessly. At last, so wearying was this, linked to the way my body felt – suspended in a moment I could not get out of – I put the letter in the mail and said goodbye to it. If Bastian could not unlock the lock that held my words, then he and I had spoken different languages.

By then, I was convinced, in any case, he would not write or call. He thought that I was married, and I had made no statements that would alter that. And as the days passed, and I heard nothing from overseas, at least the seas that were within me started to subside a bit. That felt like rest, at least for then – that I should be let go, be able to choose again who I would be in life. It was July now, and quite hot.

I loved hot days like these, since I was rarely warm except when I was in the desert. I sat one day before my desk, the door ajar, the window open to the wind. I tried to read but found the words stayed on the page, did not move up into my mind and speak to it. I smelled the wind, looked at the words, thought: *Just forget him, Emrys. It was not as you thought it was. You spoke two different languages.* But then the phone rang. I picked up and said hello, expecting that this would be a student or a colleague, maybe my partner. I heard a voice which was not his, though, and which I knew at once – a strong, rich, life-filled voice, a deep deep thing that slid inside me.

'Emrys,' Sebastian said. 'I got your letter just today. I, too, regretted that our conversation was so short. Thank you for writing.'

And as I heard this, I reached out with my right foot, and kicked my office door, slamming it shut, as I slammed shut: *It was not as you thought it was.* It was. We had not spoken different languages. The door slammed hard, because the wind caught at the wood and pushed it as it might push a canvas sail. There was a noise all down the hall, and in my mind, the slamming was a sound that marked the end of all my thoughts that I could choose to turn my back upon Sebastian. Because, with just one word – my name – out of his lips, I was again quite gone. My body sat there in my chair, surrounded by my books, but I was wet again within the instant, sailing distant seas. I felt so weak, in fact – so weakened by the wave – that I lay down upon the floor, so that I would not fall there. I locked the door. I propped my head upon some books, and said:

'Sebastian. Thank you for calling.'

'How could I not? I pick up mail on Mainland once a

week. I would have called before, if I had known that you had written. I want to see you. Can we meet again?'

'Of course,' I said, my first *of course*, I realize now; before I met Sebastian, the phrase was rare to me. But all Sebastian had to do, it seemed, was voice a wish, and I would say to anything at all, what I said then: *of course*. He was the course my life pursued now, and though I did not know, that day he called, just where *of course* was going to take me, even if I had, I would have said it.

That day, though, when I said, 'Of course,' there was a pause – a thinking far away in Scotland. And then Sebastian said, 'I must be honest. I don't just want to see you, or not just with my eyes. Is this what you want, too? That we should have a larger conversation?'

'Yes. I've wanted it since I first saw you.'

'I, too,' he said. 'I thought I knew you when I saw you in the passage. Did you feel as I did, then, Emrys?'

'I felt I'd known you all my life. I felt I'd known you since before I had been shaped from nothing into something.'

But when he said my name again, just *Emrys*, as he had, letting the first syllable linger on the air between us, it seemed a long caress that was, to me, the cupping of his hand beneath my breast, the making of his hand into a cup to hold me. And when he said the second part of *Emrys*, very quick, it was a quick command that was, to me, his palms upon my buttocks as he pulled me to him. Between the two – two hands, two syllables, two tones – it felt much more as if he owned me than that I'd merely known him always.

But I left all that out, and said just what I said, to which he said:

'It's hard to know just who we know, sometimes.'

Again, I found that odd. When we had been together, each thing he said had been so clear to me. I'd seen his face, his eyes, had felt the way desire gave shape to everything which lay inside it. But now – when I had just his voice – it seemed as if there was a place somewhere above the sea which took our words and changed them. When we had been together, time had stretched in all directions. Now time stretched just one way, a line from *here* to *there*, I thought. When Bastian spoke, there was a pause, as if the sea which lay between us contained a place which pushed our thoughts over a time-falls. What did he mean, 'It's hard to know just who we know'? I could not tell. It was as if he told me something. But as he spoke, all that I knew was that I wanted to be with him, right then, right at that instant. There was no time to lose, to stop, to pin down what he meant. What did it matter what he meant? These were just words he spoke. It was Sebastian himself I wanted.

And time was everything right now; we'd lost ten days to things delayed, because I'd been so cautious, mailed my letter slowly. Now, so urgent was my longing, I felt that I might melt – become quite formless – if I did not fly to Bastian. So I did not pursue what he had said. The words we used to tell each other what we felt seemed unimportant. I said:

'I know. We know. You know, I think. Where shall we meet? I'll meet you anywhere.'

'We must meet somewhere. Anywhere is nowhere one can get to.'

'I'll come to Orkney.'

'No. I have to go to London. Meet me there. I have to get a Jeep I bought, and bring it north.'

'I'll come to London, then. Meet me at Heathrow. Take

me to the hotel. The same hotel. The same room, if we can.'

'That would be good,' he said. And then he paused again and said, as if this were the sort of thing that anyone might say, 'I must be clear, though. If you come to me in London, you must first have left your husband.'

'What do you mean?' I asked, and meant it for the moment that I spoke. I truly could not think what he might mean by this. I had no husband. As for my partner, I had left him, in a sense, a half a year before or – at the least – upon the day I met Sebastian.

'Just what I say,' Sebastian said. 'If you would be with me, you must divorce him first. Or set the thing in motion, anyway.'

And when he said the word *divorce*, I understood that I had known, in some ways, what he had meant the first time he had spoken. I knew, too, I should say, right then, 'I have no husband, Bastian.' Or even say, 'I lied, that day in London.'

But when he spoke, his voice was all at once so short and plain, and at the same time so hedged with hidden meanings that it scared me. For, now, I pinned a meaning to the words Sebastian said, and feared, with sharp and sudden fear, he would not want me if he didn't have to steal me.

I lay upon the floor, still felled by my desire, but now with something close to terror mixed up in it. What if he did not take me? What would I do? How could I live? I heard my voice say words as if another person spoke them:

'We have a life together. He loves me.'

'I'm sure he does,' Sebastian said. 'Who could be close to you, as he has, and not love you? You must be very dear to him.'

28

'I think I am,' I said.

'You should stay with him then. You must not leave him for my sake,' said Bastian.

'But you just said I must.'

'No, I did not,' he said. 'I said that if you came to me, and I to you, that we must come to one another unencumbered. When I hold you in my arms, I want to feel no other arms around you.'

'And do you always get the things you want?' I asked.

'No, very very rarely. But I do not stop wanting them. What do *you* want, now, Emrys?'

'I want you. Only you,' I said. 'Everything else has faded.' And when, after I'd said this, I heard a kind of happy sigh, an exhalation of desire, I wanted him so much I thought I'd die of it.

'Well, then,' he said, his tone quite changed, as gentle as the sigh. 'If you want me, you'll have to give him up. I don't say you should do this. If you can't give him up, it may be for the best. I wish we'd met some other time, though. Timeliness is everything, as all folk customs demonstrate.'

And when he said this, which I had, in my own way, been thinking – of how we'd lost ten days, and now must lose no more time divided – I wondered why I did not just tell Bastian the truth, that I was his already, in every way that mattered, and that I would divorce, for him, not just this man or that one, but everything I'd known before I'd seen him hunting in the corridor.

Outside my door, a student pounded with his fist. I called out, 'Go away. I can't talk now.'

I heard Sebastian laugh and say, 'Oh Emrys, what a choice for you to make.'

The student, quite persistent, called out, 'When will you

be free?' to which I said, 'Not until the time of planting,' at which Sebastian laughed harder.

'Planting? That's in the spring,' the student said, and I said, 'Yes, I know. Just come back later, when I'm off the phone.'

Then I said to Sebastian, my voice still strange – the voice of every teasing woman who had ever spoken to a man, 'How would we live? I live on what I teach.'

'I have a little money. A tiny grant. Enough for us to eat quite long, however, on Long Holm.'

'Your cottage, is it big enough for two?'

'It's big enough for you, if you were in my arms,' Sebastian said. 'How much room does it take for two who love to sleep together?'

Well, now, this made *me* pause; I wondered if I should say to Bastian that I'd never slept with anyone. Not slept, as sleeping really means; I did not know why this was true, but it was true, no man had tempted me enough to sleep with him. I'd sleep within the bed, of course, if it were hard enough so that we would not roll together in the middle, but then, within the bed, I'd wrap myself in quilts, protect myself with any kind of cloth, or clothing, like a shroud around me. A shroud for sleep, not death. One lover, French, had pointed out to me that in the French, *to come* means 'little death', but that, to me, the *little death* was sleep. And once my partner, joking, had proclaimed that this must be the reason I loved *Gilgamesh* – when Utana-pishtim told Gilgamesh he must stay awake for seven days and seven nights if he would prove that he deserved the intervention of the gods in his pursuit of immortality, the king had gone to sleep, and maybe I believed that I could stay awake in such a circumstance.

30

But I thought, too, that now did not seem quite the time to talk of the hard time I'd always had in sleeping. Besides, who knew? Maybe at last I'd met the man within whose arms I would feel truly safe in darkness. If I'd been half-asleep – as I'd been half-asleep – when I had met him, and had woken up now, maybe in future all things would be quite reversed for me. I could not tell. I could not see what lay ahead for us. So I just said, 'I've never felt this way before. Have you?'

'No, never,' said Sebastian. 'So will you come to me, and leave him? Or would you like to think? I'll be on Mainland for two days, still.'

'Perhaps I'd better think,' I said, again surprised by words as they emerged from my own mouth, and flew the route I wished to fly, across the ocean. Sebastian said he'd call me back in two days' time, and then we cut the phone connection, though for a while I still lay on my office floor. A different student came and knocked. I said, 'Come back tomorrow if you need to see me. I'm going home now.' Then I packed my books, drew down my window on the wind, and went to tell the man I lived with I was leaving him.

That was a bad, bad time. For both of us, but more for him. He was in pain, and I had caused it. But still, he did not say the things he felt about my words. Instead he talked about the time when he'd been young. He said – in his own words – that when he'd started out in law, he had believed the world, though broken, might be mended. He said – in his own way – that then, so long ago, he'd thought the world was like a ragged coat which could, through sewing, be made whole again. But then he'd grown and seen the world, and all the ways in which the people of that world could force each other to take the hurt that all must feel, as if the sharing of the hurt would somehow heal it. And when he saw that, he had seen, as well, there was no law – no kind of law, had never been a law – which could repair the world, that only perfect faith or perfect love might do that.

So, since he had no faith, he'd chosen love, he said, the way I'd chosen words – because he thought that love, like words, could knit two things together. It was because of that, he said – that he had faith in love alone – that he believed, perhaps, I would come back to him. Then he began to drink, something he rarely did, and cry, something I'd never seen him do before. He then got angry, and asked me angrily where Orkney was. Instead of telling him, I went to fetch a globe, and placed it on the kitchen table, set it spinning. It looped round and round until my finger came to rest upon the islands to which I'd soon be traveling.

'Good god,' he said. 'Small islands. And very far up north. You're scared of water, and always cold. You think you'll like it there?'

'I'm not that scared of water,' I said defensively.

'You almost drowned when you were small. You can't swim well. You know you can't. As for the cold . . . This hardly looks a place you would have chosen.'

'That isn't true,' I said. 'Orkney is called the Egypt of the north; it has more structures from the Stone Age than any other place in Europe.'

'Well, fine,' he said. 'You can be cold, and scared of water, and it will be worth it, because you'll get to see another country that's vanished.' He sounded not just angry, but bitter, and I knew, because I knew him, all the things that lay behind this comment. Yes, *we* spoke the same language, no codes between the two of us that could not be deciphered in a moment. He meant that, in its way, each bond, whatever kind it was – bonds between tribes, bonds between people – was like a tract of land that had been set apart and called a country. He meant, as well, that those who lived within the lands believed the lines would hold them safe, until the day that they were suddenly invaded, and on that day the boundaries vanished. If there were walls, as there had been in Uruk, they fell back into the sands that they had come from; if there was law, then when invaders came the law, too, fell apart, or crumbled.

And while the law did not quite vanish – as great brick walls around a town did – it still came down, as all the books it had been written in went up in fire, and, in the House of Ashes that the fire wrote, small trace of law remained. My partner knew, in fact, that if I left, I never would come back to him.

So next he said, 'What will you do there, with this man?' He called Sebastian 'this man' as if his name upon his lips would burn him.

'I'll work, I guess. I'll have to work. I'll think of something.'

'You'll think of sex,' he said, still bitterly. 'That's why you were so wet that night, why you have slept apart from me for ten whole days. And speaking of sex, what do you know about this man? What do you know about his history?' I looked at him, as he drank whiskey, turning, still, the globe, as if to find upon it some land that would compel me now to stay with him. I had been with him, after all, not just for seven years, but for the years within those years which had most changed him. I looked at him and thought of all I owed him, how, perhaps, my brief exposure to his sister's death had been the thing that let me fully enter *Gilgamesh*. And as for him, it was a miracle that after such a death he had remained a man who thought, and taught, that in a world as cruel as ours, still no one should be punished.

But I just said, 'I didn't ask. How could I ask? I've known him for an hour.'

'You've known him for an hour. You didn't ask. Well, I will ask, then, Emrys. You're going to him now, and I can't stop you. Still, promise me you'll use protection with this man; you promise me you'll do it every single time, until he's tested.' And when he said this, I recalled, for just an instant, how she'd looked – his sister – when I'd known her. Her body was quite wasted, her face a mask of death, her flesh half burned away, like something on a pyre.

I said at once, 'Of course. Of course I'll promise that,' and reached to take his hand and hold it gently. But he did not want pity, and it made him quite enraged to think that he had even said what he had said now. He grabbed his hand away, and with it took the globe and put it back upon the shelf from which I'd taken it.

He left the house, to walk, and while I should, perhaps, have followed him, instead I went to bed, where I could think alone about Sebastian. I did not sleep, and for the next two days I hardly ate or slept at all. I was, it seemed, aroused at all times, day and night, my body on a journey to a place I'd never been before. If I did sleep, a little, I'd wake from hidden dreams to find that I was wet – as ready to make love with Bastian as if he were in bed beside me – and also that my skin was now a membrane or a tablet, so delicate, so sensitive, that my own touch was like the touch of silk to it. I ran my hands upon my breasts, upon my hips, upon my legs, and felt my fingers writing some strange text there; it was as if Sebastian's hands had entered into mine, and so, though I was so aroused I couldn't sleep, I hardly cared, especially since, when I talked to Sebastian for the second time and told him I was sleepless, he said, in that deep voice that slid right to my bones:

'Well, come to me, then, Emrys. I'll make sure you sleep.'

But that was later. First – upon the day he'd said he would – he called, and when I picked the phone up said to me just, *Emrys*. I felt the wave of passion make me weak again, and once again lay on the floor to stop myself from falling there.

I said, 'Hello, Sebastian,' and heard him say:

'So. You must tell me. Did you decide to tell your husband you were leaving him?' And when I said just, *Yes* and nothing more, Sebastian gave another of those happy, distant sighs, those exhalations.

'That's good. Poor boy,' he added. 'And did he take it well?' Now, lovesick as I was, I felt a wave of something like dislike mix in with all my passion.

'He's not a boy,' I said.

'Oh, more a man than I?' Sebastian said, his voice quite changed.

'I wouldn't know,' I said, just desperate in an instant, fearful that maybe this would all come to nothing, that, perhaps, if I let *boy* upset me, Bastian would say – as he had said upon the first occasion when we talked on the phone – *You should stay with him, then*.

'I just don't think that you should call him boy,' I added softly.

'I call all men and women boys and girls,' Sebastian said. 'You don't think that we are? I didn't mean it badly. How did he take it?'

'Well.'

'He's a good man, I think,' Sebastian said, as he had said before – or almost – when we'd talked in London.

'And do you think you're not? Not a good man?' I said to this. Sebastian said, not *yes*, that he was bad, not *no*, that he was good, but that he didn't know himself, sometimes. He said he'd been much worse, at times, than he had thought to be, and sometimes had been better than he guessed he could. He said, too, that he'd felt, when he had met me, that I might surprise him with what I would, or could, or might, bring out in him. In fact, he said that when he'd first observed me standing in the place where two halls met, he had not merely thought I seemed familiar, he'd also thought that what he felt for me was what he felt for all the things which had been made before the Bronze Age. He said:

'My feeling for you was so ancient; it was deer horns in a tomb, the garments of the Goddess, spread across the heavens.'

I thought he said 'dear horns' and so I saw *dear horns* within my mind until I got the thing untangled But when I did, *so ancient* made me think of something I had thought the day we met – that we who shared so much must be the same age, also. So now I said, impulsively, 'Oh, that reminds me,' and then told Sebastian the year I had been born. 'And you?'

'What month?'

'In April.'

'Perfect,' he said. 'At Sele, the time of planting. And I was born at harvest, in August of the same year. An older woman, then. I cherish older women. They are so wise and beautiful. Was forty hard for you, the turning?'

'Oh, not at all,' I said. 'I saw it as a triumph. In neolithic times, I would be dead by now, or at the least quite toothless. My grinding teeth would probably be left. Of course, I'd be so old I would be quite revered – the wisest woman in the tribe, the one who knew it all. They would depend on me for everything.'

'You'd have your teeth, at least in Orkney. They kept their teeth. Nothing to rot them. As for the rest would you like being depended on? Are you a bossy woman?' When Bastian asked this, once again I felt I did not understand quite what he meant – felt that his voice was fenced with hidden meanings. I thought of Gilgamesh, who says – when Ishtar asks him to be her lover – that no, he won't, because he cannot trust her. But I thought, too, that I should not attempt to read Sebastian thus, when he was far away, and just a voice, no man to hold the meanings in. I stopped myself from asking whether he really thought that *bossy* and *needed* meant one thing, and said, in answer to his question:

'Not really. But I do want to be wise. I cherish wisdom in others. I like to learn new things.'

'That's good,' Sebastian said. 'And good you left your husband. I long to feel your hands upon my body, Emrys.' At which I thought of nothing from *Gilgamesh*, except perhaps the promise that mountains and lands would bring their yield to him. It seemed to me so clear, then, that the map of the entire earth was what Sebastian and I would trace upon each other's skin soon, and that the seed of light I sought to seed the darkness of my mind had already taken root, there in the place where our two bodies spoke one language.

3

ANOTHER WEEK PASSED. I was leaving for I didn't know how long, and there were things I had to do in order to get ready. I bought my ticket, told my chairman that I needed a year off. I said I didn't want a sick leave, just a year away from this. I need the rest, I told him. This was true. I still could hardly sleep five hours a night, I was so lovesick. I'd heard this word before – before I had the sickness that is love – and thought it just a poem, all in eight letters. But it was not. Love seemed a drug, which caused an illness in which food, and sleep, and thoughts of anything but he whom I now loved became just things my body wouldn't let inside it. I tried to focus every day on tasks that must be done, but it was hard, because the whole world had become, for me, Sebastian.

Still, after what my partner had observed about the islands I was going to, I tried at least to pack for Orkney. About the water that surrounded it I could do nothing, but about the cold, I could pack clothes which would protect me from it. I always wore warm clothes, had worn them all my life – warm, simple clothes, warm pants and boots and vests and jackets – but now I went to buy the things I'd never needed in the Middle East, things made of pile that stretched and kept one warm even if soaking. I bought black pile tights, a black pile shirt, a dark grey pile vest. I had already a jacket made of this same fabric. At home, I tried on tights, and shirt, and vest, and also pile socks; when everything was on, it felt as if I wore real fur, and this felt good to me. The clothing clutched my skin just like a skin itself. It soothed the nerve ends that were so aroused there was no moment of the day or night they did not reach out for Sebastian's hands to touch them.

In fact, the last two nights before I left for London, I wore the pile to bed. I didn't sleep much more – in terms of hours – than I had slept since I had first heard Bastian say my name, but slept more soundly, went toward dreams that lay a little farther underneath my consciousness. On August 1, I woke at four, lay staring at the darkness, then rose, took off my thin gold ring and put it in a box that I would leave behind me. I'd said goodbye the night before, and so I dressed, closed up my bags and took a taxi to the airport, where I would wait for seven hours. It was as good as waiting anywhere. It seemed to me, by then, that time, which had so speeded up that day three weeks before – or stretched, at least – had now slowed down and down until I thought I knew what it would be to sit and watch the world grow old before me.

Time passed so slowly, while I sat and waited for the plane, that I believed I could have sat – those seven hours – upon the great grasslands where once Uruk had risen to the sky, and watched the city grow and age and fall, until the desert came. The time I lived in was so slow it seemed that five millennia might be a small abyss that could be stepped across, and on the flight to London – another seven hours long – the gap still seemed quite small, though now it was a gap from *now* to *never*. As I recall, I sat upon the plane and watched my watch; I tried to stop this, once I saw what I was doing, but I couldn't. The minute hand made maddening movements – exhaustive explorations of the space it had to circle – while the second hand was flighty and jerked as if it thought, then thought again, quite fickle. The hand that marked the hour had a stony disregard for what the other hands were doing and rarely moved when I could see it happen.

I watched this. Watched, as well, the wrist that time was wrapped around, the wrist bone solemn as a mountain on a treeless island. It seemed to me that underneath this mountain lay the time, and that the time had gone to sleep within the mountain's shadow. I went into the bathroom, brushed my teeth, and washed my face and hands, then sat and watched the time some more. I washed my face and hands again, and brushed my teeth, put cream upon my face, then watched my watch, while the plane hurtled forward into darkness. Behind, the sun was lost. It fell into the sea. At last, the plane began to climb down from the sky that held it. It hit the earth at Heathrow like a great lost bird that's sighted home at last; I saw the lights of London from my window. And when I did, I wondered for the first time – when, at last, the time was gone which had, until now, lain between us – whether Sebastian would be waiting for me there, if he had come for me as he had promised. What if he hadn't come?

I felt vertiginous as I stood up, and gathered up my bags, and watched the people, as they rose around me. The day flight I had taken so that I would get to England when my body thought it day had brought me in at ten o'clock at night by English time, so when we met, Sebastian and I would be adjusted to different times entirely. And not just different times. To different spaces. I would be moving from a small space to a large one. And though I was, in general, claustrophobic, and disliked any place, such as a plane, which made me feel confined, I now had a new fear to trouble me. What if Sebastian *had* come, but was waiting far too close, was standing by the door through which I'd enter England? What if he was just *there*? Now that the gap from *now* to *never* had been closed I wanted it to be – though just a little – opened up again. Now that the time had passed which I had thought would never pass, I needed a few more moments to compose myself.

I didn't think, then, just that phrase – *compose myself* – as I stood up, put on my coat and gathered up my luggage, but when my heart began to pound, my breath to quicken, and the people all around me to move forward, I knew in any case that what I wanted I was lacking. I had no time left to compose myself, if what that means is make yourself from scratch – is start creating, like a poem, the person you will be in future. I was already who I was, and could not, even if I wished, just start my life from scratch again. I'd found that out another time, with *Gilgamesh* – because when scribes had scratched with sharpened sticks upon the wet clay tablets of Uruk, they'd told an old, old tale already. So there was nothing I could do but what I did; I walked alone from where I was into another time, another space, where Bastian might be waiting, or might not be.

I had to walk, alone, right through a door – a gate – but this time pushed by those who crowded round me. I did not see them, they were there; they pushed, the men and women, while one door, then another, fell before me. In my translation of *Gilgamesh*, when Enkidu cursed the harlot – for no reason save that Enkidu would die because his life had been a life she brought him – I had him curse her with a Great Curse, and in this curse, with many other angry wishes, he had said, *May a gateway be your birthing room*. Was it a blessing or a curse that this gateway was mine, that I could not stop now and go back to the place I'd come from? I found it strange that I should feel such sudden fear as I considered what I'd done in coming here to give myself to someone who was just a perfect stranger: 'But will you know me, Emrys? What color are my eyes?' he'd said when we last talked, and laughed when I had no idea, and could not tell him.

I walked. Was pushed. Slowed down. Came through the gate. He leaned against a pillar, far behind the crowd – eyes blue, although I couldn't see that yet. His hair was brown still, but pushed back; he had the sole of one foot lifted up and placed against the pillar he leaned on. But now he saw me, saw me see him, and moved forward, not as fast as he was wont to walk because – I knew – he wished to meet me on the edge of things. So there he was again. He'd come. A man at last. And not just any man. The only man I cared about. Now that I saw him, all around me people walking dimmed, until only Sebastian was real to me. And as I went to him I realized he alone was waiting here to greet the flight I'd taken; he'd known that when I landed I would not remember I was on the wrong side of the many barriers.

And so, he'd gotten through them – who knows how? – and now was waiting where I'd needed him to be, to stem my terror. When we had almost come together, and I stood just before him, he did not look quite as I had remembered. It wasn't just his hair or that his eyes were blue – dark blue, like sky which had no rain in it. He wore his jeans, a dark-green shirt, his canvas shoes, a quilted jacket – so it was not the clothes that he wore either. He'd come and he was there, but he looked different now that he and I were meeting for a different purpose, and I was still almost as scared as I had been when I had thought perhaps he would not be here to meet me. In fact, the first words that escaped me, although I had not known they would, were, 'I'm terrified. Just terrified, Sebastian.'

He hadn't smiled before, but now he smiled, as if pleased, and said, 'Well, I'm scared, too, you know.'

To this I said, amazed that I could not shut up, 'Not scared. I'm really terrified.'

He smiled more, then passed a test I hadn't known I'd set, and didn't try to kiss me, but gathered me up to hug me. I wore a raincoat, carried bags; all this came with me when Sebastian placed his arms around my back and pulled me toward him. And as he pulled me hard, and let me lean against his chest, he also pulled me, just a bit, off balance. Because of this, I did not hug him as I wished to in return, but fell against his side, and came to rest there. He looked at me, stopped smiling, set me straight, set down my bags, then took me in his arms once more, but this time balanced. He stroked my back, hands starting at the shoulders, and ending where my spine came to a stop; he left his hands there for a moment, letting me wonder if he would move his hands still further.

But then he said, 'You came,' as if this fact surprised him.

'I told you that I would.'

'Not everyone does everything they say they will.' He took my left arm, drew it out from where it circled round his waist, and looked at where the ring I'd worn was missing. He held the hand, but lightly, touched the knuckles softly with one finger. 'I like it,' he said then, and put my hand for just an instant back around his waist, letting me hold him.

Then he said, 'Well, we'd best be off. We've got the same room for tonight, but we have lots to put you through before we get there.'

'I'm very tired,' I said, again amazed at what came from my mouth, since this was not the thing I'd meant to say to him. But it seemed somehow that, with Bastian, I must be just who I was, and say just what I felt – and just then, I felt tired. When I said *tired*, though, Sebastian lifted me right off the ground into the air, his palms beneath my buttocks. And now, I was amazed not by my words, but by his strength. He picked me off the ground, it seemed, quite effortlessly. He did not merely smile, but grinned, and said, 'Oh, oh, so *tired*, are you, Emrys?' his look reminding me of why I'd come to him. If I had come to sleep, he said – his look said, very plain – then I would need, to sleep, to come to him first.

All this he said, so simply, with his eyes, and then he set me down, picked up a bag, and led the way to where we had to walk now. This was, as he had said, through lines and lines, through forms, through customs, immigration, all the business of the world. Or maybe not the world – that business lay with us – but through the world's fine artificial boundaries. It didn't matter that those bounds, like those of love, must first be crossed, because when they'd been crossed, they could then be forgotten. The two of us were now together, and knitted up; we had a bag on either side, and in the middle, where we touched, we had each slipped an arm around the other's waist. And as we walked this way, I thought that there was not a person in the world who'd see us, thus, and doubt that we were lovers. I had been right about our gaits; we walked the same, the brisk and forward movements of our legs, the swinging backwards movements of our arms. We were now slightly slowed by bags, and lust, as well as lines, but we were clearly, both of us, quite edgy human beings.

Then, somehow, we were bumped apart; the passage went two ways, and when it did, I walked the right way, to the left, while Bastian walked the wrong way, through a gate. Alarms went off, and while it didn't matter, it seemed to me correct that Bastian would set alarms off, although he wore just jeans and canvas shoes, a shirt and jacket. It seemed correct that these plain garments would have, on him, a threatening edge of meaning. There was a part of him that was a Bronze Age warrior, after all, with all the snaps his jacket had – the soft black cotton punched with just a little too much metal. He threw his hands up in the air. He let them see that he was going out. And then we bumped together once again, and linked our arms around each other's waists. We let the business of the country happen all around us while I touched his neck, my hand unable to resist the lure of him.

And he, in turn, took up my hand, and held it like a piece of clay that he would press and bake between the two of his; his hands, I found, were hot, much hotter than most hands would ever be, and also quite abrasive, from his work. Before that night, we'd touched hands only twice, and I had not felt what a heat he held in his. I liked this heat a lot. And so, not always touching, but always causing smiles – I'd never seen before the way desire was a sun that warmed all those it fell on – we got through all the lines and

45

all the forms, the gates, the walls, and out, at last, into the world I'd gotten to. There, in early August, there was rain again, the rain of England as I'd often known it. We found Sebastian's Jeep, a dark-green boxy thing on wheels. My bag went in the back. We got inside. It was now almost midnight London time. I'd thought by now Sebastian might be tired. But he had told me, sometime when we'd talked across the sea, that he could sleep at any time, and that, after a sleep as short as minutes, he would wake up refreshed and be awake for all the time that he might need to be.

So now, as he prepared to drive from Heathrow into London, he seemed quite wide awake, as we sat down and put our seat belts on in perfect synchronicity. It wasn't planned, but happened. Sebastian reached up to his right, I to my left, and with the same quick gesture, we yanked both belts down. We pushed them in steel locks that lay between us, at so exactly the same moment that a single click was heard. I thought this boded well, and smiled at the thought; Sebastian did not notice what had happened, though. He was intent on driving; he drove aggressively, and yet with great control. He wove right in and out of traffic – still thick, within the city, at midnight. He changed lanes, thrust the stick shift forward and away, moving always in a state of taut, machined awareness, but going quite as fast as he could go, and still be safe, as if escaping from a war-torn country.

Indeed, I felt that if I should ever need to flee, myself, before the advent of a foreign army, I would want Bastian behind the wheel of any car or bus or tank that took me through the lines and guns and once again to safety. When traffic thinned, or when Sebastian was not ramming the stick shift into gear, he reached out with one hot dry hand, and rubbed me with the heat that he had in him. We got to the hotel. They knew him there. They took the Jeep away, and carried luggage to the desk. He checked us in, and while the bellman took my bags, and one of his as well, he took my hand. We rode up on the lift – the same lift he had come from when he'd appeared inside my life, this sudden man who suddenly was mine. The bellman talked, but we just leaned against the lift's too-mirrored walls, and when the lift stopped, walked around the corner of the corridor. We found our room; the door was opened, and our bags were set inside. Sebastian tipped the bellman, then closed the door and locked it. He looked at me, and I looked back and for a moment as I looked, it seemed to me that he was just a perfect stranger. My partner had been right. I knew him not at all. Who was this man who I had fled my country for? And what should I do now that I was with him in a land that was a new land now that I was with Sebastian there?

But then he sat upon the bed, and took his shoes off, and his socks – a thing that I might do myself. I was relieved to have a task to undertake, and sat down on the couch, removed my boots, and tucked my socks inside them. Then, while Sebastian took his bag across the room and set it near the closet, I also took a bag, and zipped it down so I could find the clothing I had bought for Orkney. I wasn't cold – although I could have shivered, if I'd let myself, from all the ways the moment made me feel, the wondering-what-would-happen-next a kind of force that was as fierce, in truth, as any cold that might seep down into the bones of me – but though I wasn't cold, I thought that maybe later I would need these clothes to sleep, and so I set them neatly on the chair where Bastian had sat while I poured out the tea and longed to strip him naked. Once they were set there, though, I had exhausted all the things I knew to do until I realized I should take a bath. But first, I walked across the room, looked down on London – all the lights that shone like beacons and would shine, thus, all night long.

Sebastian came behind me, put his arms around my waist, then turned me gently toward him, and kissed me. I hadn't meant to kiss him yet. I'd really meant to bathe. I thought I needed water on my body. But when he kissed me – not quite kissed me, nibbled me, like deer, just tasting grass – I kissed him back; I could not stop myself. I wanted to stop, to bathe, but though I held on for a while to this idea – that I must climb into the water like a seal, and let the water make me new again – the thought at length went to the place where all thoughts go at last, a place to which there is no following. Sebastian's hot hands held me by the waist, and now they tugged my shirt loose from my pants and slid beneath it. I moaned, I couldn't help it, when Sebastian touched my skin. I moaned again when he then moved his fingers. Sebastian did not moan, he never moaned, he never made a sound. He took my shirt between his hands, my camisole, as well, and slid them up and off my head and dropped them on the floor behind me.

We still stood right before the window in front of which he'd sat, three weeks before, and thought that he should say, 'Can I take you to bed now?' At last, he did just that. I felt like something that, if seeded, would be carried by the wind, and after flying miles would fall to earth and land there, not too planted. I moaned as he took up his hands and placed them underneath my breasts, just made his hands into small cups to hold them. He held them for a moment, then he left them, took me by both hands, and led

48

me to the bed, which I sat down upon. He put his hands together now upon my clavicle, his two thumbs touching, so that the hands, like two spread wings, brushed lightly on the bone so close there to the surface. He then just drew them down, across my breasts, across my waist, all of the skin that he had bared, until he reached the place my pants were fastened. He pushed my knees apart, but gently; it felt light, as light as those two wings. He kneeled upon the floor, and zipped my pants down, drew them off me.

'My god, you're beautiful,' he said. 'Who would have thought this body lay beneath those clothes you wore? Here. Lie back upon the bed for me.'

Three weeks before, I'd dreamed that it was I who would bare him – who would first make an inventory of all the things that I'd discovered. But now, I let myself just fall away into a place where what might happen was not the thing I had imagined. I had not lied, though, when I'd told Sebastian I was tired; I was so tired I cannot recollect each separate moment of the night that followed. The later times, the other times, each one comes back to me in all its detail when I call on it. But that first time, I was so tired from lack of food and sleep, it is as if it were a rocky island I see through drifting fog. I see the moment I stood up, and Bastian stripped my shirt off, the moment when he cupped my breasts, and then, as tender as a man could be, kept cupping them while he kissed me. I also see the moment when I lay, now naked, on the bed, and Bastian, still clothed, lay right beside me. I took his shirt off, found, upon the chest that lay beneath, a little hair – not much – and nuzzled into it. But then there came the moment we were both unclothed, and rolled together, hip to hip, to find our hips just fit.

And I was, at that moment, so wet, so tired, and also so enchanted by the way our bodies fit, it would have been quite effortless to come together. We almost did, but then – out of a place which lay beyond the place I was – there came to me a thought like fog, just drifting. I did not think – not quite – of him whom I had left, who'd made me promise not to throw myself into the chasm of death; I did not think – not quite – of her whom he had lost, because she'd trusted, far too much, a man she'd trusted. But I did think that it was strange that if this man, Sebastian, was *my* man, he would not know me well enough to know I'd want the question. If nothing else, he could not know that when the two of us made love, we might not risk a child – and there was always, now, the other issue, also.

He did not ask, though, and, as a result, from the far place which lay beyond the place I lay, the words came to my mouth: 'No, wait, Sebastian.'

Sebastian held my hips and looked at me. He seemed unable to discern why I might stop. He murmured, 'Wait?' and I said, 'Time,' but meaning more than that. Time, time, I'd thought there was no time, but now it seemed that time was all there was – all we were given, all that might be lost or taken from us.

I said, 'I think that we should use protection.'

To this, Sebastian said, 'You will not need such things with me,' and turned away a bit.

'We'll both get tested, soon,' I said. 'Why not?'

'I want you now,' Sebastian said, at which I loved him.

'I know. I want you, too,' I said. 'It's just . . .' What could I say? If I said more than just enough, then time would stop, and what I wanted most of all was to move on. I said, 'It's just . . . I promised I'd be careful.'

'You promised *him?*' Sebastian said. 'What does he have to do with us? You told me you had left your husband. If it's not true, then go home now. I want him gone forever.'

His tone was hard. His eyes were hard as well, and now he rolled entirely away from me. Since I could feel the hurt he felt, and since I hadn't said the thing I really meant, in any case, I tried to turn the tone, and said, 'Don't you believe that we must make the proper offerings for happiness?'

'Yes, to the gods,' he said. 'Not husbands who you claim you've left behind you on another continent.'

'He thought I must be mad,' I said. 'Perhaps I am. But even mad, I try to keep my promises.'

At this Sebastian looked at me, and laughed a little, then said, 'What promise shall *I* take, then? Something quite hard, I think, if you like fairness. Perhaps I'll ask you to make sure I'm buried in my tomb. Or that my thigh bones go there, at the least.' And then he kissed me, said, 'All right. But just for now. And just for now, I'll help you keep your promise. I think I could make you forget it, Emrys, though, if I should really try someday.'

And that, too, I remember clearly – how those words excited me. But then, what followed – which was long and full and mostly rich – is blanked out by the fog that blows in front of it. I do remember how he held wet fingers to our lips; I do remember how – before – he spread my legs apart with just one hand, then took that hand, and touched the place that he had opened. He touched it lightly, oh, so lightly, and was pleased at what he found, wet all his fingers, brought them to our lips and fluttered them. He seemed to know at every moment just what I would want before I knew myself, and knew that that was what I

51

wanted most – that he would be quite sure, at every moment, what came after. That doubt should lie beyond us. And it was all like that until he took my hips, and let me down, as lightly as he could, upon him.

Though he said, then, 'No, slowly, Emrys,' I was not slow, and found that he'd been right – this thing I'd brought between us was, though thin, as cold and foreign as any grave before it knows you. But even so, we came, and almost right away. We could not *not* have come, no matter what lay there between us. He smiled, I laughed, and then, when I felt that he was still hard, I lay down carefully upon his body. He said, first, 'No regrets?' and I said, 'No regrets,' and then we just held on to one another, smiling. It was then that he said:

'I knew this, from your hands, when you were pouring tea. You should have worn gloves, if you wished to hide from me.'

'I didn't want to hide from you,' I said. 'I wanted to undress you. I wanted you to hold my hips. I wanted you inside me.'

'Well, now, that's where I am,' he said. 'You lucky woman. Do you always get the things you want?'

'Oh, very rarely. Never.'

'Well, now you have,' he said. And then we fell apart. Sebastian got up, came back, and took me in his arms; my head was now half on his arm, half on his shoulder. It was then, as we lay, not quite replete, that he told me about the words *cunnus* and *cunte*, and the Kunta Cave in Orkney. He told me, too, of all the other words that *cunt* had made, still in the OED for anyone to find there.

'*Cunabula*,' he said. 'The cradle, earliest abode, the place where everything is nurtured, in its beginnings. *Cunina* was

52

the goddess who protected children in the cradle, in Rome. *Cunctipotent* is still a word, which means all-powerful, exactly like omnipotent, but better. Or *cunicle*, a hole or passage underground. As for the tombs in Orkney, since they are chambered tombs, with long long passages, open at one end, they are – a favorite word of mine – *cuniculate*.'

'Are those long entries narrow?'

'Why do you ask?' he said, and laughed. 'I'd think you wouldn't care. That's my department, surely.'

'No, no, in the real world, I mean. I'm slightly claustrophobic.'

'You are?' he said, amused. 'Well, we'll cure you of that. They are tight, some of them, the best of them – my tomb, and Cuween Hill. Maes Howe, the Vikings broke in through the roof, of course, but they would not have needed to. The entry passage there is really huge.'

His tomb, he'd said again, and I was more than slightly claustrophobic. My partner had been right about my fear of water – which had expanded since the time I'd almost drowned. Since then, I'd been quite frightened of confinement anywhere, and did not go to places which, like tombs, could keep me tied to any air one instant longer than I wished it. *His* tomb, though; he would wish to take me there and, I saw now, would laugh at me if I resisted it. I liked that he would laugh. It seemed that all my fears might vanish if they were merely laughed at.

'I like that word,' I said. '*Cuniculate*. That's in the OED?'

'Oh, not just that. The best of all are *cunne* – obsolete – which means to prove, to test, make trial of. To taste, as well. And *cunning*, in its earlier sense – to know, possessing skill. A broad word, in its meaning, before things grew so dull. Like dexterous, clever, expert, able. Even magical.'

'And so,' I said. 'You're cunning, aren't you?'

'I hope so. You're the one to judge.' He laughed again, and I did, too, and then we lay and touched some more. His touch was silk to me.

But then, I had to sleep. Of course, I couldn't sleep, like that, all wrapped around Sebastian. So now, after the thing that I'd already put between us, I had to tell him, too, that I could never sleep with men – not if the bed was soft, as this one was. I'd brought my sleeping bag, I told him, and would take some cushions off the couch, and put them on the floor, right there beside him. Then he could sleep, and I could sleep, and we would try, and some night soon, to sleep together. He looked at me.

'I always do this, really,' I explained.

'I thought you said you wanted something new.'

'I do want something new. Everything new. I just need one night's sleep, that's all. I can't sleep touching anyone.'

'There seems to be a lot that you can't do,' he said, though trying hard to mask the way he meant this. 'You're here, you've left your husband, risked disease, made love with someone you know not at all, and now you won't just *try* to sleep with me?'

'I could just *try*. Of course I'll try. I just won't manage it, that's all. I would. Of course I would. You think that I don't want to?'

'Just sleep,' he said. 'You take the bed. I can sleep anywhere.' I looked at him, amazed, but he just nodded. Then he took up my sleeping bag, some pillows, kissed me once, went right across the room and made his bed upon the couch. I got up, too, and took the clothes that I had put upon the chair back to the bed with me, where I pulled on the tights and shirts and socks, to sleep in. Sebastian smiled a sleepy smile, and said, 'Oh, Emrys, what have we done? I can't live long like this. Sleep well, you wretched girl.' And I did sleep, as well as I had ever slept, that night – a deep, deep sleep that slid deep down inside me.

And when I woke, and looked across the room, I saw Sebastian wide awake, saw that he had not stirred from where he was, so that he would not wake me. At that, I truly loved him. Before, I had been so in love that love had not, in truth, come into it. But now, when he had been so careful, patient with my sleep, I looked at him and smiled, and thought two things. One, that if I left him now, went back to where I'd been, and didn't do this, after all, it might be better in the end for Bastian. The other was the same, but backwards – if I left him now, and went back home, and didn't do this thing, it might be better in the end for me. I didn't know, of these two thoughts, which was the real one, and which came to cover up the truth. Or maybe both were real, both true.

I took my clothes off, threw them on the floor, looked at Sebastian, loved him, called him to come to bed. When he climbed in, I wrapped myself around him, naked, saying, 'Sebastian, I've been thinking. Maybe I should go home. Maybe this wasn't such a good idea for us.' But as I wrapped myself around him, I no longer wanted to go home; his skin was silk upon my soul. But I had said it now. It had been said; perhaps I should go back. And he said, Yes, perhaps. Well, this upset me. That he should be eager to say yes, and not to ask – as I had thought he must – just why I said this. And so, without him asking, I told him anyway. I said that, though we had made love, I had not yet let go, and that, at least for women, there was a moment when you made a choice to do that. I'd had no choice about the way I felt, and no choice but to come to him, but that what lay ahead now still seemed a choice that I could make. I said I cherished choice.

Yet while I spoke, Sebastian moved his hands across my buttocks, as if he knew that he must say goodbye to them; he ran his fingers up and down the place they came together, as if already they were something that was past to him. Yes, yes, his hands said, it was sad, but he and I must part, must make the only choice that made us human. Yes, yes, his hands said, holding my buttocks tight, no doubt I would prefer to dress in clothing, not Sebastian.

'But why for women?' he then said. 'For men, too, that is how it happens.'

'I don't think so,' I said. 'I think it's different. For women, when you make the choice, and let it go completely – just trust completely – who the man is hardly matters. Afterwards, he can control you.'

'Oh, surely not,' he said. 'Or, if he can, the same is true the other way around. I am a man. I know. We, too, give up control when we give in to this.' And then he slipped a finger past my buttocks, there between my legs, and dipped it in, and took it out, and dipped it in again.

I groaned. What happened next? He stopped. He said, 'Well, we should eat. I do think that it goes both ways, but that is not the point now. The point is you alone can know what you should do. Whether you come with me to Orkney or you don't, we must check out soon.' So we got up and bathed, and then we dressed and walked out into rain, and found a small café, and had a breakfast there. We went back to the room and packed. I didn't know, still didn't know, what I would do, what I should do. Would all this come to nothing?

'What will you do?' he said. 'Will you go home?'

'I just don't know,' I said. And found I didn't. We had just twenty minutes left before we needed to check out. Our bags were by the door, the bed was made, the room was neat. I sat down on the bed to try to think.

And as I did, Sebastian came and sat beside me. He said then, 'Really, Emrys, all these clothes. I thought I took them off you.' He said, 'You slept last night, I think. You were a seal. You looked a seal, in all that fur you wore. If you must go, then I would like to see you once again as you might be if you would be, for me, a human woman.' And as he finished this, he put four fingers to his lips, but not as if to say, *Be silent.*

He thought, then bent down, took my boots off, reached behind us, found pillows, gently laid me down on them. I let him do this. I just lay there, while Sebastian moved beside me. I thought: *We must check out. We have just twenty minutes left.* I thought: *There is no time for us to do this.* But then I felt, through clothes – a heavy shirt, a vest, my pants – the silk that was Sebastian touch my skin again. He put his hands upon my breasts as if he owned them, but owned them as you own a thing you love. A china cup. Through all the cloth that lay between his hand and my silk skin, he owned them, and his hands said that they knew this. Oh, I could sleep apart from him for all the time I wished, and all the time that this might last – which would, his hands said, not be long – and I could make him put a skin between his flesh and mine, which would, no matter what I might believe, protect me only from the things I could not catch from him, and I could also say that I had not yet made the choice I had to make if I would stay with him, but he, his hands said, knew that he now knew me, and that

57

this had been choice enough – to let him know me, so he knew just how to take me now.

And I had made that choice? To let him know just how to place his hands flat on my breasts, through cloth, holding them there as if to say to them: *I know you*. He left his hands there for a time that was in time, but timeless, as if he said, *Yes, we have time. Time loves us*. He then unbuttoned everything so slowly that it was as if time had been, in truth, arrested. He moved the pillows he had placed beneath my head, and let my head lie flat upon the bed now. He didn't say a thing, just held me flat against the bed, with one hand underneath my shirt, holding my stomach there. He moved the other hand below, and with a single tug, had taken out the button of my jeans and zipped them down again. Now, holding me in place, he slipped my jeans around my thighs, and to my knees, and then he took my shirt off. He kept one hand at all times on my stomach, palm to skin, and holding me as if he pinned me there.

Yet as he did, I felt like something light – like paper, maybe, on which one word, and that word *hope*, was being written. Or like a tissue-thin bright cloth, a silken pennon, or a sail, that would have blown into the sky had Bastian not secured me. And now that I was naked – he still clothed – he moved one hand beneath me. He placed the hand beneath my nearer thigh, then slipped two fingers into me. Two fingers, why two fingers, not just one? I didn't know. He knew, and left them there, not moving them, or just a little. And then he laced his other hand across my thigh, and touched the top of me, these fingers moving. They were a slow, slow question that he asked me. The moments passed, but in a place where moments passed without the clock that ran the world beyond us noticing. By

58

now, I was quite gone, and felt that time had gone to sleep beneath the sail of hope that was my body. It was as if, with his two hands, Sebastian had unlocked the gate of time, and taken us to stand within its gateway.

And there he asked, though not aloud, and not in words: *This choice, will Emrys make it now? And if she does, what will I do to her? Perhaps I'll love her. Maybe not. Maybe I'll kill her.* This is her choice, he thought, and I did, too, because I knew that when I'd made it, there would be no returning to the place I'd come from. What was this choice, then? That I trust, that I leap out in space and time, and see if, there, a perfect stranger would catch me. That I believe that if I risked what was much more than other risks – the risk of being known – the risk would let me know the world around me. And now, I saw that this was something I could choose – that no one else could choose – to let Sebastian take me. I felt his fingers touch me like the pulse of time itself – the pulse of everything which makes us long to be immortal. It was as if I stood there at the gateway of two worlds – the worlds of life and death, the worlds of past and future – and if I'd said, *No, no, I cannot make this choice, I won't*, it would have been the same as saying, *Kill me*.

I didn't say it. I said nothing. Had I formed words, with mind or voice, the words would have been just the opposite. They would have been, *Oh, live me, please. I'm going to trust you, Bastian. Trust you to hold me in this world I've blown to.* But I did not form words with mind or voice, because the world had now become a formless place for me. And in that world, there was a brightness up ahead, like some white sun seen through a mighty gateway. I was drawn toward it, realized I had made the choice to move into the future that lay beyond the gate ahead of me. And then there came a moment when I was myself, the gate; I was thrown wide, and thought: *At last, thank god, I'm opening.*

So there it was. I lay upon my back. I felt a sense of bliss like nothing I had felt in all my life until that moment. I thought: *Well, there it is. The thing is done now.*

Sebastian thought this, too. He didn't say it, though. He said, instead, 'We'd better go. You're too alluring, Emrys.'

'What time is it?' I said.

'It's almost noon. So, are you going back?'

I said, 'I'm coming with you, now, Sebastian.'

To this, he said, half-smiling, a secret happy smile, 'But maybe I won't let you, after all. Such doubts deserve some kind of punishment.'

Just like a girl, I said, 'Oh, let me, please. You must, now, anyway. You have to.'

At that, he took my clothes up from the place he'd put them on the bed, and set them next to me, then ran his hand from my bare neck to my bare stomach.

'Well, all right, then,' he said. 'I won't force you to beg me. Or anyway, not yet. I'll take you to my tomb on Long Holm.'

4

BUT WE WERE NOT there yet. We left that day, and driving in
the Jeep, took the long miles up through England. I felt so
rested from my sleep – the best I'd had in weeks – and also
so wide open, still, that everything that day was wondrous.
It rained as we went north, and though that must have
made the driving hard, Sebastian still drove fast – through
wind, through rain, through thunder. He drove, in fact,
quite savagely; we went at speeds I hadn't thought the
British ever took, and in and out around the cars ahead of us
– while water poured behind, a sheet blown up by wheels
onto their windshields. Sebastian had a habit, when he got
behind a slow car, and could not pass it right away, of
talking to its driver.

'Oh, yes, they let you out today from hospital?' he'd say.
Or: 'Let me get this straight. You are conducting tests at
just what speed a car will stall?' To some old soul who
blocked his way – an ancient driver with shrunken
shoulders, creeping on the road, peering through rain –
he said, and more than once, 'Remember Death. Remember Death, my girl,' as if he quoted something. And then he
shot around her, while she cowered in her seat. I watched

him, laughed, said nothing. I loved each thing he said, each thing he did that day; at one point I lay down, stretched out across the bumpy part between the seats, to place my head upon Sebastian's lap and look up at him. He glanced down, touched my head, looked at a car we passed, shoved the stick shift away from him as if he shot it at a target, then – when the car had been quite drenched by what his wheels had thrown behind us – looked down at me again, and smiled that secret, happy smile he'd smiled in London, which seemed to say, 'I've got her now.'

I didn't care. I loved it. Loved the having come to him, the coming that was still to come for us. I loved the fact that it was raining, that the wind blew hard, so that the trees beside the road were bent by it. They threw their branches down, then lifted branches up, and bent again, their leaves a thousand whirling bracelets. I loved good storms, in any case. They were, though not the kind of tearing in the fabric of the world that had occurred when I met Bastian, still like a window in a wall you'd grown too used to seeing. That day it seemed quite indisputable that storms could help you see that, right behind the solid plane of ordinary life, there was a world more like the world as it had been in the beginning. I said this to Sebastian. Said that storms could show the way creation myths had all – though long ago – come to be written.

'You like these myths?' Sebastian said. I lay, still, on his lap, and now he looked down at my face, in asking.

'Don't you?' I said. 'There are so many different cultures which had the same idea about the start of things. That the beginning of the world was like a mighty storm, and then, eventually, an island coalesced, at which a god or goddess pinned it into place from heaven.'

'I like this, too,' Sebastian said. 'And when you get to Orkney, you will see that there are really islands which will seem to have been pinned that way.'

I looked at him and loved him. I still lay within his lap, so now I turned and cupped my hand between his legs, quite lightly. His legs were spread apart, to reach for both the pedals of the Jeep. He spread them slightly wider when I cupped him with my hand, though he did not appear in other ways to notice that I touched him.

'All stories of the Flood are just creation myths, transplanted,' he said. 'The second forming of the earth was how the men who wrote the Bible tried to placate those who hated their hard tales of losing Eden.'

'I never liked that second forming. How sad it must have been, after the Flood, to have those birds all flying around looking for earth to land on.'

I thought Sebastian would smile at this, but he did not. He said, 'Yes, it was sad. All birth is sad, I think. What will be lost is never clearer than at that instant.'

'*All* birth is sad?' I said. 'I don't agree.'

'And do you not?' Sebastian said, then said, 'Go on. Undo me. It's only fair that you should have the chance I had.'

And so I did. He drove still like a lunatic, quite savage, weaving in and out of cars; the rain had lessened just a little bit by then. 'Death waits us all, my dear,' he said, as he left one more old, old soul upon the road behind us. That he could pass like this, and brake, and then race north along the earth as if he would just lift into the sky if he could manage it, and never pause in his pursuit of something far ahead, while I undid him, freed him from his pants, and took him in my hands, did not seem somehow a surprise to

63

me. With any other man I'd known, I would have thought that such a thing was dangerous. With Bastian, I just said, 'Of course,' and lay upon his lap. In this position, in a car, so that his lap was all the world I saw, it felt as if he was a piece of clay I molded. In fact, it felt as if my hands might be a kiln with which I'd bake the clay which took its shape before me.

'The way it grows under my hands,' I said. 'What power, to make a thing as hot and filled with life as this.'

He looked down, smiled slightly, said, 'You like to babble, don't you?'

'Not usually,' I said. 'Just now. I feel as if it's me who is the made thing, really.'

'Oh ho,' he said. 'A great responsibility for me, my girl. Don't take me in your mouth. But do, please, shut it.'

I didn't laugh, I giggled, but shut my mouth and did what he had asked. In fact, I said, 'Of course,' before I lay there and just played with him. I drew it out. I made it long. He didn't groan, but when he came, his foot grew weak on the accelerator. My hair was there already, so I wiped his semen with it. His eyes had been half-closed, but when I did this, he looked down and murmured:

'Mad, quite mad. I had to get a woman who wipes my semen in her hair, but likes to dress up in the night like some great fur seal.'

We drove on north. We stopped quite late that night, and by the time we stopped, I'd gotten past the sense that I had slept enough to last a week, and fallen asleep within his lap – or, at least, dozed there. It was eleven o'clock when I woke up, because there was a sudden silence. Sebastian nudged me, and said, 'But why can you sleep here? Your head within my lap like that? You're touching someone,

64

right? In any case, we're there.' *There* was a pub just west of Edinburgh, and Sebastian knew the people who ran it; they'd kept the pub lights on outside, and waited for Bastian to arrive, although they otherwise were shut up tight by then. We got some bags, and walked across the gravel, where there had been no rain that day; the storm had been down to the south of us. But here it was quite cold, and though I'd known that Scotland would be cold, I hadn't known I'd feel it quite like this. I shivered.

Then, as Sebastian knocked, I said, 'Bbbbrrrr. That's quite a breeze.'

'You're cold?' he said.

'It's cold.'

'Oh, hardly cold. You'd best get used to this. Orkney is much, much colder.'

He knocked again, and when the man came to the door and greeted him by name, he seemed surprised Sebastian had a woman with him.

'Sebastian,' he said. 'Come in. But I'm afraid . . . I didn't know. We only have a room with twin beds in it.'

'That will be fine,' Sebastian said, the words much more for me than for the man who ran the pub, or owned it. They had a tone; the word is hard to find. As if the thing that really made a lunatic of me, in Bastian's mind, was not the other things he'd said, but this – that I could sleep within his lap within a bumpy, moving Jeep and yet had never slept with any man within a bed. But since I knew the publican would hear the words, not read the tone, and since I wanted him to know just how things were, I said:

'We'll put the mattresses on the floor, and side by side, if that's all right,' at which the man inclined his head politely. He looked at Bastian, said, 'Come in then.'

Sebastian paused to let me enter, and shook his head at me, in what appeared mock disapproval. This made me feel aroused and powerful. The man, over his shoulder, asked if we would eat – just sandwiches, he said, but he could make them. At this, Sebastian looked at me, and asked me with his eyes if we could eat again. We'd had an early supper. I said, 'Of course.'

'I'll take the bags up and come back,' he said. 'You stay and have a drink. Order whatever you like for sandwiches.' I did. There was a light above the bar, and I sat on a high stool on which the light was falling like a puddle. The publican drew me a pint of lager and set it down, and then went off to make the sandwiches. I sat and sipped, and thought, of all things, of the verb *to come*; it had been used three times since we'd arrived. It seemed to me that you could scarcely say a sentence in English without the word *come* coming into it. To come to where, exactly? Where had I come to when I'd come that morning, when I'd felt that I was blown right through the gate or door which was myself, and then had found myself as I had never been before? When I had not yet come to England and had talked to Bastian on the phone, I'd felt that I would melt if I did not just fly to him. After coming, though, I'd felt as if I had new hands, new feet, new limbs, all formed, all made, all perfect. Indeed, the coming was a giving-form-to; it was the making of a thing which had been, previously, quite formless.

Just then, Sebastian returned and sat beside me at the bar, slipping an arm around my waist, sipping my beer.

'I like the verb *to come*,' I said.

'Oh, do you?' he said, tightening his arm. 'It's good, but I think *bring* is better.'

'It's not so rich.'

'I don't agree. What could be richer than the way I brought you off, or you brought me? That's bringing, isn't it?'

'I guess it is,' I said. I fell back into silence as the publican returned, now carrying a plate of sandwiches. He set the plate down on the bar, then drew Sebastian a glass of beer and pushed it toward him so that foam poured down the side. I'd been aroused enough before, with Bastian's arm around me, but now I felt quite weak with it, and sipped my beer in silence, while Sebastian ate sandwiches. He drank his beer, and then another, chatting with the man behind the bar, but keeping one arm tight around my shoulder. And then at last we said good-night and went upstairs, and there I found that Bastian had already put the mattresses on the floor, and heaped them up with blankets.

We were both tired, now, and sleepy, from the beer and from the day – both tired and sleepy, they were like two separate things that night. I lay down on one mattress, closed my eyes, and held my arms out wide, to take Sebastian in them. He got down on the floor, then stretched himself beside me, to let me take him in my arms. His eyes closed too, and we just held our bodies close for quite a while. I smelled his skin. I felt his hair upon my face. It was the softest hair. At length we sleepily, and tired, turned off the lights. Then, in the dark, we touched again, enwrapped ourselves, and this time, took off one another's clothes. We had not spent much time in anything but stripping one another before Sebastian said, 'I won't forget my promise. But then, is it all right if I just get inside you straightaway?'

To this, I said, 'Of course.' He made all ready, kissed me

once, letting his lips dance lightly over mine, letting his hands fall down my front like rain. He spread my legs wide with his hands, and when he did, I pushed my arms above my head and to the sides; I felt like something spread to catch him, like a net in which he would now gladly be entangled. He paused, then slipped inside me, lithe as a fish in oceans – the oceans that had ruled the world before the world was made – and I was there, a starfish, maybe, spread to catch him. He slipped inside, then out, then in again, quick thrusts that I felt gladly, each one separate. I did not move, or speak, just lay there, pinned upon the ocean floor, and felt him. I didn't think, then, of these things, of nets, and fish, and oceans. I think them now. I rode the waves right to their ending.

It was a gentle coming, a gentle bringing, for us both. We rolled away, pulled all the bedclothes over us. Sebastian took me in his arms, and seemed to fall asleep within a second. He fell asleep, and then he twitched; his legs twitched, feet twitched, arms twitched on my arms, against my back, around my waist. I knew he was asleep – his breathing told me this – but all his muscles suddenly were taken with this twitching. If he had never known a woman who could not sleep entwined within his arms, then I had never known a man who slept like this. The twitching just went on. Or rather, it would stop, for two, three minutes, then it would begin again. It was as if each arm, each leg, his back, had all been held by something, taut, and now had been released by it. We thought dogs dreamed of hunting and that the reason why they moved like this was that their paws were trying, in sleep, to push the earth behind them.

Was that what Bastian, too, was dreaming? I'd thought that *I* slept poorly, since I had to wrestle with the letting go of consciousness. But as I felt Sebastian twitch within my arms, I thought this must be worse, to keep this wrestling up in sleep – to find that there was no escape from it. At last, I slipped away. Slipped from his arms, and found my bag, got out my pile clothes, and dressed in them. Went back, and lay beside him, though under different quilts; I crawled as close to him as I could get and still be separate and then fell asleep. And I slept well – not quite as well as I had the night before, but still the sleep was deep and restful. I had bright lovely dreams, of sea birds flying, just like sea birds I would see, and not in dreams, in Orkney. But these were not just white and brown and grey, as sea birds were; they were bright scraps of color. They seemed, in fact, like cloth, light cloth, just borne up by the wind, in blues and crimsons, rust and green, cerulean. And dancing, they were dancing; clouds of birds just twining in and out of one another as they flew. And more, they spoke aloud, or cried, as sea birds do, but in the dream in language that I understood.

They didn't speak to me, but to each other. Said, 'The dry land's gone. We're hunting worlds of water.' Said, or so I thought, when I woke up, 'We're wet, wet, wet. We're water birds, we love it.' And I was, as I always was these days, wet too, when I woke up, and turned to find Sebastian and make love with him. But Sebastian was not there. He'd dressed and gone downstairs. He'd even packed his bags before he left. And when, two minutes later, he came back up the stairs – I heard his footsteps, thrilled before I saw him – he seemed in such a rush to get me up and out of bed, so uninterested in love this morning, that I was hurt by it.

'I see you put your clothes back on to sleep,' he said.

'I'll take them off now, if you'll come to bed.'

'I can't. We have to go,' he said quite tersely. 'We have a lot of miles to cover today.' And then, 'Did you sleep well, at least?'

'Oh, yes. I dreamt of sea birds.'

'Really? I never dream.'

'You must. Everyone dreams. Besides, you twitch as if you're dreaming.'

'Yes, others, too, have told me this. But what you can't remember is not real. What did your dream birds do?'

'They spoke in English.'

He laughed, but very shortly.

'Well, that's convenient. Do you ever dream Akkadian? Let's go,' he said. 'Get up now, Emrys. I want to put the mattresses on the beds again, and make them.' So I got up, although I wanted just to stay in bed, and make love all day long – not speak of dreams, but make things I could dream of. I got up, took my pile clothes off, got dressed for the long ride, then packed my bags while Bastian made the beds. I longed to say, 'Please, let's stay here and have more sex; I want more sex.' I said instead, 'I've never dreamt Akkadian. But if I did, it would be quite important that you help me to untie my dream, as Enkidu helped Gilgamesh.'

Sebastian stopped what he was doing, just a pause, and said, 'Untie your dream? And how untie it? Was it first, then, tied? And tied by whom?'

'The dialect that Gilgamesh was written in has the verb *pasaru*, to untie. In the epic, dreams are dangerous, and it is always necessary to untie them. The verb is used three ways. First, just to report a dream, second, to have the dream interpreted by the person to whom you tell it. Last, *pasaru* means that magic – cunning – will be used to take away the evil consequences.'

'Yes. I remember now,' Sebastian said. 'Let's go, let's go. We have to go now, Emrys.' And so we went, and drove all day again. I couldn't help but wonder what the rush was – why it was so vital we get to Thurso. But I said nothing since I knew that if I waited, night would come again, and we would stop. The sky was clear today; it still seemed very cold to me, but luckily the heater in the Jeep was working. Sebastian's mood had changed just as the weather had. And while I had no thought to ask the rain why it had blown away, I wondered what had happened in the night to make Sebastian rush like this. He'd rushed the day before, but had, it seemed, done it from habit more than will. Now it seemed his will which drove him; and he seemed only sometimes to remember that I was with him as we drove, and did not sense at all how much I wanted him.

Yet I was hungry for his body – so hungry I could hardly believe we'd made love only hours before. This was the hunger that was fed by what it fed on. We drove. Sebastian talked, from time to time, when he glanced over, and saw me sitting there beside him. He talked about his tomb, and how he'd found it in a place where he had thought, from studying maps, a tomb might be. He talked about the way that megaliths all over Europe were set on ley lines, since the man who first had drawn them on a map, and linked them up – long lines drawn through stone dots – had noticed that the lines were drawn like ropes through places which, in modern times, had names which ended with a *ley*. He'd thought the lines had first been drawn in minds, and then upon the earth; he'd thought the neolithic peoples had traced them on the land, and then had pinned them to the world with standing stones and tombs and mounds and other earthworks.

71

But though, Sebastian said, he had been right that there were lines that megaliths were found to lie on, these lines were really paths of energy. And this was not made up, but something that, for sixty years now, had been tested by dowsers who felt, under the place they walked, blind springs that felt like water.

'There's water underneath them?' I asked, now lying on his lap, as I had lain the day before, but now, so ravenous for Bastian's body, I would have had him enter me while he was driving if such a thing were possible.

'Not water, no,' he said. 'That's what's so strange. These are blind springs. The dowsers call them that, as if it is the water which, on looking up, cannot see *them*. It feels them walking with their dowsing sticks, because it tugs them down. I've seen this done. I did it once myself, and felt the tug, as if a rope had caught the stick, then let it go. Quite strange and wonderful.'

'But there's no water? None at all?'

'It's something else. They think there may be deviations in the local geomagnetic fields. At megalithic sites, but most particularly at henges, these fields of energy converge. The standing stones seem like a kind of needle, acupuncture for the earth, which, set where energies are strong, will channel them.'

I listened to this, liked it. But my energies were strong enough so that I wished Sebastian would stop talking. Stop driving, too, and park the Jeep, and let us go off through the moors, cold as it was, to find some blind springs of our own and lie on them. Sometimes he did stop talking, and looked down on me and smiled, or touched my arm; sometimes he reached out to take my hand in his, then place my hand upon his knee, and with his hand above mine, mold it there.

And when he talked of getting back to Long Holm, he said, 'When we get home,' quite unselfconscious about the way he chose to phrase this.

But then he talked of something else again, of querns, and how he'd found a quern on Long Holm, near his tomb. He talked of how the grooved ware which was found at Skara Brae – the Unstan ware as well – must have been baked in quite a hot kiln. He talked of Skara Brae, where we would go before we went to Long Holm. A hundred years before, the sands of Skaill Bay had blown off, revealing underneath a neolithic village. Each house, Sebastian said, was shaped just like a body; he found it strange not everyone could see this. Each house had, as its center, one big room, square-round. He said this was the dwelling's penetralia.

'Its what?'

'The inmost parts, or recesses, of a building. Especially of a temple, where the inner shrine or sanctuary is. But at Skara Brae, each house was its own temple. There was an altar placed in each – some idiot archeologists call these altars "cupboards." And around the penetralia, the outer rooms are arms and legs, but curled up – curled up just as you are.'

And I was, then, again. Curled up upon his lap, and hoping that he'd stop the car. But we drove on and on, Sebastian tearing toward the north, and talking to the drivers whom he passed and left behind. And not just where there was a sign which said, as these signs said, 'This Is A Passing Place,' but any time he wished. 'Get on with it, my boy,' he said, screeching round a curve, or, 'There's an end to all things, isn't there, my girl?' And then, the cars behind him, he would slow down just a bit, and glance down, or, if I was sitting, over at me. He glanced at me as if he half remembered me from somewhere.

We got to Thurso; *god*, I felt, *at last, an end to all things, after all*, and then went on to Scrabster, upon the Pentland Firth. We checked into the pub where Bastian always stayed when he was there. And though I wanted to go right up to our room and rip our clothes off, Sebastian, who had hurried all day long, now seemed to lose his urgency. He asked me if I'd like to take a walk down to the sea, and though I had no wish to see the sea or anything but him – naked before me – I said, 'Of course. I'd like to stretch my legs a bit.' So we walked down, together, striding, as we did, as if one stride had been designed for both of us. Sebastian took my hand, and at the beach we stopped and looked out at the sea which we would sail tomorrow. The sea birds were just buff and brown, and did not speak in English, but they soared up against the sky, dropped down, and grabbed bright fish, then flew away with them.

I saw them, saw the sea they took the fish from, saw the sky they flew against, as if they'd pin the fish to sky like scraps of bunting. And as I saw them, though I did not lose the lust I felt, I also felt a bad, bad memory start to nudge me. I didn't want it. Pushed it away. Ignored the birds, and watched, instead of birds, a line of white across the bay. It went from land to land, with inlet in between. Perhaps a reef lay underneath it. As ocean hit the rock, it circled back, creating foam that was a line of white which went across the inlet. It smashed against the cliffs, the waves there seeking entry in the wall of stone they suddenly confronted. But as they were refused this, they curled sideways, reaching out like a paintbrush, dipped in thick white paint, and then drawn right across the edge of rock it painted. I showed this to Sebastian.

He said, 'Yes, it's a reef. There are a lot of hazards here to shipping. The skerries are the worst of them; all skerries save the one off Long Holm twice a day become invisible.'

And as he said this, *hazards*, I found that I could not – as I had wished to – push the thought right from consciousness. It was the birds that did it, the birds against the sun, which now moved toward the west, with red around it. When I'd been five, the sky had looked like that, the night I almost drowned – although the water had been lake, not ocean. At five, I could not swim. I wore a dress that night, a white dress, lace around its hem. I had on small black shoes, white socks, a necklace. There'd been a dock which led out from the land, and I walked out onto that dock, planning to take my shoes off. I got distracted, walking, when I looked up and saw, against the setting sun, some birds that seemed as if they had been pinned there. I lifted up my hand to point to them – my hand went toward the heavens – and so I walked right off the dock.

Yes, even though it ended, I walked on, as many walk in dreams – as legends have it silkies walk on islands. But I was walking water, treading time as I went down, and as the water closed above my body. I was quite young, and therefore not at all afraid; I treaded time, and looked up at the lake above me. And it was just so lovely; the world, in one bright spark, became a great round tub of light, a perfect mirrored thing of silver. I saw it, thought it lovely, but noticed that the dress had floated up and now pushed on my eyes, my mouth, my nostrils. And it was then I noticed that a kind of holding started. I tried to push the dress away with both my hands. But at the same time, I was

75

forced to hold my breath. I held and held my breath until it hurt, and then hurt more. And now the lake above me, which had been a perfect circled mirror, became quite hateful to me. It was no longer a great shining pot of light, but just an ugly tub of time that I was held by.

And not just held by, tied by: I knew there'd come a time when I would suck it toward my mouth, and it would force its way into my body. I held my breath, though, held my breath until the time I could not hold it any longer. I had to breathe. The air rushed from my body. It seemed to me that all the breath I'd ever drawn was leaving me, as bubbles, and then I choked on water, on stale and fishy water, on horrid water, pushing into me. And though, just then, my father pulled me out, by just one wrist – he jerked me, and I lived – I would remember, all my life, that choking feeling. So many fears had come from that first fear that I had felt when I was five, and now, tomorrow, I'd take my first trip in a boat, and tell Sebastian he could add a fear of water to the rest of them. For now, I wished to just forget it, and go up to our room, where Bastian would take my mind off anything but him again. When we were just the two of us in bed, there were no fears for me, except the fear of losing Bastian. And that fear, I believed, would soon be left behind, as he and I set sail for land that Gilgamesh called Faraway; that land would have new frames, a brand-new way to hold the world, and there would be things contained in it. Our love, I thought, could heal all wounds, all pain, and fix the world so it would be unsinkable.

5

THAT NIGHT, THOUGH, BASTIAN drank. We walked back from the sea, and I was wet, as I was always wet then. I wanted him to take me hard and fierce as any danger which, so long ago, had threatened me. I wanted him to take away the hurt I felt remembering the lake, by covering it with joy, and burying it forever. As we walked up, still holding hands, our strides alike, I thought it odd that he, who knew my body almost as if he'd made it, did not know that same body had almost drowned once. Oh, well, I'd tell him when the time came. Now, I merely wanted him. I felt that I had earned him, through the long day I had waited. But when we got back to the pub, he pulled a chair up to a table; he seemed to know the people who sat drinking. And though he gestured to the chair beside him, he did not introduce me.

Instead, he ordered food and drink for both of us without first asking me what I would like, then said to one man, who sat with us, 'How is Sarah? Is the cast off?' and to another, 'What was the catch this week, then, Charlie?' How could it be that Bastian would not know how much I wanted him? It made me almost sick to watch the way the women at the table – one fat, one thin, and both quite homely – smiled at him, and seemed to flirt, while he encouraged this. He said, 'My girl, not *really?*' And though some people at the table tried to include me in their talk, I felt unfriendly. Sullen. Indeed, I sat and brooded. The food came quickly, and I ate quickly, thinking that, if I did, Sebastian would take me up to bed then. But now a new man joined the table – a man called Tait – who seemed to know about Sebastian's work on Long Holm. He said, 'So have you found another knuckle bone?' to which Sebastian shook his head, and said, 'I don't think I deserved the one. It was a kind of miracle.'

But when he said these words, his mood appeared to shift yet more – and not in any good direction. He drank his drink, and did not talk, but stared into the lager as if he sought to see a secret in its bubbles. What secret could there be? I thought. And yet upon his face was that same bright blank look that I had seen in London the first time we had met there, when he had asked me if the man he thought my husband was a man who truly did not think that people should be punished. It was a hooded look, the kind of look a bird of prey must cast down on an empty ocean. I said, 'Sebastian, let's go up,' to which he said, 'I think I'll have another, just to untie my dreams a bit.' He seemed to think this funny, but to me, to joke of *Gilgamesh and Enkidu* seemed a thing he'd only do to hurt me. And I felt hurt enough by then, as he had lager after lager.

I just could not believe this. For one brief moment he'd been mine – or so I'd thought – when I'd been his, but now he seemed to be deserting me. Whatever secrets he might see within the beer he drank, I thought, he did not see the secrets *I* was keeping. The next day, I must tell him I was scared of water, I had never sailed on any ship, and when we got to Long Holm, I must tell him I was scared of tombs as well – that I had never entered one. I'd thought he'd care, that he would help me with these things, but now he seemed – had seemed all day – indifferent to me. I hated how this made me feel. It hurt my throat. It made it ache. It made me feel just desperate, just savage. And when at last I'd coaxed him from his final drink, and up to bed, and we had put the mattresses upon the floor, I felt a way I'd never felt in bed before. Quite cunning. He'd said, as we came up the stairs – he was a little drunk, though he could hold a lot of liquor – 'Perhaps we should just sleep tonight.' To this I'd said, 'Yes, probably.'

And then, when we had reached the room, I'd changed into my pile clothes, as if I would just sleep as he had said we should. I lay beside him, facing him, not touching. His eyes were closed. Outside, the lights of the pub's porch were glimmering through the window, so that I saw Sebastian's eyes, his beard, the broad planes of his cheekbones as he lay naked. We kissed, a light kiss, he reluctant – or punishing, I thought, though I could not think what I had done to anger him. And I, so cunning, knew that I could use this hard reluctance – could make it serve me just by tugging it. I gave him one kiss, then another, and with each quick kiss went deeper, but still not touching him with my body. I flicked my tongue into his mouth, and then I flicked it out again. I moved my body oh-so-accidentally, and brushed him on the thigh. 'Oh sorry,' I said, and pulled away, wondering how much of my cunning he sensed, and how much he could not sense – dulled, then, by liquor.

'You do drive hard,' I said, and stopped the kisses,

putting out my hand to touch his beard, and then his lower lip, as if to say goodbye now.

At that, he pulled me to him. Said, 'My god, these clothes again. What woman comes to bed in clothes?'

'I thought I would just sleep,' I said.

'But not in all these clothes. Just take them off, for god's sake, Emrys.'

'All right,' I said. 'The room is warm. I think we're right above the kitchen.' I took my clothes off slowly. I let him watch me through half-closed eyes, then lay down beside him once again, and put my head upon his shoulder, at which he touched me on the neck, as if he wondered something. I let him touch my neck, then moved my neck so that the place my throat hurt took his hand upon it. His hand, in falling there, constricted, just a little, the flow of air into my body. He felt it, knew that it had happened. He didn't move his hand until I sank my head against his chest. At that, he touched my hair with the same hand he'd held against my neck. He laced his fingers through it, and tugged it lightly, and when he did, I pulled away, so he would know it hurt, this pulling.

He pulled again, I pulled away; it did not hurt at all, I was so hot and wet, so savage with the lust I felt. He liked his women bare? I thought. He'd have me bare. Untie his dreams by drinking? No, I didn't think so. I realized that I wanted him so badly that I wished to hurt him. But I knew, too – so cunning – that if I were to get what I most wanted, it would be better if I took the hurt on me. And as he pulled my hair – my hair like seaweed on a rock, and tugged by tides, quite hard – he felt the hurt, as he felt everything that lay in hidden places. Then he let go. I moaned against his chest, and he let go my hair, then said, 'And if I take you, will you sleep with me tonight? Right in my arms?' to which I said, 'Of course, Sebastian.'

At that, he moved away, reached out to where his bag sat on the floor, did what he thought he must, then pushed inside me. And there was nothing slow about this push, and nothing gentle; he pushed hard, just filled me suddenly, so suddenly it forced my breath from me. I heard this, heard my breath, my own breath in my ears, and loved the sound of it, a shout of triumph. I stretched my arms above my head again, but this time did not feel as if I were a starfish, or a net, but something which might catch the wind in it. I felt, perhaps, a vessel, a sailing ship so strong, so balanced on the sea, it could take any wind that might be thrown at it. And now Sebastian was the wind, pushing inside me, while I pushed my arms above my head, wide open to him. I wished he'd take my hands, and pin them there, in place, as if he tied me to a mast, or made me be a sail for him from wrists to ankles.

But he had something else in mind. On one hard thrust, he paused, then stopped, and raised himself, upon his arms, above me. He looked at me, and smiled, and said, 'You are so hot,' and then went in again, but slowly, now. 'For someone who is always cold, you have the hottest cunt I've ever entered, Emrys.' I laughed a little at this, quite surprised. No one had ever said a thing like this to me before, yet it seemed somehow likely to be true, though sounding so unlikely. 'A furnace,' said Sebastian. 'The peat stove that I have on Long Holm. A kiln to make a beaker in.' Then he slid in again, as if to warm himself within this fire he spoke of, and this was slow and sweet, until he stopped, rolled off, and said, 'Turn over, Emrys, on your tummy.' I did, and felt Sebastian lift my hips in place, and wait for me to get my knees right, to balance on my elbows, let my hair fall in my palms, and then he put himself inside me once again, and this time he just filled up every part of me.

I moaned, as he was once again within me – moaned so loud it might have been a shout that carried to the rooms below us. I could not help it, pub or no pub, men below us drinking, men gone home, the breath that was inside me must push out now. He held my buttocks in his hands, held them in place, and then he pushed, as deep as he could push, inside me; it felt he pushed right to my core, as if he were the strongest wind that ever took a vessel. Had I been that – a ship upon the rocks – he would have knocked me back to sea again, but as it was, he held my buttocks, kept me anchored. Each time he pushed, I moaned, a great hard exhalation of desire, as if the breath that filled my lungs now filled more than just lungs, the breath was everywhere. In fact, each thrust, each gust, each hit was breath that was exhaled like all the winds of earth, which, now a storm, had first been gathered in a single valley.

'Oh god,' I said, and then again, 'Oh god,' or maybe it was something less articulate, less formed, less molded than two words together. I did not think then, but think now, that Bastian that afternoon had spoken of the quern which he had found on Long Holm. He'd spoken of the way the turning of the pestle on the stone below would grind the grain to powder, and over time the stone itself would change, as year fell into year, and grain was ground on it. He thrust and thrust again, and since I'd never come that way, not once in all my life, I thought I could not, not without Bastian doing something more than thrusting. But although he, as I discovered, was not good in every sea, he knew this one as if he were Poseidon. And when he came, I came, and almost shouted, 'God, I came,' and then collapsed beneath his body. He lay upon my back, put his mouth near to my ear, and said (a mirror answer to the thing I'd really said), 'Of course you came. Did I not say you were a kiln to me?'

That night, Sebastian thought I slept with him. I let him think it when he woke, and did try, when he went to sleep, to make it true. He rolled down off my body, running his hands over my back, and then, as if he were a child upon a harvest hill, just falling off me. He took me in his arms, putting one arm beneath my neck, the other around my waist, as if he had no doubts at all that it was he who was cunctipotent. And then he fell away to sleep, as he had fallen from my back, and right away was dreaming. At least he twitched, his body jerking like a dog's when hunting in its sleep again, although this time, as I thought of the sea-crossing we would make tomorrow, I thought that maybe sleep, for him, might be a kind of drowning. And if it was, no wonder that he wanted someone else's company when he must thus go underneath the water. For me, sleep was, quite often, all too light, not deep enough; that was the reason why I could not sleep while touching someone. But if, when darkness dropped across your eyes, you fell into a trough from which there might be no returning, then what you needed most from someone else would be to know that they would lift you safely from the place you'd fallen.

I could not sleep, though, with the twitching. I slept alone. But that night I was naked, and woke to find Sebastian still asleep beside me. So I moved into the half-opened circle of his arms, and when he woke, he thought I'd been there all night long. He grinned, a true grin, maybe the first true grin I'd ever seen from him, then said, 'I told you so. I told you you could sleep with me.' He pulled me to him, smelled my hair, and said, 'So now we cross the water,' and though I felt quite pliant, quite relaxed, like something that had yielded for all time, I also wished the time had not arrived when I must tell Sebastian I feared water.

In fact, I put it off, still. We got up, dressed and packed, then took our bags down to the desk, had breakfast, paid, and packed the Jeep. We drove the Jeep onto the ship, and left it on the car deck, then walked above to one great open deck from which we could observe the sea. We once again saw sea birds wheeling, saw the line of white that went from shore to shore, but this time also looked at great steel plates and bolts, at great steel cables. We walked through gleaming doors, and through the cabins which had been named the Viking Lounge, the Hoy View Grill, the Noost. Sebastian picked a place they'd named the Skerries Lounge for us to sit upon two facing padded benches.

'It may get rough,' he said. 'The Pentland Firth is wild. It's called a dirty sea in Scotland, and is famous for its weather.'

'How did *they* cross it, do you think? The neolithic peoples?'

'With sail, I think. The puzzle was how they could know that, though the country to the south – in what is Scotland now – was just a mighty forest, hard to work with stone, Orkney did not have a single tree upon it. They must have been quite brave to sail this sea on just a dream, in any case. They knew they were unlikely to get back again.'

'Me, too,' I said.

'What do you mean? You think I won't let you go back?'

'No, no. I'm scared of water, Bastian. I almost drowned once.'

He looked at me.

'But you can swim?'

'A little. Just a little. I'm like a dog, but not. Dogs like the water, I think. They don't just panic.'

'And you do? Well, now I see where your obsession came from. But these are not the Waters of Death, my dear. This ferry's safe as houses.' He said this very kindly, though as I write it down, it doesn't seem that kind without a tone to it. He added, as the ship began to move, 'You *are* brave, Emrys.'

At that, I touched him on the head and said, 'Not brave. Just crazy about you.'

He chuckled, said, 'Or maybe simply crazy.'

Yes, maybe simply crazy. Because, although a little time went by when the great ship was stable underneath us, once it had crossed the bay and turned into the sea, all things were changed in just an instant. I looked out of the window, saw a mist, or fog, which seemed suddenly to have blown there. It was not fog exactly, but the wind out on the Firth, blowing across the waves so hard it cut them. Yes, cut them like a knife – Sebastian told me this, that wind could slice the waves so that they looked quite flat beneath it. Above the waves the water looked like smoke or fog, although it was just ocean torn from where it lay, and tossed up skywards. And as we moved into this smoke, the ship began to twist; it was a huge ship, yet it tilted first to one side, then the other. It had become as light as paper, as light as tissue-thin fine cloth – a silken pennon or a sail that, on the next roll, might be tossed up into the sky just like the water. It tilted, then came down, and was not paper, or cloth, but stone; it fell upon the sea like a tree falling there.

The ship first pivoted, then fell, then pivoted again until, in just five minutes, it felt as if my insides, too, had been unmoored, as if my organs floated freely. We were still in the lounge. Sebastian sat beside me and read; he really read, it was incredible. I groaned, and fell against him. He put out one hot hand, and steadied me, then put his arm around my shoulder. He said, 'Remember something. Think of something, anything at all. It helps to try and keep the mind in place, when you feel seasick.'

'I can't,' I said.

'Well, try.'

'How can I?'

'We've two hours ahead of us. This storm will last until we're past St John's Head, into Hoy Sound. You have to try to tie your brain to something.'

'Well, talk to me, then. Talk.'

'All right.' He put the book down. He said, 'Did you know *Pentland Firth* means Southern Sea in Norse? It . . .'

'No, never mind. Don't talk to me. Forget it. Hold me. Help me. Oh, my god, Sebastian.'

'Not god. The Reverenced. From Greek. That's all it means.'

'Well, shut the fuck up, then,' I said. He laughed at me. But though he laughed, he held me, told me to lie down, to put my head upon his lap, look through the window, try to fix my eyes on the horizon. This helped, or sometimes helped. Fix eyes upon the place where sea and sky meet, then take up any line of thought and follow it. I tried, but the horizon was not there, or was obscured by all the water that the sea had smoked. As for the line of thought, the only one which came to me was dark; it was, again, of drownings. Not mine, this time, but ones that I'd encountered long ago, and that I had not thought about for thirty years or more. As I lay on the ship, and tried to think, I found them there, within my mind, like great wrought cables not quite cast from it. For thirty years I'd dragged them with me, and now upon the day I'd told Sebastian about the day I'd gone into the lake, I found myself returning there. To deeps, old memories, times when I had been a child who had not yet discovered the tale of Gilgamesh. When I had not yet seen him safely over the Waters of Death, ships had been things which always sank for me.

This was because I came from inland, where no one ever saw the sea, but tales of shipwreck were quite common. And not just tales, but songs, and children's books, and all the history of war; all these had come to me, because I was a reading child. *This ferry's safe as houses*, Sebastian had said, but feeling how the ship now fell away beneath me, I doubted that. I thought of how a ship, when it went down, created a great vortex with its passage from the air to water, and how, into that vortex, went the whole great crafted house that was the house of any voyaging. I'd read a book when I was young, about a girl who had been sailing, in a century now gone, to meet her fiancé and marry him. And then, the story went, the ship had hit a hidden reef, just one short mile from the harbor, and she'd never made it there.

She'd seen the lights of rescue, but had been borne upon the rolling tide of oceans, until she was too heavy to be borne by them. Her mouth was pushed by water, and I, a reading child who'd almost drowned herself, had dwelled upon that moment, the moment when she lay there, her hair like seaweed wet upon her cheek, the night as black as pitch, though lights did prick it. Nor was that all. For just as she, that girl, had gone down in the sea, so, too, I now remembered, had a cabin boy. He was the song; it all came flooding back, the cabin boy who'd wished to win a bride and had been fooled by his own captain. And so he'd drowned – after a feat of strength which saved his ship – and then he had been sewn into his hammock and thrown back in the sea again. Was this, then, how to keep the mind in place? I thought. The girl, the boy, both drowned, both tied, both falling like stones into the water?

I clung to Bastian, who, in turn, held onto me – one hand upon the book that he could somehow read, one hand upon my stomach where the sickness was. Oh, god, I thought, please stop this. Oh, god, I thought, please stop. And then the ship lay flat again for just a little while, but long enough so that, this time, the greatest ship of all came sailing, from the place it had been moored in me. The greatest ship and greatest shipwreck, the ship named after Titans; who could have thought its name auspicious? I groaned. Sebastian patted me. But there it was, and sailing once again within my mind, as it had sailed when I'd first seen the night time stopped for it. I saw it now again, the moment when the women, with the children they had borne, set out in boats, and left the men they'd loved behind them. That moment made me sick because I felt that it *was* sick, that people who'd been joined by love itself should do this, should choose to come apart, that one should live and one should die, when they had promised, once, to die together.

I clung to Bastian, still. Black thoughts, and now I knew, as I had not known as a child what it would really be to leave the person who had lifted you from some deep sunless place to which you'd fallen. I'd been with Bastian just four days, had known him just three weeks, and all my life before seemed like a sea-smoke I would die before I'd sail back into. And now, in thinking about shipwrecks, deaths at sea, I thought that what was worst about a death by drowning was that, until the very end, you could feel hope you would survive it. Hope that, against all odds, the night on which you floated would be lit by lights of rescue. Hope that a hand would grab your wrist which stretched, still, toward the sky, and that that hand would jerk you back from where you foundered.

Yes, that seemed harder than all else, that there was hope, and hope, and hope, and then a moment when that hope was wiped out, razed from the world of light, like something sucked into a final vortex. And having Bastian now was having life, and hope; he seemed the only thing in all the world to cling to. I'd never felt like this before, not once, with any man – that if he were to leave me, I would die without him. And now, as I just clung to him, I thought of when he'd said, *What woman comes to bed in clothes?* and when he'd said when I had told him that he twitched in sleep, *Yes, others, too, have told me this.* I'd seen, I'd known, both times – had known before he spoke – that he had had, before me, other women. But now, this scared me badly; I went from black sick thoughts of drowning, shipwrecks – deaths that I had long forgotten – to something else now. I clung to Bastian, still, but now I thought of how, although he'd saved me once, he'd also brought me here to this wild sea, then told me I was crazy to come with him.

But was I crazy? No, I thought. I knew what crazy was. It was to have the life you loved just cut in half for you. And when I'd been that way, half-crazy – halved in every way there was – I'd had no way of seeing that up ahead in my own life there might be some new gateway. But now I knew there was. Now I had met him, my male self. Like someone lifting a swimmer from the sea, he had revived me. But now I felt so sick it seemed less good that Bastian was the only place where I could take the rope that was my mind and fling it on a spike which would, if I was lucky, hold me. He'd saved me once, but would he do the same again, if I should ever need it, or would he leave me, as so many lovers had been left upon the deck of the *Titanic?* He'd gotten drunk the night before, had flirted with the women at the table where we sat, had said to me, *Perhaps we should just sleep tonight*. And now he'd brought me out upon this sea that was as wild, as dirty, rough, as any sea upon the face of heaven. Indeed, for all that he had said, *This ferry's safe as houses*, I knew that no ship that went out upon the Pentland Firth was safe; a thousand thousand ships had beat themselves to death on Orkney's shores, some people – few – surviving.

The ones who had survived had not gone home again, but stayed, to live forever in the islands. A galleon wandering from the great Armada had made it this far north, and had been wrecked upon the rocks of Ronaldsay. Each splintered board and tattered piece of sail which chance had washed up to the shore had brought a gasping man from death to life again. And then, with time and care, the Spaniards had grown whole, to marry women who had once been Norse, and then been Scots, and now were pure Orcadian. They had been changed, those men, by the great crossing that they'd made; they knew that they could never go back home again. And there was no thought, either, of a trip back to the south for all the neolithic peoples who had made it here. They'd known that they were here to stay, the crossing of the Pentland Firth a grave for any thoughts of going back to shores that they had come from. Could I, I wondered, if I wished to, cross this sea again? Or did you get to cross it one time only?

And I felt sick, just oh-so-sick, at this dark thought, and others – *Others, too, have told me this* – that I got up from where I lay upon the bench. I stood, unsteadily, while Bastian looked surprised. He asked me where I headed. I said, 'The sea.' I walked across the tilting deck, then felt that I was climbing it as you might climb a mountain. But I got to the doors and pushed outside and headed toward the rail. I thought I'd vomit there, if I could make it. The ship slipped sideways, drew the finger of its hull right through the trough, then hit the bulwark of the sea beside it. A wall of spray arched overhead and broke, then fell like stones around me.

It hurt, this water, as it hit me, hit again, and hurt, and I – in opening my mouth – could taste it. I turned around, bent double, to lurch across the deck again, wet to the skin now. The water fell still, stones upon my head. The swells the ship was hitting were like mountains. But I, with struggle, opened up the gleaming silver doors, which closed behind me, bringing silence. I still was sick. The ship still rose and fell, the deck within like the deck without, a thing that had to bend and change beneath me. I thought I'd find a bathroom, but the ship now pushed me up, and sent me falling toward the wall beside me. And there, as I put out one hand to catch myself, I found the hand which caught me also pinned me. I could not move, just leaned there like a starfish spreading wide, resisting all the force of oceans.

Now, as I leaned there, hand on wall, my eyes followed my hand to where it spread, and as it spread, it pointed. I saw that I had fallen on a map of Orkney under glass, a map which seemed quite lit by all the light around me. Indeed, as I was held there, pinned by time, the map seemed like a shining silver lozenge. For just a moment, it was like a great round tub of light, and I, a drowning child, looked up at it. And as I did, two words sprang out at me like sparks of light, or ten bright bubbles. Bring Deeps, they said. Bring Deeps seemed all the world at that one instant, and then the ship was tilted back, the ocean freed me, and I lurched across the room, and lay back down upon the bench which Bastian still was sitting on.

My head on Bastian's lap, the words I'd caught, Bring Deeps, went with me. I held my hands upon my stomach. Sebastian placed his hands on me, to soothe me, but it seemed to me by then I would have chosen death over this sickness. I closed my eyes, then opened them again, and looked, and saw our four crossed hands upon my stomach; they seemed just then a sculpture we had made, the top of a stone sepulcher. Bring Deeps, I thought, what did that mean, Bring Deeps? It was, I'd seen, a channel in the sea of Orkney. Bring Deeps, ten bubbles I'd exhaled once; Bring Deeps, two short black pennons which had been caught upon a reef, the reef of me. And when, at last, I vomited, in a paper cup, and brought forth, with a different kind of bringing, what felt like things that I would die to lose, Sebastian held me tenderly, and said, 'Poor girl. But it won't last forever, Emrys.'

At this I thought: *I know it won't, oh god, I know it won't. What I don't know is what I'm doing here with you, upon a sea so wild, and filled with deeps which fall like stones around me.*

6

BUT I SEEMED ONCE again to know why I was there when we had reached Hoy Sound and passed the Ness into the harbor. The water there was calm as if it never had been rough, and Bastian was even calmer. Except when we were making love – or eating, sleeping, packing – he had been driving ever since he'd met me at the airport, and driving fast and hard. Now, as we walked down to the Jeep, Sebastian seemed relaxed, as if some alchemy had changed him in the ocean crossing. As if – at home at last – he had no need to hunt, since what he hunted he had landed on. Indeed, it seemed that Orkney was the place which was, for him, the lodestone, hub, the center of the four directions. He pulled the Jeep down off the ramp, and onto land, and said, 'Well, Emrys. Here we are. I hope you like this place.'

And I did like this place. I liked it most because it suited him – because it seemed the landscape he was made for. The landscapes I had known had all been hotter, drier, harder – bigger, somehow, when you looked across them. They also had been treeless, as Orkney was, but there on Orkney it seemed as if the land had not been measured off against a too-great space. I think it changed the way I saw it that, when we landed, I was emptied out – the three weeks of my love and sickness left me blank and clarified. As a result, all the impressions that I had of those green islands were so strong that they rushed into me and took up lodging. Indeed, it seemed, that first day that I saw it – and seems still – that Orkney was the place that other places came from. Or should have come from, anyway, a sort of clay all other places in the world must carve their names on. Because it was four things, just four and intermixed, so that the patterns seemed to mingle. It was the sea around it, touching it with many-fingered hands; it was the sky above it, which kept it pinned in place; it was the rock, grey rock, with long green hair; and last, it was the wind that blew it.

Indeed, the wind rarely stopped blowing, and the clouds, if clouds there were that day – and there were clouds most days, though sunlight also – never stopped throwing moving shadows. The air was clean and clear, the coastlines long and empty, the hills seemed higher when you'd climbed them than you would think they were from seeing them. And green. Orkney was green, a land with western hills and lowlands on the east, the lowlands running down to sheltered bays – broad, cultivated lowlands, with sheep that grazed on all the green stone walls around them. The mighty cliffs were all upon the west, where weather hit, and they were quite alive with sea birds. And on the east, a lot of geos – natural harbors for small boats. Noost Geo, many of them were named, I found. The Viking history of Orkney was not visible on the land, but it was everywhere in names, and once I knew what things were called, the landscape took on different shades of meaning.

Like Pentland Firth, or Southern Sea, it hooked the ocean back to memories of empire. That empire had, for a short time, ruled all the seas that it encountered. Before the empire fell, the islands had been given to Scotland as the dowry of a princess. That day, I saw or learned a part of this as we drove south. When we got off the ferry, and onto land again, all my sickness left me. And when it did, I felt quite filled with love again, and ready to do anything that Bastian suggested. He had a room for us in Kirkwall, which wasn't far from Stromness, and we could reach it by the west–east road in less than half an hour. Despite the crossing we had made, which had seemed endless while it happened, it was not even noon yet, and now Sebastian said he'd like to show me Mainland. To show me Scapa Flow, perhaps, and then, perhaps, the henges.

'I'd love to see the henges,' I said.

'I bet you would,' he said. 'You're made for them.'

So he drove south, and not as he had driven us before, but slowly, while I rolled my window down to breathe the cold clear air of Orkney. The first place Bastian turned was at a bay just named The Bush; from there we headed down to Orphir, Place of Ebbing. We parked and looked back west, where we could see – as I saw from the map Sebastian held before him – Bring Deeps again.

'Why do they call it that?' I asked. 'What does it mean? I like it.'

'I like it, too.' He gave me half the map to hold, then pointed at a spot on Hoy called Bring Head.

'They must have named Bring Deeps from that,' he said. 'You'll find that Orkney's very sexy.' Then he took back the map, and folded it, and put his arm around my shoulder, and we both stood and looked at Scapa Flow, its vast vast waters, ten miles square, before us. We were quite silent for a minute, then Bastian said, 'You know of Gunther Prime, who made it through? That's sexy, too, I think.'

'You find death sexy, Bastian?'

'Not death. Just men like that, who risk it all and make it back alive. Even Churchill said that he was very brave.' And then he looked at me, and smiled, and there was no look in his eyes – not then – which said, *So, OK, Emrys, prove it*. Why would there be? With one word, *death*, I'd proved I knew the story he was thinking. He smiled, I smiled, and it was one of those rare moments when you know that someone else's thought, unspoken, is the perfect mirror of yours. We turned back, smiling, to the Flow; it was so flat, so large, and so enclosed, that once Great Britian's warships had felt safe here, within this harbor. They'd thought, as they looked all around them at the walls of land – like brick walls, but no need to make them – that there was not an enemy in the world who could get through and harm them here. But Gunther Prime, a German U-boat captain, had taken in his submarine through waters it could not be taken through.

Yes, who could have imagined it? It was a thought that no one else had had, since Holm Sound was so narrow and so shallow. But Prime, on a dark night when there was no moon in the sky, had taken in his submarine. He'd sailed above the water, and once he'd made it through he'd sunk an aircraft carrier. A thousand men had died that night. At first, the other ships thought there had been a rupture in the carrier's engine room. But no. Just one torpedo blew the ship up. And Gunther Prime had turned around and sailed back through the Pentland Firth to Bremerhaven. After – only after – had the Churchill Barriers been built, too late, as was inevitable. So when, that rare sweet moment, Sebastian and I both smiled, our eyes one eye, it wasn't because we thought death was sexy. Rather it was because we both thought it quite wondrous that, out of all the world, we should have met another person who saw the sea we looked at as a symbol of vain hoping.

Then we drove north to Stenness, that vision still within our minds – that safe, safe haven that was not safe at all, in fact. When we arrived, Sebastian parked and we climbed once more from the Jeep, at which I noticed right away that everything at Stenness was circled. Because there were no trees, the circles could be seen for what they were, just clear as clear, and moving inward. At Stenness, there were hills on every side, around a shallow bowl where the stone slabs stood. The loch made semicircles, pushing at the land, the white-caps tiny semicircles of water. And there were also clouds which threw round stains upon the land, before they hurried on to paint another island. I stood and breathed the air, and looked at sheep, rock walls, and hills, but mostly at the mighty standing stones which stood like magnets for the mind and body.

Sebastian took my hand. He said, 'Come with me, Emrys,' and led me to the circle that was waiting. I walked into this circle, Sebastian at my side, his hand in mine, and felt the earth just turn me, like a sail, into a thing which had a new direction. It was the place, the circles, stones, Sebastian, too, although Sebastian was a man – a man who walked, and threw up both his hands, and walked away, and then walked back, and said, 'Turn here. I want you.' He had two hands which could be, if he chose, like butterflies just blowing at our lips, or could be, if he chose, like weights upon me. The Stones were stones, though, and

97

they may not be so easy to explain – in words – as any man, or any woman either. There were long legends all through Scotland about walking stones – as if no one could doubt that standing stones were almost human – and it is true that at the instant that I came within their arms, I felt they were a part of my own species. I felt that they, who had been pulled by men from where they'd lain quite flat within the earth, and then had been brought here into this circle, had known the men who brought them here as well as anyone could know a person.

But they were stones, not men. Real stones. They did not walk. They were real stones, they'd stood here on this land for five millennia. They'd stood, near to the loch, near to the firth, and feeling on their backs the shadows of the clouds that moved above them. Their tops were cut diagonally when they'd been carved out of the ground, so that they looked like fingers pointing up to heaven. Toward stars that pricked the night like needles sewing a black cloak; toward clouds that painted clouds upon the earth below them. And toward the sun as well, a sun that, when it rose and set, might stain the sky blood-red, might make the birds that swam before it look like pennons. The stones had not grown tired, not fallen asleep, but had, instead, let time run off them like water. Some of the stones had fallen. Four of the twelve remained. Yet where the eight had been, there was, still, something strong, a field of energy so great it was like speech – the ley line. But some who had encountered Stenness had not heard this speech, since, in the last hundred years, some men and women had carved graffiti on them.

We walked around, and looked at this. Sebastian grimaced at the names and dates, the strings of letters. To him, it was just desecration. To me, it seemed pathetic, since the people who had carved their names, initials, dates had not perceived that as they did they merely showed their deafness to the ages that had come and gone before them. They showed – could not have shown more clearly had they tried – that they had come to Stenness and heard nothing, babble. And as I thought this, I thought, too, that Babel came from *bab-ili*, which means the Gate of God in old Assyrian; from that meaning came the famous city which had been built at one time in the land of Shinar. At that time, we were told, in what is called the Bible – which means just Book – the whole earth spoke a single language. And all the people on the earth said, 'Let us make us a name. Let us build us a city, and a tower, whose top may reach right up to heaven.' But their god, a jealous god, a Viking god of sorts, saw them start to build this gateway, and then stopped them. He did not want them reaching into his domain; he'd thought that if they did that, nothing would restrain them. So he had sowed confusion, scattered peace, destroyed the place where things could be imagined, then accomplished. He'd done this by creating different languages for all; if people could not speak, they could not build together.

My god, what a cruel god, I thought; who'd worship such a god? I asked Sebastian. He said, 'Idiots.' And then we walked around the stones again, this time looking at the tale that had been carved into the stones not by a person but the planet. One stone I stood by – standing by the standing stone, while Bastian stood and held my hand beside me – had, on one side, gnarled bark, a kind of bark of stone, that showed where rain had, for millennia, tongued it. Another stone was like a sycamore, so flaky that it seemed it could be easily picked off by hand, then let to fall to ground like something seeding it. On both ends of that stone, the bark was pockmarked, almost like volcanic rock might be – as if the rain that had kissed and licked it all these years had been so hot that it had really burned it. In all the stones that stood, still, there were, as well, great cracks, like knife marks made in still-wet clay. And all the stones that stood, still, though their tops were cut diagonally across, had four flat sides below, the two large sides facing the inside and outside of the circle.

I saw this, felt this, looked, and then leaned back, quite close to one great stone, watching it, as it swayed above me. Or seemed to sway. It towered. And as I looked, it seemed that it was surely moving, although it was the air above that moved, in fact. I moved as well, leaned backwards until I leaned, or fell, against Sebastian, dizzy. He put his arm out, steadied me, then let me lean some more against the air that fell behind me. To look way up and tilt my head, to see the stone against the sky, and moving; to me, it was not that the stones might walk at night, but that the earth was like a ship I'd boarded. And this stone, maybe, was the sail, the ship in calm, calm seas; I felt the earth beneath me, like a cradle rocking. I knew then that the air and rock and earth and sky above would hold me if I wished. The choice was mine to make. Would I now live upon this earth-ship, where air would hold you up if you would lean on it? Or would I die, on this hard moving earth below my feet – lie flat, and let the clay forever absorb me? But I had made that choice. I'd made it in the room where Bastian had first led me through this gateway.

'I've never felt a sacred place as strong as this before,' I said.

'It's the cunabula,' he said. 'Where all was born and held

against the sky. Can you imagine coming here and not imagining that?'

And he was right, I couldn't. It was a sacred place, a place where all the people who had ever lived here walked around us still. They came up from the loch, and from the sea, as if they walked onto the earth straight from the other side of nothing. Sebastian let me lean, and look up at the sky, until I was too dizzy. Then, his arm around me, he led me to the center of the stones where we sat down and leaned on one another, and looked around us. The sheep who grazed this circle loved the stones, I saw; they'd scraped the earth upon the leeward side of each of them. And I, as quite contented as I'd ever been in life, just sat and felt the presence of the stones, and watched the sheep, and leaned against Sebastian. I watched one lamb go down right next to a great stone, scraping a little in the dirt, to mark it. It put one knee, and then the other, in the scraped place, leaned its head against the stone, and went to sleep that way, just leaning.

Behind another stone two lambs were standing, peeing hard, intent upon the feeling, happy. When they looked up, they'd lost their mother, and they got into a fright – baaing, screeching. Time had slipped for them. They saw their mother, raced right over, had the slightest lick below, and then, abashed, looked sleepily around them. One sheep I watched looked so much like a sheep-dog it was hard to think it was, in fact, a sheep. It looked most like a wolf wearing sheep's clothing, since it had black legs, black coat, black face, and blue-green eyes, which stared at us. Sebastian, too, observed this, and pointed to it, smiling.

'That's what you're like. Who'd know, to look at all your horrid clothes, what lies inside them?'

'They're not horrid,' I said. 'They keep me warm.' I said it softly, smiling. I felt contented, safe. Quite held within the ship that was the circle where the stones were clearly towers meant for heaven. But not through futile labor, brick by brick by brick; instead, a finger simply pointing upwards. I sat and thought this, watched a lamb, now chewing on some grass. The bottom of its mouth went sideways. The top went sideways, too, but quite the other way, so that the back and forth was like a grinding. Like a mortar and pestle, almost, but not quite – more like a quern, the grass the grain it held within it. To the lamb, quite contented, grass was all, the only language that it needed. To me, with Bastian, in the circle of the Stones, a question came to mind now. And that was this: what would the people who had set these stones in place have thought of that which we called writing? When it had been invented, they'd been dead, and only their Great Stones had seen the day when language had become not only sound but object. They'd been here, these mute stones, when things had changed forever, when language had been pinned to clay by hand by people.

Before that day had come, however, there'd been a long, long time when not a single living person had known that language – written down – was missing. They'd been here, here on this earth; they'd come, then they had gone, and when they'd lived and loved and thought and built their tombs, they'd known that all was gesture. They'd known that words were words, and time was time, and that the clouds that hurtled through the sky just painted shadows on the earth below them. They'd known that time and space were things that could be stretched or shrunk, grow large or small, depending what they held in them. And when they

102

told their tale – those long-gone folk who had no Babel, and lived in houses shaped like bodies – they spoke with stones, and were contented.

And as for me, although there'd been a time when only *Gilgamesh* had taken me to a place which had been large enough to hold my dreams inside it, that time was gone now. I put my head down in Sebastian's lap, looked up at moving clouds, and thought that seals could become women and women seals, here. And there could be a moment when a woman, half-alive, could be translated by a man to something whole again. I knew this was the time that I had wished for all my life. I could now say: *My book was written on my body, Bastian. Read it.* But I did not say that. Or not aloud. I just lay with my head upon Sebastian's lap and looked up at the sky. He looked down at my face, and touched my hair. He placed his hands upon my breasts, right through all shirts, all covering. He said, 'You know the legend of the standing stones? That women taken at their feet will bring forth bairns? That standing stones will make them fertile?'

And as he said this, something stirred within me, a longing that was not for any kind of power. I wanted no containment, of any kind, to anything. I wanted all things now to slip from where they had been held and into something else, as if they slipped from rock to ocean. And now, although I'd never wanted children, and had always found it strange that anyone would bring into the world a thing that she could not make safe there, I wanted all the rest of what Sebastian could bring so much I thought: *So what if children also came of this?* For there was nothing safe. All things were dangerous when they were born into a world they would be lost from. Only the

Stones were safe, the Stones which stood and did not sleep, but let time run away from them like water. And just as the gap from when they had been set here on the earth to *now* was very small, so was the gap between the thing I'd once thought I might want and what I wanted suddenly.

I wanted him. Just him. I wanted him to take me then and there, to bed me, plant me, seed me. I wanted him not as I'd wanted him the day before, but as I'd wanted him the day we met in London. I'd wanted just one thing, then, for him to rise out of his chair and take me; all of the things we'd spoken of were held inside that. In fact, my want was something that could contain all words; gold treasure, harvest hills, and gates had been as bright and vivid as they'd been that day because my longing gave its shape to all that lay within it. And now, the stones that stood around us seemed to give their shape to us, although it was to me unclear whether the stones, more, held our love, or whether our love had made the way I felt about the stones. They seemed one thing, perhaps. It was as if, and once again, I saw beyond the fabric of the world, and saw you could not know just what you'd make at any time – because the time you made it in was what would make it for you.

And so, I let him touch me. Hold me, own me, stretch out one hot hand and help me to my feet, and lead me from the center of the circle. He brought me to a standing stone, the scraped place where the sheep had been, and sat me down and knelt between my feet, undid me. One part of me thought: *This is madness. The sun is in the sky. The road runs by the stones, the cars go by it.* One part of me thought: *This is life. This is the life that I have always longed for, although I did not know how I could find it.* And so Sebastian undid me. I moaned. He pushed his finger deep inside, then took it out, but slowly. It felt as if a fish had slipped from earth to sea, and then Sebastian said, 'So, Emrys? Shall we seed you?'

It was the words. The words he spoke. I wanted, then, no words; had he not spoken them, I would have let him come inside me. But when he spoke I looked up, looked into his eyes, and saw that look he had of challenge, that look of OK, *prove it*. Perhaps I read it wrong. Perhaps his eyes, just then, were but a babble to me. But then, although his finger in my body felt like every pen that ever put life on a page, I said, 'No, wait. You know I promised.' I heard these words as if they had been spoken by a woman I had never met, but – just like his words – mine were out upon the air, too late to take them back. I didn't care at all about my promise. Why did I speak? Why did I say, 'No, wait'? It was that look, the look of a man who believed that men who risked it all, like Gunther Prime, were sexy. A man who thought, perhaps, that death was just as good as life, if there was victory involved in winning either.

I don't know what I thought. It was the day; I'd crossed the Pentland Firth, had found that I was dragging memories of death behind me. And all the deaths that I had dragged had been of ways in which both men and women had had their hopes of love betrayed for them. The girl who had gone down upon the sea would not have drowned had she not gone to seek her lover; the boy had drowned because he'd tried to win a bride, and had been fooled by someone who had never meant to give him that. And all the men and women, boys and girls, who'd been betrayed not so much by the ship which sank beneath them as by one another. I do not know. All that I know is that I said just what I said, and added one more lie to all the lies I'd told Sebastian.

And that was that, for then. We did not fight until we got to Brodgar. I zipped my pants back up, got to my feet, and led the way back to the Jeep. We both climbed in and pulled our seat belts down. I heard not *snick snick* as they closed upon the locks which held them, but just one *snick*, the two together. And then Sebastian drove to Brodgar, only a few miles away – a bigger circle, much bigger, than Stenness. It had, still, sixty stones, and it was dark, with heather growing in it, because the farmers here had feared, for many years, to plow inside it. I think that even if I'd seen it when I didn't feel Sebastian's anger growing, I would have thought Brodgar too big, too broad, a circle stretched too far, its stones too thin for what they tried to hold. Sebastian drove us there, and parked, then said, 'I'll stay here in the Jeep. I've seen this.' He did not unsnap his seat belt.

'Oh, Bastian, please, I've been so happy. Please come with me,' I said – though feeling anger start to grow inside me, too. Sebastian stared at me, his eyes quite hooded, hands upon the wheel; he then took out the key, and did not fling wide the door he climbed from, but pushed it carefully out, and just as carefully closed it. And then, quite fast, as fast as he had driven up through Scotland, he walked, strode, ran ahead of me. He stopped.

'So here it is,' he said. 'You like it? Happy now?'

To which I said, 'Oh, for god's sake! Sebastian!'

'No, no,' he said. 'You can't have it both ways.' His voice was loud against the hillside as he said this. A tour bus pulled in, then, and parked beside the Jeep. I saw a crowd of people pouring out of it. Sebastian did not stop, however. 'You felt them, felt the dead, and yet you said, "No, wait, Sebastian, I promised."'

When he said that, he flung his hands into the air, palms outwards, knuckles at his shoulders.

'Well, all right, then, my girl. I don't believe you really think I am diseased. Perhaps you think I am your toy, then?'

'That's ludicrous,' I said. 'I've run away with you to Orkney, I've left my job. That's just absurd.'

'Perhaps,' he said. 'I really wouldn't know.' And then he took one palm from where it was, leaned on the air, and pinched his fingers all together before him.

'Like this,' he said. 'Like this. You think me something you can take between your hands, and pinch like this, and have me when you want me. You're wrong. I have my work to do.'

'*I* think that? *I*?' I said, quite stung, and now, not caring for the people climbing toward us any more than he did. 'No, you're the one who thinks *that*, Bastian. That you can have me when you want me, have all of me. That I have no work of my own that matters.'

'I will not do this,' he said, still pinching with his hand. 'You'll have to choose your path now.'

'Oh, no,' I said. 'You will. You said you would get tested.'

'I never said that. Never,' said Sebastian.

'Oh, so you won't?' I said. 'That's smart. That's sensible. Why not?'

'Because I just don't choose to. My blood goes to the women whom I love, not to some test tubes in a lab. You want me, you want all of me.'

'I don't want all of you,' I said. 'Why should I want a man like you? I'm used to . . . something else.' I stopped myself, and just in time, from saying, 'better men.'

Despite my stopping, Sebastian heard the words I hadn't said, like something broken from a tablet. He said, 'You're used to something else, indeed. And so am I. You'd best remember that from now on, Emrys.'

'Don't threaten me,' I said, standing within the Ring of Brodgar. 'Don't try those tricks on me. They just won't work.' But they did work, because what he had said had hit me hard as something that had slapped me. *My blood goes to the women whom I love, not to some test tubes*, he'd said, as he had said, *What woman comes to bed in clothes?* and, *Others, too, have told me this*. I saw them all, those women, crowding round me like the ghosts that I had felt within the Ring of Stenness. But these were not kind ghosts, not gentle ones; these were the ghosts of women, Bastian's women, who'd fallen by the wayside, but who still hoped that he'd return to them. I hated them, those women, felt them crowding round, their ghosts around me like the dead, although not dancing. I hated Bastian more, though, his stance, his threats, his voice – his thought that he could, like a tablet, break me.

7

THAT AFTERNOON, WE BOTH stayed angry; we could not stop, although we wished to. Language had led us to a place from which we could not wake at will to fly from it. How could this be? I think perhaps because our bodies spoke so well we failed to notice that our mouths spoke different dialects. We failed to notice, then or after, that our words could turn to stones, or were like ropes we had drawn forth and then become entangled in. And though our conversation in the Rings needed to be untied as much as any dream in *Gilgamesh*, it never was, and there's no magic that can change the evil consequence. We drove to Kirkwall, checked into the house where Bastian always roomed when he was there, and then, since it was three o'clock by then, had early tea, down in the parlor. We said few words until Sebastian said, 'I have to get my mail. I have to work today.'

And I said, 'Fine. You do that. I'll take a walk and see this ugly town you've brought me to.'

'Go and see St Magnus,' said Sebastian. 'I've been there one too many times. I've had it up to here, in any case, with Viking savages. They went on the Crusades and slaughtered everyone in sight, then on their way home, stopped off at

Orkney to break in through the roof of the best Stone Age tomb in all of Europe. When *that* was not enough, they scrawled runes on its walls, claiming they had removed the chambers' "treasures". Liars. There was no treasure.'

'I know,' I said, as short with him as he had ever been with me. 'I know a lot that you don't think I know.'

'I'll see you later, then,' he said, and he was gone, and I was left enraged and desolate.

I pulled myself together. I felt a total fool, but put on a down vest, canvas jacket, boots, a woolen hat, before I went out walking, and that was good, because that way I wasn't cut in half by the cold wind that gathered at each corner. Kirkwall wasn't ugly, as I'd said. But neither was it like the rest of what I'd seen of Orkney – clear and cold and high and bright and welcoming. It was complex, with taut stone streets, and towered, tiered walls of stone, which seemed to have their windows peering darkly through them. Nor was it true, I noticed, that, as Bastian might imply, I felt the cold here more than other people. The day was August 4th, and from each chimney that I passed, smoke rose, although it was high summer in the Orkneys.

And in the air from all this smoke, there were two odors, coal and peat – two smells upon the chilly wind they blew in. As each fuel burned in hearths around the town, before dispersing in the sky, it heated well, I guessed, the house that it was burning in. But still, they were so different, coal and peat, you'd never think, to smell them, that they could be kin to one another. The smell of peat was lovely, sweet and rich, the smell of something that had once, perhaps, been lilies. These then had gone into the bogs, three thousand years before, created by the changing Orkney weather. The peat bogs had grown up where once there had been grass; and now, the great dark blocks of crumbling earthy peat, when set alight, still smelled of meadows.

The coal, though, smelled of fear. It was a bleak, depressing smell; it made it hard to feel much joy in any place where coal smoke blew around you. And you need not know anything of coal, and how it forged itself within the darkness of the earth a million years before, to feel this. You need not know how miners, even now, were sometimes killed, so far away from light and air, and chipping off black blocks of burning. The smell in any case was bleak; it smelled of places where you'd once been trapped, from which – against all odds – you'd managed to escape. It smelled of times that you would rather not remember, when the things you loved had been upended, loosed by someone's hand and broken. And yet these two smells, intermixed in Kirkwall – now flowers, wafting on the air, and now the hard and hurting memories – came from two fuels which each had lain within the body of the earth in graves, one shallow and one deep, and which had each been then brought forth out of the deeps to give a bright bright gift of ease.

I walked, and thought. Tried not to think of Bastian, although I thought of little else. Though I was angry, still, I longed for him, and wanted him beside me as I walked the streets of Kirkwall. I felt defenseless in the face of all these new impressions, which I drew in as if I were a sponge, attached to firth-bound rocks, and water-hungry. On doors and windows, I saw notices of funerals. And not just on the doors of flower shops, or undertakers, but on the windows of the grocers, bakers. On the same windows, there were notices of celebrations, revels; the daily paths of life announced the dying. I longed for Bastian to explain, to point

111

things out, to bring me fully to this place he'd brought me. As he was not there in his body, I tried to think what he might say about these things. I thought of how the people whom Sebastian studied had had no fuels like coal and peat; in that way, too, their time was different. They had no written language, no notices announcing death, and as for fuel, just wood which drifted onto Orkney's shores, or oil derived from whales and seals and fishes. All surface things, however. Nothing to burn that came from down below them.

And what had that been like? To live upon an earth whose skin had never once been torn? Where only shallow plows had tickled it, and little spades had nudged it, to let it take into itself the seed of things to come? The world had been, I thought, quite like an infant child, kept dry by its earth swaddling cloths, and those who'd walked upon it had never dreamed that this would change, any more than they had dreamed that, after they were gone, there would be written language. Then everything had changed. Then bronze had come, not quite as strong as iron, but still drawn forth out of the body of the earth as copper. And no coincidence, perhaps, that as the bronze had come, the climate changed, and peace and plenty vanished. As people tried to move to better land, the people who lived already on that land built stone towers – brochs – to stand within and fight, and those stone brochs, signs of the age when neighbor had fought neighbor, still stood in many places in Orkney. All that because of changing winds, and bronze, torn out of secret places in the virgin body of the earth, just like the peat and coal that blew above me.

And as I thought that, I thought, too, of Bastian. He was right there, in any case, inside me – had not been pushed away by any thinking. The way the two smells intermixed upon the air seemed, at that moment, quite like the feeling that I had for him. First peat, the flowers wafting in the air, then coal, the hard and hurting memories. I loved him; he undid me with the pen that was his hand. I also feared him, feared him deeply. I feared the part of him that said, *It's hard to know just what it is we know*, the part that said, *All births are sad, I think*. He *must* know it was not his blood I feared, but him. Not that I'd catch some dread disease, but that I'd catch Sebastian. And that, if I should catch him, he might kill me when I did. The thing we'd talked about had come to stand for something else – for pain, for sorrow, for the coal he burned within. If once he slid inside me, I would, in having all his flesh, have everything his flesh was wrapped around. His past, his women, all his years on earth, the brochs he'd built, about which I knew nothing. All of the places where he'd ripped into the world, and brought forth something that was hardly treasure. Indeed, if once he slid inside me – him, just him – I felt that I would catch from him the things that troubled Gilgamesh so much that he had crossed the Waters of Death to try and lose them. But I, no more than he, would find that easy. I wanted peat, not coal. If they were mixed, they might undo me.

And then I saw St Magnus. I was still angry, also sad, and, sad, decided to go inside it. But what I saw was not, I think, the church that Bastian saw. I saw a lovely stone cathedral, wrought of both red and yellow sandstone, mixed until each color seemed to make the other brighter. I saw a church that, with its arches, reached, as churches should so reach, up to the heavens. It wasn't like the Stenness Stones, the sacred lines of land, but there was still a kind of dancing

113

in the dome of it. Yes, it went up and up, the dome, and then came down, fell sideways – was, in its rise and fall, almost miraculous. And when I later saw, with Bastian, for myself, a chambered tomb, I saw this arching was the heart of what both tomb and church – though not the Stones of Stenness – seemed to say to us. In fact, in the long reaching overhead, and the long hand that stretched down to the earth again, the dome of Magnus captured, on a bigger scale, what chambered tombs had done so many years before. The corbeled roofs the neolithic people had created had spoken to builders in the centuries that followed.

But if the Vikings had, as Bastian said, tried to destroy Maes Howe, or at the least to thrust into its heart, with words, what they would have there – treasure – then they had also built this church, and had, here, written sense, a sad and final kind of sense that did not skirt the thing that Magnus had been built for. On every tomb – and it was filled with tombs – they had, with labor, carved at least two words, *Remember Death*, the same words that Sebastian, accelerating through his life, had said through gritted teeth on roads in Scotland. *Remember Death, my dear*, he'd said to some poor soul, so old she looked interred already. He'd shot the Jeep right past, not even waiting for a sign which said, as those signs said, *This Is A Passing Place*. And here in this cathedral which he claimed to hate so much, I found its source; almost each tomb that had been set within these walls remarked this.

But many said much more. *Behold the end of life*, some said. *Corps rest in peace until archangels sound sole joy above*, said others. *Death waits us all*, the words quite often read. *The hour none knows. Behold the end of life. Remember Death*. This took me back to *Gilgamesh*, to one great line from that

114

first text that ever had been written; I had not liked my own translation of it. It was the one place in the epic I'd found it hard to see the words that should be put where the first words had been. *The sleeping and the dead, how like brothers they are*, I'd written. *Do they not both create death's image? Death's time is hidden, but the time of life is plain.* This could have been, instead: *The face of death cannot be shown to us.*

But here – here in St Magnus – the face of death *was* shown; on many tombs there were not words but pictures. There was an hour-glass on some, the sands of life all running toward the bottom. On some, a kneeling woman, hands clasped before her breasts, and legs entangled in her dress so that she seemed, almost, a mermaid. On some, a spade and shovel, crossed as bones are crossed by pirates. On all, or almost all, there were the bones themselves. Two thigh bones mostly; that, too, Bastian had said when we were back in London. He'd said, *What promise shall I take? Something quite hard, I think. Perhaps I'll ask you to make sure I'm buried in my tomb, or that my thigh bones go there.* These thigh bones, on these tombs, were crossed so that, if they'd been turned upright and fastened off with lines, they would have seemed, themselves, an hour-glass. Some held in the crossed place, where bone touched bone and made a kind of barrow, not grain, but skulls, instead. And not just skulls in stone, but skulls that had a look about them of something, someone, trying still to speak. Some skulls were turned quite sideways, yet the eyes were still both there, as if they'd journeyed round the skull to look at you. On other skulls, set straight, there was a long thin ridge of nose, with nostrils that seemed from a monkey's skull. Some skulls were smiling, eerie; one, painted on a sign that hung above an aisle, not only smiled, but dipped its head, quite sprightly. It held a spade and hour-glass, was wrapped in a white shroud. Above it were the words *Memento Mori*.

I wondered where these bones had come from. Why so many bones? The hour-glass, the spade and shovel, did not surprise me. As for the mermaid woman, tangled in her dress, she seemed a cross between a silkie and a supplicant. But bones, such bones, sheaves of them, like grain. And sad, sad tales of loss. Lost children, mostly. *Agnes nine children bore unto her mate, six died before their sire, by cruel fate*, one read. *Death waits us all. The hour none knows. Remember Death*, it read below that. I placed my hand upon the tomb, which did not have real bones behind it, still knowing, as I'd never known before, that there was something about bones which was quite beautiful. In the same passage that had given me such trouble when I'd translated it – in which the sleeping and the dead had been portrayed as brothers – there had been one line that was clear, and could be read just one way: *From the beginning there is no permanence*.

But bone was, if not permanent, at least a thing that lasted long – a long, long thing that was, because it lasted long, quite beautiful. Yes, bone was beautiful, as Bastian said, who worked with bone, and brushed it, and took it from the earth where it had long been buried. It was a kind of fuel, but for the mind, and for the heart, of all of us who lived but would be bone ourselves someday. It was, although not death's sole face or image, a thing you saw behind the thing you saw, just standing there. If death was image, bone was memory, and it reminded us that there was something about facing death that was also beautiful. To face death fully, meet it with your eyes, just as the eyes of all these smiling skulls did; it was to know that it was like a deep deep thing that slid inside you. And more than that. Once it was in, it took you from yourself, and made you null. The self just vanished. The world you'd lived in when you were alive slid forward, though, and you, if you were lucky, would be bones at least, and someone like Sebastian might, through finding you, remember you.

The whole thing made me happy, made me feel a kind of joy – that I remembered death, but was not dead yet. It was joy and relinquishment, and modeled on the church, on everything that had been mixed, like life and death, there. Two odors, black and white, were coal and peat. Two notices on windows, the funerals to come, the celebrations. The red and yellow sandstone, intermixed, and set alight, so that the colors seemed the colors of flowers. And then the way the arching of the stone reached far, far up, but then began its long climb down again. My anger was quite gone. I just wanted Sebastian. I wanted him right now, and for as long as I could have him. So he'd had other women. So what? Had I believed that he, this man, my man, at forty, would be a virgin? Had I believed that he would wait for me to wash up on the shore of him? I was here now, that was what mattered, and if I'd once written a book called *Gilgamesh and Enkidu*, the time had come to read the tale of Emrys and Sebastian.

So I returned to where we stayed, and lit a fire in the grate, and started up the heater that was in the room also. I went down to the parlor, and brought up tea and cakes, then lay down on the bed and waited. Sebastian came at last, an hour later, but he was still quite angry, as if the time that had gone by since we had fought was held within his fingers. He came into the room, threw down some letters on the desk, then greeted me quite coldly.

117

'Hello,' he said. 'You're back.'

'Good mail? Did you get work done?' I said, quite careful to surround each word with all the tones that it should grow in.

Sebastian noticed, but just said, 'I have a lot of work ahead of me.'

'When do we go to Long Holm?'

'Day after tomorrow.'

'That will be nice. I want to see your tomb. I visited St Magnus. I was so struck by all the bones that had been carved there.'

'Yes, there are lots of bones. My tomb is better, though. The bones are real. I've found, as well, a lot of dogs' skulls. I think I told you that.'

'You did. What does your dog think of those skulls?' I asked.

At that, Sebastian started finally to soften.

'Oh, Corbin. Well, he doesn't judge this. He likes the tomb. He puts his nose between his paws and waits outside for something yummy to come to him.'

'Does something yummy come?'

'Rabbits, sometimes. Not from the tomb. There's a huge warren right beside the tumulus, with little sandy places. If you look you can see footprints, front and back, and little tiny rabbit droppings.'

'And rabbits.'

'Yes, and rabbits. They wait and wait and then they bolt, just panic. Corbin is more patient.'

'Corbin,' I said. 'He's black, then?'

'A great black water dog. How did you know? Of course, Old French for *raven*.' I saw that this was working, and that Sebastian's anger was being drawn away from him by words that did not need to be untangled.

'The raven Noah sent, to bring him word of dry land. No dry land, though. Hardly the raven's fault.'

'No, hardly,' said Sebastian. 'Shall we have supper?'

'I'd like that.'

'I don't suppose you brought a dress to wear?'

'I didn't. We could buy one, maybe.'

I listened to these words, and liked them, as they fell upon the air, although they quite surprised me when I heard them. They surprised Bastian, also. He smiled a tiny smile, as tiny as a rabbit's footprint. Then he stopped smiling, and said, the smile inside him now, 'Well, yes, we could. The shop will still be open, for the tourists.'

And so we went out in the streets again, and though the wind was cold, Sebastian did not have to do too much to warm me. He tucked me in his arm, and I leaned on that arm, feeling his heat pass through his arm and into me. Good god, a dress, I thought. I'd never worn a dress in all my life, not since I was just a child and almost drowned in one. But Bastian led me through the wind, and to the shop, which was quite good, since tour boats from Denmark and Norway often docked in Kirkwall, setting on land a host of stylish women. There at the shop, he had me stand and wait while he looked through the racks, and picked three dresses that he wished to see on me.

'These three,' he said. 'I want to see them all.'

They were all different, but all tight, all long, I saw.

'Why long?'

'Not to the ankles. Not that long. I like your ankles. I like your bones. Such fine bones, on your face, your arms, your hips. No one can make such bones. They come with you, or don't. They did, with you, and you should show them off.'

Around us, women listened. Tourists, without their men,

119

and women from Orkney who worked selling dresses. I heard their listening, and more, was dazzled by their listening, since they, too, smiled, as our desire blew to touch them. And I thought: Why that anger? Why that fear? *This* was not coal, interred too long within the earth, a low-grade illness. This was not even peat, which, though it came from flowers, could crumble in your hands before you lit it. No, this was something else, the thing that all who came upon the earth, were born here, longed for. And so I put on one dress, and then another, then the third; the third was the one that we both most liked on me. It was a deep green, made of silk, with shoulders cut away, and tight tight sleeves, a tight tight bodice. Then, just at the hips, the skirt blew out around. I saw it in the mirror, not quite blowing. I saw me there, as well, and saw myself – as I had never seen myself in any mirror – before the mirror of Sebastian. I walked out past the curtain, and he looked at me, quite hard. No smile this time, a look just far more subtle.

And I, again a stranger, heard the words upon my mouth, the words of some now-teasing woman. 'Well, this one shows my bones off. But if all you want is bones, why not go back to Long Holm now, and find some?' But Bastian, still unsmiling, and ignoring those around, came toward me, ran his hands across my shoulders. Then he moved his hands, so hot, so dry, so hard, and slid them over silk down to my hips; he took me by the hips, and pulled my hips to his. And then he held me, firmly, saying:

'This is no joke, my darling. I'm holding now the part of you that will, with any luck, remain upon the earth five thousand years or more. I've found such hips in tombs, and wondered who the lovely ladies were who wore them under skins. The skins of deer, perhaps.'

And then he said, 'Dear bones,' and looked me in the eye with something more like love than he had ever shown before. I thought he said, 'Deer bones,' and said, 'You've found those, too.'

He said, 'Never as dear as yours.'

And when I heard that, knew what he had said, knew that he'd said it, I wanted him to take me on the floor; I wanted him to just blow back the green silk skirt of waves, to push it to the hips he held, and take me. I wanted it so badly that I swayed within his hands; his hands felt this, and holding harder, steadied me. He said, for all to hear, 'Not here. Just wait,' then said to one bright listening woman, 'We'll take this dress. She'll wear it. Wrap her clothes up.' The woman nodded, as if she loved to hear such orders and obey them. Sebastian said – to me now – 'Don't fall down. I will be back,' and then he left me for a moment, swaying. I almost did fall down, but leaned against a wall that was nearby, put out a hand, and stayed myself. It felt as if the deck I rode on was, once more, now tilting. Bring Deeps, I thought. Bring Deeps. Was this, then, what it meant? But then the dress was paid for, and Sebastian returned to me. He took the bag that held my clothes in one hand, took me in the other, and put his own black padded jacket around my now bare shoulders. I swayed, still, but I let him lead me out into the wind, out into the street, and not toward dinner.

He said, 'Just walk. Here, lean against me. I can steady you.' He steadied me until we reached the boarding house, and walked up the stairs there. Then he threw wide the door, and tossed the bag that held my clothes onto the bed, then kicked the door behind him. He still held onto me, and said, 'Now, Emrys. Here we are. And you look lovely in your dress. Let's leave it on you.' I swayed, as I had swayed when I had looked into the sky above the Stenness Stones. I felt, and for the first time in my life, the thing you feel, when, as a woman, silk is stretched across you – the way that it is warm as skin, the way it holds your flesh tight to your bones, and seems, in holding them, to love them. I swayed, and once again Sebastian held me up, would not let me lie down. He said, 'No, stand. I want to stand now.' He took me to a wall, leaned me against it, said, 'Stay there,' then went to close the shutters.

And now, half-light fell through the shutters, since the sun was in the sky, and high; this was still August in Orkney. So half-light fell in long thin lines across the rug, the walls, across Sebastian's body as he walked toward me. I leaned against the wall, my silk dress off my shoulders, so that my neck was bared to Bastian. He kissed it, kissed it lightly, nothing in his kiss of threat, or force, or power, or anything but tenderness. And then he took his finger, ran it right across the place where the tight dress held my bared clavicle. It seemed to seek an entry like a wave against a cliff, a long hot finger reaching sideways; Sebastian seemed to be just painting that broad bone that held me up, from which my body was drawn down below him.

He murmured, 'So, and did you like St Magnus, Emrys Havers?'

I could not speak, so I just nodded yes. He took his finger, then, and let it slip an inch inside the dress that he had chosen and then had put upon me. He slid it right across, the finger, east to west, then back, returning over ground he'd covered; he seemed to think my breast bone was a cliff that he would climb, or maybe, like the Marwick Head, would fall from. He kissed my neck again, let one hand slide, like rain, down the long standing stone that was my arm. He held my wrist then, lightly, pinching it between his thumb and the four fingers that had bones in them so light, so subtle. Then, holding my wrist, tugging my wrist, tugging it down, as if to hold me to the earth I stood on, he took his other hand, and placed his palm against one breast, just as he'd done when we were still in London. And I felt, as I'd felt that morning, *This man is silk to me. The dress is silk. My skin is silk, just binding me.* His hand upon my breast said, as he touched me through the silk, *I own this. This is mine*, and then he moved his other hand beside it.

And as he did that, I swayed again against the wall, and slipped. My wrist within his hand no longer anchored me. He said, 'Stay still. Don't move,' then slid his hands right down to where the green silk skirt still waved above my ankles. He touched it, touched my ankles, took my shoes off. Touched the skirt, and pushed it up. Kneeled at my feet like someone worshipping. 'Don't move,' he said again, then slid the waves right up across the bones that were my shins, my knees. He did this very slowly, as slowly as a tide might move in waters far away from Orkney. A tide where, twice a day, the water climbs the rocks, but slowly, in no hurry to attain the top of them. And once there, in no hurry to retreat, to slide back down and lose themselves again in oceans. 'Don't move,' he said, as with one hand he held my skirt, a rush against my hip, a rush of green silk, bunched and waiting. With one hand he pulled off the pants that were beneath, and tossed them on the floor; he was still at my feet, just kneeling. Then, with the hand he'd freed, he took the skirt again, and shifted it so that it stretched across me. He tucked the skirt into the silk where it came taut across, so that my hip bones were the hook he hung it on.

He then took both my wrists and pinned me to the wall, clothed from the waist up, bare below it. Quite like a lamb, he knelt, just nuzzling at the place where my legs met, as if he sought a reassurance there. He slid down, sat, and nuzzled, sniffed, and held my wrists. 'Don't move,' he said again. 'Not till I tell you that you can.'

He licked then, licked me, held me in his mouth and sucked, not hard, not so it hurt, but so that I felt held by it.

'Now move,' he said. 'Move both your legs out.'

'I can't,' I said. 'I'll fall.'

'You won't fall. I'm right here. I'll hold your legs. Let them slide out.' And they did slide, a little. He held them with his hands around my ankles, hard in place, so that I stood, legs spread, while he sat right beneath me.

'Yes, there,' he said. 'That's right. You are a standing stone. Now stand, while I converse with you.'

And the slow conversation that followed upon these words was like the conversation we had not quite had when we were at the Stones of Stenness. It felt as timeless as the rock the earth was made of, took me to a place where, though the waves were crashing on the shore, the waves were suddenly suspended. In this place where I found myself, there wasn't any word, spoken in silence, which lacked a multitude of meanings. Yet each meaning was clear. Each added something new to what had come before, without erasing it. I felt: *He loves me*. Felt: *He knows that I am his*. Felt: *He is mine, why would he kneel before me?* Felt, as he put his tongue out, and ran it through me like the rain running through cracks in stone: *I wish no word to come of dry land, raven*. Felt, as he slid his tongue between my legs as if he marked the birth of language there: *So where is Babel now? And how could Babel come from this, though it*

124

might cause a standing stone to stumble? And felt, at last, as he just made his mouth into a door that I could clamber through if I wanted to see the things that lay beyond it: *Oh yes. Oh yes. He, too, knows of the vortex in the sea, the time-falls we must ride. He knows time flees for us.*

I came. I almost fell. He held my ankles tight, did not betray them. But even so, I slid right down the wall and came to rest, the skirt still tucked onto my hips where he had tucked it. At this, he let me go, and my two knees now fell apart. I looked at him, as if to say, 'Let's go to bed now.' But he said, 'No, not yet. Rest for a moment. Then kneel at my feet,' and reaching out, he pulled the silk from where he'd put it. He pulled it out and down, so that it spread across my wide-spread knees, green waves climbing upon the rock of them. Then he stood up before me, did not lean against the wall, but stood, and said, 'Come. Kneel. I want your mouth around me.'

And so I knelt. There was a rug. I placed my knees upon it, felt my knee bones through the rug touch the hard floor. I knelt as if in church, and wore the dress that in some age I might, perhaps – although with shoulders covered – have worn there. The dress, so long, so full, got tangled round my feet, so that I had to reach behind me to untangle it. Then I put both hands up, brought them together as if in prayer, unbuttoned all the buttons that were before them. Each button was quite slow, a dancing circle of time, but Sebastian was not impatient, standing over me. He touched my head with fingers that were light as blowing air, until I had him all unfastened. And then, once I had freed him, I put my mouth upon him; I did not think of any promises. I thought, if I thought something, that I must look quite like the women who'd kneeled upon the tombs I'd seen within

St Magnus. They'd been like mermaid women, tangled in their dress; they'd seemed a cross between a silkie and a supplicant. But I was just a silkie, something that had slipped up from the sea, and was about to be land-seeded. And when Sebastian moaned, the first time he had ever made a sound when we made love, I knew how much he needed me. I put my hands upon his hips. I held his hips quite tight, and then I took him, not too deep, inside me. I tasted him. He moaned again. Then said, 'So *cunne*, Emrys. You taste me. Do you test me, also?'

'Oh, no,' I said, freeing my mouth, holding my hands around him. 'No, I don't test you, not at all, Sebastian. This is a little different.'

'It's not that different, Emrys. In either case I reach the secret chambers of your soul. Your penetralia.'

'So shut up then, and reach them.' At that, I took him in my mouth again. This time, he did not interrupt me. And as I held him, tasting him, and licking him, I felt a hunger I'd never felt before, a kind of hunger hard to call with words. Perhaps because it was not hunger, more like thirst, and here I find the words that will allow me to call up the feeling. It was the thirst of grass for rain when months and months have passed; it was the thirst of tired men for drink, not just for drink, but for the warmth and laughter that go with it. The thirst of dogs for bones; they do not need them, they have eaten, but something of them smells wonderful. When I saw Corbin, later, waiting outside the tomb on Long Holm, with both his paws crossed, that was the kind of thirst that he had in him. A thirst that was for drink that you would wait for, that you'd savor, and that you'd hold within your mouth until you were replete with it.

And so I did not think, just not at all, of promises, or of

how safe I'd been before I'd been with Bastian. I did not think of all the things that I had left behind, when I had shed my clothes, put on this green silk dress for him. I thought, in fact, of death, but in a way that saw it plain, that saw that seeing it could only bless you. At last, I felt quite safe, because I'd seen that there was nothing in the world that you could wait to do, if you remembered that your death awaited. *So, and did you like St Magnus, Emrys Havers?* I'd liked it. I had seen there what I'd never seen, not once, when I'd been writing *Gilgamesh and Enkidu*. That facing death was beautiful – facing it head on, instead of trying to find the ways to turn it sideways. There was no way to make it anything but what it was, and even bones could not have immortality. We had, just now, this joy. How could I catch my death? I'd caught it long ago, when I'd been born into the world forever.

But then, when he grew larger, or, more likely, thrust a little deeper down inside me, there was a moment when I felt quite breathless. I felt my throat constrict, and for a moment, almost close; I felt a child again, who'd fallen in water. And here it was above me, the circled, mirror thing, which was a lake I had thought lovely before the holding started. But when it had, and I'd been drowning, I'd felt the lake was hateful, forcing me to take the water in my mouth, when I rejected it. But Bastian – now the lake – felt this, or something like it, and took my wrist from where it was, and lifted it. He tugged it, just a little, lifting me from where I was to somewhere just a little further off of him. He knew what I had felt. He knew. I loved him for the knowledge that he had of me, for what he did once he had gained it. I took my wrist back, held both palms around the place where I was drinking, drank again, a deer back to the water

127

hole. And as I did, he came, the touch of both my hands the final touch that let him go wherever he was going. I felt his hot seed in my mouth, felt it push and push, the throbbing like the throbbing of the heart that pushed it. His heart's blood, in my mouth. Was this what he had meant? *My blood goes to the women whom I love*, he'd said. I tasted it like tea, tea held within a cup, the tea that we had drunk the day I'd found him. And while this may sound strange, I let it run around my mouth until I felt: *Well, now I truly know Sebastian*, and then I let it slide back to my throat to vanish there at last, into the time-falls that we both were riding.

8

THE NEXT DAY WAS a good one, all day long; Sebastian again believed I'd slept with him the night before. I was too tired, though, from the sea crossing we had made, and all that followed it. We went out late to eat, and when we got back to the room, I took a hot, hot bath, while Bastian put the mattress on the floor. When I climbed underneath the covers, I found that here in Orkney the beds had heated mattress pads, so I could sleep again quite naked and be warm. Sebastian fell asleep at once; I rolled away from him and did the same. I had no dreams that I could bring to mind when I awakened. I woke again before Sebastian did. I rolled within the circle of his arms, to let him hold me, so when he woke and found me there, he smiled and said, 'But what is this? Twice in a row? Twice almost makes it true. It is three times in fairy tales. Once more, and you will win me.'

We rose, and ate, and then Sebastian took me to Maes Howe. I told him that I only wished to see the place it stood, and save the crawling-into for his own tomb. I said, in fact, that I had just one tomb within me, and that it had best be his on Long Holm, to which he answered, 'Now that you've slept with me, you could go into any tomb you cared to enter.' But he knew, now, that it was true that I was scared of space enclosed upon itself. And so we merely parked, and looked at all the people pouring from their buses, and racing over the green fields where hay was being cut. We looked at how Maes Howe rose up, a perfect mound, a perfect hill, in the flat landscape all around it. The oval platform that it stood on was encircled by a wide and shallow ditch, just as the henges, too, had been placed in these earthen circles. I looked, and as I did, it seemed to me that the long-vanished people who had built this passing place might have had no written language in which to say, *Remember Death*, but even so, had said it very clearly.

Then we were off again, to Skara Brae, an hour or so north, and past the Loch of Stenness and the Ring of Brodgar, and as we drove, the clouds all blew away, the wind died, and the sun came out. The sun was shining, and it felt almost like the August that it was, when we arrived and parked. Uncovered, literally, from the sands of time, a hundred years before, the village had been found when a great storm just peeled the dunes back off it. As Bastian had said, the houses there were shaped not like the squares that we are used to living in, but like our bodies. Each one had a core room at its center. And on the sides, to right and left, at top and bottom both, four limbs – though these were round, curled inward. I crawled inside one while an ancient Scotsman, with hair protruding from two cauliflower ears, stared down at me as if to say, 'You're not Scots, are you?' The earth was banked around the houses, so as we walked, we could look down, and see our own dark shadows playing in them.

It was that kind of day. Sunny and bright, with dark,

sharp shadows, and also everywhere we went, with animals. At Skara Brae, quite near to the great arm of Skaill Bay – an arm which swept white sands within it – some arctic terns were nesting, and when we walked on those white sands, the terns came swooping overhead, one following us much farther than the rest of them. That one, a male, we guessed, became quite aggravated, darting at us, then darting much closer, until Sebastian threw his hands into the air, like someone telling armed intruders that he would not fight with them.

'Oh, go away,' he said. 'We won't attack your children. Don't punish us for walking underneath you.' The tern ignored these words, the hands as well, and pushed his chest down under him. He slid upon the wind, then wheeled, and climbed back up, then slid back down, and this time closer; and when we turned and walked away, retreating, as he saw it, he didn't simply let us go, but pressed his victory. Indeed, he chased right after us, crowing in his pride that he had faced down such intruders. I laughed, but Bastian didn't. In fact, he ducked his head, then turned and pinched his fingers all together, gesturing. 'You won,' he said. 'Be happy now. Leave us alone.' At which the darting bird flew back toward those he thought he'd saved from death, and we walked on to Skara Brae again.

We were there hours. Just hours and hours. Looked at each house, went back to it. The tourists came and went, running a race as if the tides of time were speeding them. But somehow, in between their pushing tides, there were long times when there were just a few real travelers. Some tour guides, too, whom Bastian taunted mildly – though taking care they should not hear him. When they referred to the big square tanks made of flat stone set on end, as places where the neolithic peoples had kept fish-bait, he could not keep his mouth shut, turned to me and said:

'Oh, yes, I'm sure. Just where I would keep fish-bait. Right in the middle of my living room, right next to where I ate and slept and took my woman to my bed and worshipped. I'd keep some smelly limpets just in case I wished to fish, during the night, perhaps in my stone "cupboard".' I laughed, he laughed, and then, when a Salvation Army band arrived, and set their songs up right next to the settlement, we left, pausing, however, to hear the singing and to watch the way the Scots who'd come to hear on purpose sang along with it. They sang quite silently, their faces red and worn, their mouths like fish mouths, opening, and closing. Beyond them were some seagulls, hoping for a treat, and people in the crowd provided one. I gave some water biscuits to the seagulls farther on, and watched them, scared, skitter away from me, until I'd moved beyond them, at which they crowded toward the food, enormously excited. Sebastian said, 'Well, they're not picky eaters. Whatever's on the menu, they're hungry for it.'

Then we walked on, up to a cliff where fulmars nested. They made flying look so effortless, came up the cliffs with such sheer joy, and then hung in the air, riding the currents, that watching them was almost dangerous; they made me feel that I could fly, as well, if I just spread my arms, and leaned as I had leaned at Stenness, and followed them.

We saw seals, too, that day, the first seals I had seen. They bobbed their heads up in a line, and watched us from the sparkling water. They raised their noses, barked like dogs.

'They say that barking seals mean rain,' Sebastian said at that. 'But I think that they bark when they feel horny.'

And when we left Skaill Bay, and drove up north to Birsay Brough, the animals continued to present themselves. A horse right by the road had a penis so erect it almost grazed the ground, three feet below its stomach. We saw a bull, as well, who had a scrotum sack with balls in it the size of melons. We saw another bull, a bluish white – quite blue, in fact – who looked like one of those portrayed on old Greek vases. This bull was lying down, his front hooves tucked beneath him, his back hooves tucked as well, everything folded. Behind him was a cow, a blue-white cow, much smaller than he was, and far less muscled; she was standing. She leaned and scratched her head against the bony mound below, from which the bull's short tail was sticking up. She scratched and scratched, and then, as if to thank the bull for giving her this spot to scratch her head on, she licked him on the hindquarters, and then licked up the back. The bull lay regally, as if beyond contentment.

At Birsay Brough there were more birds. The brough was near to Marwick Head, where birds just wheeled and circled in the air, then circled back in clouds; that day the birds were clouds, the sky was blue and clear. The cliff was high and, at the top, was slick with grass and moss, and when we stopped and walked there, Bastian stood, I thought, too near the edge. He stood, just looking down, and standing upon moss, on wet and mossy rock, as if he contemplated more than birds there. I almost called, 'Sebastian, come back,' but there was something in me that told me not to do this, that he would be angry. The day had been so lovely, Bastian in a mood that seemed quite new to me. He wore it as I'd worn the dress he'd bought – as if he

133

knew that though he was not used to it, it showed him off – and I wished to do nothing that might disturb this. I thought, in any case, I knew how he was feeling as he stood upon the edge of Marwick Head – that we could fly like fulmars if we wished to.

And on the Birsay Brough, a tidal island, the birds were nesting. The tide was out, so we could pick our way across the path of stone, still glistening wet. Dark seaweed bladders filled with air were flattened by the air they lay in. Upon the brough, sheep grazed, some of them white, some of them black, some of the black with white lambs, white with black ones. One sheep had such a heavy coat that when she first knelt down it seemed those narrow bony knees could not support her. And when we climbed the brough, the barren hill that was flat one way, upthrust the other, I knew just how she felt because it seemed the sky was on my back, my knees not quite supporting it. But at the top, the brough was flat and grassy, home to birds, some of them nesting, some of them fleeing from us. There was one eider's nest I came to, where the bird had gone away, leaving two eggs, crushed flat and dry, behind her. Maybe a sheep had crushed them; before she left, the duck had covered the crushed eggs with down to keep them warm. I picked some up, and saw on each small feather a hook that took firm hold of all the feathers next to it.

We also saw some geese. They ran away from us. A flock of adults, and a brood of dark and tiny goslings. When they first saw us, they were in the thrift, and there they ran and ran to get ahead of us. They did not fly, and it seemed clear that, among the grown-up geese, there was some disagreement as to action. Was it quite necessary, some asked, to run, or would it be all right to just lie down and take a rest now? So some lay down and rested, while the others ran ahead, and then, of course, the resting ones, not wishing to get left behind, ran also, tiny goslings following them. And there were guillemots, small black auks, which looked like tiny penguins, standing on the cliffs, then flying. More fulmars – big white birds with yellow bills – and kittywakes, with black upon their wings, as well. We looked for puffins, did not find them. They'd left a month before, Sebastian told me – told me, too, that, though they nested on land, after they left it and took their young back out to sea, no one was quite sure where they went. They seemed to live almost entirely on water, a very private species.

I asked, had no one banded them, put small radios on their backs? Sebastian laughed and said, 'My god, Ms Emrys Havers, you're American after all. Why don't you organize the signal party?'

It was that kind of day. Just normal, no black things, but only what was bright and filled with living. Each animal we saw seemed nesting, mating, nursing, intent on what was *now*, intent on sunniness. We went back to our room, and there, as he had done in London, Sebastian took me to the bed, untangling, as we went, my clothing; he tugged at this and that, tugged at my hair, my pants, and made things fall apart again before him. We made love, and it seemed to me that Bastian was a dowser seeking hidden springs, at which I tugged him to me. But he tugged me to him, as well; we made love twice that night, once with Sebastian on top, and once with him beneath me.

'Why can't we do it side by side?' I asked.

'It doesn't work that well,' he said, but we did try before we gave it up and tumbled round again.

That night, I laughed in joy the second time I came.

'Sssshhhh, sssshhhh,' Sebastian said, though he laughed, too, and pulled me down into his arms.

That night, I really slept with him. He wrapped me in his arms, and slept, quite quickly, as he always did. His mouth was on my hair. It took me longer, but I thought of birds, just wheeling, thought of how fulmars, leaning out against the air, trust that it will support them, ride on it. That way, I fell asleep. Riding the air that was Sebastian. And slept with him, so soundly, in between the times he twitched at me, that I would wake, with twitching, quite bewildered, wondering why I'd woken, until I felt him there beside me. And then I slept again, and woke only when he, with his whole body, pushed at me, each arm, each leg, like something throbbing. That time, I lay there sleepless for most of the next hour, watching the light come to the sky, though it was still the middle of the night in latitudes below us. I lay and thought of *Gilgamesh* in my translation – how his second dream upon the journey to the cedar forest had been one of the things I had created for it.

In the middle of the night, his sleep came to an end, so he got up, and said to his own lover: Enkidu, did you not call out? Why did I wake up? Did you not touch me in the soul's dark chambers? Why am I so disturbed? Was it a god that passed us by? If not, why are my muscles trembling? Oh, oh, I've had a dream, a dream that needs untying, because in it I grappled with a bull out in the wilderness. I sank down to my knees. My tongue hung in my mouth. But then, I drank some water from my water skin. Yes, I had written that, had seen it in my mind where the words that had once been there had gone missing. Adapted it, in part, from an old Babylonian fragment – from the place Babel was, which God had thrust on humans. I lay and thought, and then I slept, still there in

136

Bastian's arms, and now I had a dream myself, one to remember. In my own dream, which did not wake me, I held an infant in my arms. A girl, I saw she was a girl, with hair the color of wheat. She wore a green silk dress, as green as grass or moss, and flowing right down to her ankles, which were tucked inside it. I saw, within my dream, her body dark against the sky, which was lit up with all the colors of sunrise. She was still very young; she had a sleepy face, but big bright eyes, lit by the sun which rose behind her. Against the sky, birds flew; they seemed to make an arch, almost a gateway that the infant might have passed through. And then she spoke, not with her mouth, but right into my mind. She said, 'Can I come in, now?'

At that, I woke quite up, and lay and thought about my dream. I knew, when I woke up, I'd dreamed a daughter. The other time I'd thought of having a child it had been in passing; when we had been within the Stenness Stones, I'd thought that yes, that, too, might come of this. But this was not *that*, *too*. This was just *this*, that child, that girl I'd dreamed of bearing. She had, in one brief dream, become as real to me as anything that I had spent my whole life never seeing. Bring Deeps, I thought, Bring Deeps; those words, as well, had entered me, then bubbles of air, each bubble one bright letter, when I could not resist them. Was this what they had meant? This seemed the time for something new to enter. And not just enter me – enter the world, and enter it through me; I would be God's great bright and babbling gateway. I would be like the sunset that the birds framed with their wings, allowing what was bright to fly right through them.

It seemed quite right that there would be a time like that, when all one had to do to bring a child to the world was to throw wide the world's gate, bid her enter it. Sebastian, too, must want this; what else could he have meant when we were standing by the Stones of Stenness? He must have meant that we should turn to one another, throw wide the gates that had been closed, and let our child run through them. Not in my dream, but in my waking mind, she ran up from the loch, then paused and walked between the standing stones. Not in my dream, but in my waking mind, I thought she laughed to see what lay upon the other side of nothing. Then it was morning. Bastian woke. By then I'd moved away, and lay upon my back, staring at what I saw inside my mind. I smiled and turned to him, but when he saw me, I could see that he believed he'd been deserted on the deck of sleep that night. He did not mention it, but said, straight from his own dreams, maybe:

'How are we different from the other animals?'

I said, 'What do you mean?'

'From birds. From sheep. From cows, perhaps. I've always thought that it must be because we, men and women, have principles.'

'Well, so we do,' I said, just soothing him, and filled with love for him – this man who I now thought might be my child's human father.

'But do we? Really? What of you? Why did you leave your husband? What principle is there in that? Just animal.' At any other time this might have made me angry, or ashamed, but now, the girl still held within my arms, against the sky that was a summer sunrise, I tried to think what he had dreamed that had brought him to this mood that he'd awakened in. I couldn't guess, but said:

'I thought you said you liked men who, like Gunther Prime, would risk it all, and make it.'

'I do. I do like that.'

'What principle did he serve? That he should kill, *en masse*, for Hitler? Or that he should be loyal to the country of his birth? You have to choose the way that you will see it.'

'And you, then? Do you choose?'

'I've chosen. Choose to love you.'

'How can you love me, Emrys? You do not know me,' Bastian said. 'How can you love a perfect stranger?'

I had moved closer, touched him, and now I held him tight, still not disturbed. 'There are no perfect strangers. Just imperfect ones. But I don't care. And anyway, I know you better than you think.'

'What do you know?'

'I know that you have secrets.'

'Well, everyone has secrets.'

'No,' I said. 'Not everyone. We do. And I think we should talk to one another about ourselves in words, soon.'

'Oh, do you really?' he then said, but rubbed my back, with fingers soft as wings.

And when, at this, I said, 'You know, I slept with you last night, I really slept with you,' he stroked my face, though his was sad. He found his watch, and looked at it, told me we had to go, or we would miss the morning ferry to Shapinsay.

We rose, and dressed, and packed, and after we'd had breakfast I helped Sebastian load the Jeep with food that he had bought when he had gone to get his mail the day that we arrived. Sebastian kept his boat on Shapinsay because a ferry stopped on Long Holm only once a week, he said. That morning he seemed rushed again, though this time with some reason; if we missed this ferry, we would wait eleven hours until the next one. Once we had packed the Jeep, we raced off to the harbor, searched for the proper ship, and then drove onto it. Through all this rush, I held my memory of my dream, and of Sebastian's hands, like wings upon my back. But he, as I could see, had gone beyond his dream – whatever it had been – and past our talk, to something that now seemed to him more important. It was again as it had been the second day that we drove north – that he seemed hardly to remember I was with him.

In fact, once he had turned the engine off, and climbed out of the Jeep, he left me in it while he strode out toward the rail, and stared across Wide Firth to Salt Ness. *There are no perfect strangers*, I had said. *Only imperfect ones*. But Bastian seemed just then like five or six of them. Where had he gone, the man who had been with me the day before, who'd joked of limpets, cupboards, waved his arms at birds? Each of the men he was was like a spoke that held the rim of the great wheel that his whole self was wheeling on. When the wheel turned, and a new spoke was uppermost, the rest seemed somehow lost deep in the mud beneath it. I got out of the Jeep and watched him as he watched the sea, and felt a little troubled, as I thought of my dream-child. A dream was one thing, even a bright dream such as the one I'd had; a living, breathing child was something else again. And one thing was for sure; to have the child, I'd have to have Sebastian first, not just the blood, but what was in his blood – what his blood stood for. What were his secrets? In our first meeting he had said that words had always been a love of his – that each was like a secret waiting to be learned, a passage waiting to be dug so you could see what lay beyond it. But I did not yet know what would slide in with all the rest – his women, brochs he'd built, his hard and hurting memories.

The sea air, just then, changed. Grew colder, cleared his head. He seemed now to remember I was with him. We climbed the stairs, and went into the lounge and while I sat upon a bench, hoping this crossing would be calm, Sebastian looked at notices stuck on the walls there. After a while, he took one down, and brought it to me, smiled.

'Look at this competition. The British influence in wild Orkney.'

I read the notice: 'August Competition. 1. Flower Arrangement in a Candlestick. 2. Longest Stick of Rhubarb.'

'Something on their minds, you think?' asked Bastian.

I smiled, but did not laugh, and so he tickled me a little, as if the wheel had fully turned again, a new spoke uppermost. And then we got to Shapinsay, in less than half an hour, drove the Jeep down onto the island, and in the sweet bright air of August – another sunny day – drove past a place called Balfour Castle, all turrets and towers. It was, Sebastian told me, not a true castle, at all, but something Balfour had had built in 1850. It held the strange obsession the mid-Victorians had with time – or rather, with how time could be, through buildings, organized. The windows, doors and towers displayed, in how they had been numbered, the days and weeks and months of Roman calendars.

'Quite mad, they were,' said Bastian, but indulgently again, as he had been indulgent about rhubarb. 'They had the right idea, that dwellings should be tuned in to the earth, they just had no idea what earth they lived on.' We passed the castle, Bastian waving to some people in the fields – one field was bright, bright yellow, growing rape, for oil – and then he pulled up to a small and isolated cottage, off a dirt road which we now bounced along. He turned the engine of the Jeep off, said, 'Corbin's here,' then said, 'You wait. I'll only be a moment.'

So I unrolled my window, and breathed the air, which was now scented with alfalfa, cut and bunched in long heaped rows and drying in the sunshine. Then Bastian came back, a great dog leaping at his side, its black hair tight with curls, and gleaming.

'Here's Corbin. Corbin, Emrys. Emrys, Corbin,' Bastian said, as Corbin leapt into the Jeep and sat beside me. He sat on top of me, in fact; he was a young dog, maybe two years old, and now he took his tongue and scrubbed my face, as if it was his job.

'He likes you. Good,' said Bastian, and then said, 'All right. Get in the back now,' an order Corbin followed, though reluctantly. He started toward the rear, then stopped, came back and licked my face some more, as if he was intent on finishing the job he'd started. 'Just push him. Shove him off you,' Bastian said, and so I did, at which Corbin regarded me with hurt black eyes and did as Bastian wanted.

Then once again, we drove. Came to a small landing on the northwestern shore of Shapinsay. A few boats bobbed in the water, off a pier that was the only protection this shore offered. One boat was big enough so that I thought it must be Bastian's, but it wasn't; Bastian's was smaller. Corbin, who knew the boat, ran to it, sniffed it, and rocked it as he placed his paws on its gunwales, then jumped in and landed on the floorboards, while I stood and stared, amazed. I'd seen from maps that Long Holm was at least two miles from Shapinsay. Two miles, that is to say, across the Stronsay Firth – and this was what Sebastian made the crossing in. The boat was not just small, it was a shape I'd never really seen before; the prow and poop were raised, and it had sail and engine both. A single mast which took a square sail, and an outboard engine.

'It's called a cock-boat,' said Sebastian, amused at my expression. 'In Welsh, it's *cwch* boat, but in English, *cock*. *Cock* is a funny word, quite new for what it often means now. It has a hundred other meanings. The best is god; it means god. Did you know that?'

'God help us, if you think this boat is safe to cross this sea,' I said.

'No, no, it really does. It's a perversion, clearly. The intermediate form was gock, and it was used for exclamations.'

'Like what? I'd like one now.'

'By cock! they used to say. Cock's body! How would that one be?'

'Cock's body! And cock's bones?'

'Cock's heart. Cock's pain.'

'Cock's passion. How about: Well, good cock, Bastian Ferry!'

We laughed at that, the first time we had laughed together, freely, at a joke that one of us had made. Then we got the boat loaded, or Bastian did; I carried bags and boxes which he stowed, with great care, around the cock boat. Corbin helped by interfering. When everything was loaded, Sebastian checked the Jeep; he didn't even lock it, there in Orkney. Then he gave me some oilskins which were stored up in the bow, and put on the long oiled coat that he had worn the day we met in London. It was the first time he had worn it since the day we'd met, and it thrilled me to see him in it; there'd been a time when I had not

143

known whether I would ever know what lay beneath the pieces it was sewn from. He told me that he rarely used the sail – that it was there in case the engine failed him – so as I put the oilskins on and took my place up in the bow, the mast thrust up before me, and I wrapped my hands around it.

I didn't need to, though. The sea was calm, and when Sebastian pulled the cord to start the outboard engine, it caught immediately; the boat shot forward, at which I found that Bastian drove his boat just as he drove his Jeep, quite hard, and with a good deal of abandon. Not recklessly, however. Once, he swerved from side to side to demonstrate how stable the boat was, really. But mostly, we went straight, and though the firth was all around us, I did not think, this time, of shipwrecks, losses, drownings. No, this time, it was lovely, to be right on the sea, watching the way the boat carved water. And there were sea birds wheeling all around us as we plowed – guillemots, ospreys, fulmars, even puffins. They all dived after fish, and took these in their beaks or in their talons, then carried them off to eat them. Corbin was happy, too, watching the way the boat threw water out behind it, carving trenches. He thought, perhaps, that as with Bastian's chambered tomb, if he just looked and waited, there'd be something yummy.

And then, I saw Long Holm. A low green hill, not only treeless, but with no plants of any kind upon it. Just grass, and at the tide lines, seaweed on the rocks. A skerry about half a mile to the south, on which some seals were sunning. I'd learned when we had been in Scrabster that what made a holm a holm, and rocks like this rock – where the seals were sunning – skerries, was that a skerry was completely covered over, twice a day, when the two high tides rose and erased it. A holm, however, like Long Holm, was a place that always flourished, green and treeless, since tides, though climbing holms as well, just climbed them to their tide lines. 'Skerries,' Sebastian had told me, 'are a hazard to all shipping. You cannot put a lighthouse on one. And if you're any boat abroad in a strange sea, a skerry could well sink you. We have one off Long Holm.'

This, then, was it. A rock which, at low tide, as it now was, was maybe a hundred feet in length, I gauged. And as we chugged on by it, Sebastian slowed way down, so I could see more clearly the seals that lay on it. They watched us with large eyes – large sleepy eyes – and then they lifted up their bodies, stretching. They had grey fur, and yawning mouths. Some lifted both their tails and heads, so that they bent right up, on both sides, like a cradle. Sebastian, seeing me smile, took the cock boat in quite close to where the low rocks met the tide line; he said that this was safe only at low, low tide, because the rocks fell right off to the deeps then. When the tide turned, there would be danger. But now he could, and did, take the boat in so close that I could see whiskers on the seals' astonished faces. I saw, as well, the seaweed and the thick dark slime that grew on rock when it was mostly covered with water. I also saw a spike right on the skerry's top. Perhaps at some point, someone had tied a boat to it. It wasn't a large spike, perhaps three feet in height, and thick as one small finger pointing toward the heavens.

'Why put the spike there? Right on top? How could you moor a boat to it?' I asked Sebastian, who'd cut the engine now to idle.

'Some Englishman,' said Bastian. 'He claimed this rock was his. He didn't even want to moor his boat to it. I think

I told you that this skerry is quite unusual, since at high tide, two or three feet of rock still stick out of the water. He saw this, and he claimed he had inherited it from someone who'd also left him other lands in Orkney. But he knew English law, not udal law, which rules these islands. In Norway, farmers own the seaweed, the fish, all of the treasures of the deeps which might be thrown up on their land sometimes. In English law, the Crown owns everything right up to the high-tide mark. This man thought he would claim a foot of ground or so.' Sebastian laughed. Though he was English, he seemed to think the English had been put on earth mostly to amuse him. 'He left, though, after finding that Long Holm itself was not, as he had thought, his, too. His name was, oddly, Martin Havers.'

And when he said that, *Havers*, though he said it casually as one might say, *The longest stick of rhubarb*, I felt a slight, uneasy tightening in my chest, for no good reason. Havers was quite a common name, I knew, in Britain.

'Some relative, perhaps?' Sebastian added idly, his tone matching the idling of the engine.

'Oh, I don't think so. Hardly.'

'Just as well. The name is not marked on the map, but this is called, in Orkney, Haverskerry.'

'Haverskerry? How odd.'

'Well, it's an insult, really. Your name, you know, in Scotland, means to babble. To talk garrulously, or foolishly. Orcadians say, "How she did haver on!" or, "Havers! What a mouth he had on him!" ' He said this, still, quite idly, as if he did not mean an insult, or threat, or anything at all by this.

'My name means "wild oat" in Norse.'

'Yes, well. The words do change. So this was named after a foolish man, that's all.' And then he gunned the engine, and we shot away from spike and rock, and seals which clothed the rock like its fur garment. I could see all of Long Holm, green and long and bare, and could see, as we passed around its southern shore, the cottage Bastian lived in. And as I watched him driving the boat hard again toward shore, I felt the tightening in my chest grow worse, as if some great hand squeezed it. Who was this man I rode with? A man who could just take my name and throw it back to me; it seemed to me that he had said that, like the other Havers who'd come to Long Holm, I, too, might be foolish, greedy, foreign.

And while I'd spoken of our secrets as if I thought they were a thing that could be easily disposed of, it seemed to me right now that maybe secrets were the thing – the only thing – you never could get rid of. I'd told Sebastian I feared water, and boats, had almost drowned, and yet he'd brought me to this distant island. I'd told him I feared tombs and yet, aside from his own house, a tomb was Long Holm's only habitation. And he had told me, what? Nothing at all about himself, except that maybe – this by inference – he thought people should be punished. And I thought of that moment in the Jeep, and heading north, when I had put my head upon Sebastian's lap and looked up at him. He had glanced down, and touched my head, looked at a car he passed, and shoved the stick shift into gear, then brought it back again. He'd smiled a secret happy smile, as if to say, *I've got her now; I took her with my hand. I let her come to me, and then I made her come.* What if he'd thought more than I'd guessed, this man I didn't know – had thought, perhaps,

147

She chose to come. I'll give her Haverskerry. By which he had meant, what? A place where nothing grew, and nothing could be born, and nothing stayed, but all was buried, finally, in deep water.

9

THAT NIGHT, A FOG blew in. We had unpacked the boat, and taken all our things up to the cottage. It was a half a mile from the geo where we'd dragged the boat onto the sand up to Sebastian's home and the small sheds he'd built to house his stores and artefacts. The path was quite well worn, but it still took some time to get the luggage and supplies from beach to dwelling. The task, however, calmed me, let me feel that I had made too much of something that Sebastian said in passing. And when I saw his cottage, a crofter's cottage, one big room, all painted white inside, with spots of color, I let it all just go – that moment of deep fear – because a home is, in its way, a language. This home might have no power, no phone, no heat, but it was still as clean and neat and bright, and fully placed within the place it had been built as if it shared the virtues of the past and present. I knew that Bastian had lived there for a year, and in that year he'd made a home which showed that there was something simple at his center. If Sebastian was a wheel that turned through time from one thing to another, unexpectedly – at least to me who watched him – then he was also the small place the wheel was centered on, the place where all the spokes met in the middle.

And here, it seemed, the spokes met; it seemed almost as if this house lay, as the Stones of Stenness did, upon a ley line. Indeed, perhaps it did – the tomb above it on the hill, the sea below, the house itself looking toward Stenness and Brodgar. The cottage had stone walls, which either Bastian or someone else had painted white, and wood floors polished till they gleamed. All of its windows had two panes, one on each side of a central mullion, and set into the stone, with hand cranks underneath, so that each pushed out into open air. The bed was high and fairly wide, built in, a platform set beneath the western windows, piled with thick down quilts. On the floor beside the bed there was a Turkish kilim, fairly large; the color came from that, and from bright pillows, some strewn upon the bed, some large ones on the floor before the fireplace. The fireplace was for peat, not coal. The peat stove, too, was there. There was a plain desk, a solid door on legs, that faced the windows looking south; on this desk, books were stacked, with more books set beside it on a plank-board bookshelf.

And on the walls were photographs, unframed, but matted. Nine of them, all black-and-white, and each, in its own way, more like a painting than a photograph. One was of Bastian, young, his beard and hair quite blond, his whole demeanor softer, different. His eyes looked at the camera, and in his eyes I saw no hint of that look he now had, that look of OK, *prove it*. He smiled a sleepy smile, like someone freshly come from love, although he sat in a wide-open, rocky landscape.

'Where was this picture taken?' I asked.

'Shetland,' he said.

'Oh, you've done work on Shetland? At Jarlshof or where?'

'Long, long ago. You look. I'll get some dinner ready.'

So I did look, while he went out to the small shed where he kept peat, then brought a load in for the stove, another for the fire. When we'd arrived, the cottage was quite cold, and I was cold, so while Sebastian lit the fires, I stood close to them. Then he put food away, and started to prepare an early dinner. Corbin was leaping in the air in happiness. I went back to the pictures, looked at each of them in turn, and found that only one was of Sebastian. The rest were all of megaliths or artefacts, but they, too, somehow had the look of love about them. There was one of an ax-head made of stone, and lying on some rocks right by the ocean, which was blurred out in the background. There was one of an awl which lay on wrinkled cloth, and seemed to have been made of something's leg-bone. There was a dolmen which was filled with hot, cupped sunlight, a menhir, too – a single standing stone, but rounded at the top. And there was one arched megalith, two standing stones, flat-capped, that looked like something one might see at Stonehenge, but had not been taken there, I thought.

And I thought, too, that, with these photographs, what they portrayed was not as crucial as what stood out of sight – what lurked right at the edge of vision. These were an artist's pictures, in which the edges of the world had been a little blurred, and that small blurring made each picture like a fulcrum for what lay beyond it. It was as if, behind the thing portrayed, you could see – better – all the things you could not see there. Or more, as if the picture, though it was of something still, was moving through the time and space it photographed. They were great pictures, truly. I asked Sebastian who the artist was. He said, 'Oh, just a woman I knew once.'

I looked at him, but left it. Went on to look at other things, the things that he had placed upon the windowsills. A feather from a gull. An ancient tooth. A polished ring of hard black stone. A necklace of bone beads, which might be modern. He'd done this. Bastian had. The walls, the floor, the kilim rug, bright pillows, quilt, the gull's soft feather. The whole just came together to be him, the him I'd known I knew. All thoughts of Haverskerry vanished. And when the tea was done – tea was what Bastian called it – I found that that had come together, too. Mashed potatoes, yellow courgettes with garlic, a salad with scallions, a hard-boiled egg, some cheese and diced tomatoes in it. Lamb chops with home-made mint sauce. Sebastian could cook, it seemed, as well as he could love and make a home and find a woman to take there.

And that was me. That woman. We had been heading here to Long Holm for so long that it had not been hard to doubt, at times, that we would ever get where we were going. But now, we both were here. This was our home. Sebastian had called it that when we'd been driving up from London. I'd come here, somehow knowing it would be like this, and I'd been right, and now, as the meal came to an end, and I felt so contented, I wanted to give Bastian something in return for what he'd given me. What did I have to give, though? I had brought nothing for a house gift. But Bastian had no need of those. He had his photographs, his kilim rug, his polished ring of hard black stone, his necklace of bone beads upon the windowsill. But now I thought about my dream, and what I suddenly had in mind was far, far better than a house-gift, because it was the thing he really wanted, and it seemed the proper moment for me to want to give it.

But then, Sebastian said, 'Well, shall we walk now? Get some air? Perhaps you'd like to see the tomb?' And I said, 'Yes, of course, Sebastian,' while Corbin leapt into the air at the word *walk*, which he had heard, and Bastian said to him, 'Yes, Corbin, walkies.'

He then tamped down the stove, set a wire screen before the fireplace, took up two quilts, and rolled them quickly in a bedroll. He tied this up with rope, told me to put a jacket on, and put one on himself – his black one with the snaps. When we were warmly dressed, he took a lantern, slung the bedroll on his shoulder, and when we went outside, the air was cold and pure, the purest air I'd ever smelled. My house gift – which would be as much a gift to me as to Sebastian, after all – could wait. We'd come, now we had time. The island said this – rock and grass and sea and sky. They all said we had time. *Time, time,* they said, *time loves us.* But then I saw that fog was blowing in from the northwest.

'Look. Fog,' I said.

'Oh yes. We often get fogs here. That one will miss us for a while, I think. See, there's the tomb.' He pointed up to where a mound was set, quite nicely placed within a semicircle of valley. It wasn't a made ditch, it was a natural feature of the landscape where a hillock rose and then fell down into a trough. From down within that trough rose up the mound that held the tomb the ancient people had made, setting the narrow entry passage westwards. With many of these tombs, including this one, Bastian told me, the passage had been set so that the last light of the sun upon the winter equinox would fall directly down the entry. In fact, the sun, in setting, would cast its golden light against the back wall of the tomb which stood to catch it.

Sebastian smiled as he remarked this.

'You've seen that?'

'Yes, I have. Last year. Corbin and I both. We spent the night within the tomb together. Oh, no, I have no matches. This is a Coleman lamp. Stay here. I'll get some matches.'

And so he hurried down, with Corbin at his heels, the bedroll swinging on his shoulders, while I stayed where I was, and watched him walk. I watched the fog as well, which now, as I was left alone, blew in. It wrapped me up, then blew away, then wrapped me up again. It tore, then cleared, and then it closed around me. I'd never seen a fog come in so fast and dense before; where I was from, fogs did not fall like thunderbolts. This blew in like a thing that covered meaning up. 'Sebastian?' I called, but there was no response. And though he'd said to stay right where I was and wait for him, I saw no way that he would find me in this fog when he returned, and so began to climb up toward the tomb, which was two hundred yards above me.

I walked, though, quite a while. Farther than I thought I should to get to where the tomb was. The fog did not blow out again. It got quite dense. I saw my hands and feet and saw the ground, the grass where sheep had grazed; I saw the rocks that thrust up through the grass – not standing stones, just rocks, but somehow in that fog they seemed to have a quality of looming in them. But that was all. I walked and walked; I tried to stay quite calm, but I felt panicked, like a dog who swims in seas too far from home. The cottage was below me, the tomb was right above, and yet this was like drowning on dry land. My god, where was I? Fog tore into my throat. I felt it choke me, push down like something

154

trying to ram into the heart of me. Where was he? Where was Bastian? This time, when I called him, I could not even hear my own voice coming from my mouth; my voice was strangled. Oh, god, where was I now? Sebastian could not love me, or he would never have abandoned me like this.

At that thought, things grew worse. I tried to run downhill, tripped, fell, and clambered to my feet again. I was unhurt, but terrified; I'd never been in fog like this before, so I could not have known what it might feel like. I was a child lost in too-big waves now. Sebastian knew this land. I didn't. How could he have left me here? And as I thought this, it seemed then, right then, that all this fog, this fog around me, was just the fog that I'd been living in. What was I doing here, upon this tiny island, where, as small as Long Holm was, I could just lose myself in fog? I didn't know. I must be mad, quite mad; at this thought I *got* mad, mad at the fog, and mad at Bastian. I thought: No, I won't have this, I'll take control myself, walk down and find the boat, the path above it. And though it took a moment to compose myself enough to walk again, I did, and made my way, through fog as thick as dusk, down to the sea. And there upon the beach was the cock-boat, in its geo, the well-worn path above it. By then, I was composed enough to stop and sit and breathe until my breathing had returned to normal.

Then I climbed up the path, and found the cottage. Sebastian was not there. He must be at the tomb, then, waiting for me. I found the path to that, and climbed it, too. I had been right. He sat there at the entrance to the tomb, the lantern lit, his hair and beard bejeweled with drops of water.

'You went for a walk?' he said. He said it lightly. Could he possibly be serious?

'No, Bastian, I got lost. You didn't come and find me.'

'Lost?' he said.

'Yes, lost,' I said, and threw my hands up in the air. 'You make it sound like I'm an idiot, or a child. Fog does that sometimes, though. It loses people.'

'But this was not that kind of fog.'

'What kind of fog is that? The kind you don't come looking for me in?'

'You're angry,' he said, as if perplexed.

'You're right. I'm angry. I've been here on Long Holm about four hours, and already I've gotten lost here and you haven't come to find me.'

He said, 'Please don't be angry. I want to show my tomb to you.' At this, he set the lantern on the ground, rose to his feet and caught my hands where they were still held out in front of me.

'You look like me,' he said. 'Don't look like me too much. You are so much more beautiful than I.' He took my hands in his, and rubbed them as if they were flints, and he the spark that soon would fly from them. And then he put his arms, but loosely, around my waist, and put his lips to my lips, kissed me lightly. He looked me in the eye as he drew back, not far, and said, 'I really am sorry, Emrys. Please forgive me.'

At this, I felt the way I'd felt the night he put the dress on me, and pulled my bones to him. Like something that the flint had sparked already. It took so little for Sebastian to make the past become the past for me. I felt not quite aflame, but warm all through, as Bastian leaned his knees to me, and touched my knees with his, my thigh bones with his thigh bones. I kissed him back, and now he kissed me fully, and it felt once again as if the whole world was a map

Sebastian would trace on me. Indeed, I felt I knew, as I had never known before, just how correct creation myths had been. Perhaps my getting lost had been for this – this finding after. Space might have four directions, but for me, they all led one way now, toward this. Just as this tomb seemed to me his, Sebastian was my center now.

'All right,' I said. 'Forgiven,' and I came close to saying, *I love you. I love you more than life itself, Sebastian.* But I did not, just let him slip his arm around my waist, as the fog cleared a little and blew away from us.

'It's nice, this place,' he said. 'You think? It's quite peninsulate.'

'What does that mean?'

'Just as it sounds. But here, the peninsula is made by land, not water.'

'And there are blind springs underneath?'

'I haven't doused this land; if you can bear to come into my tomb, we might just see if we can feel what springs may lie beneath it.'

'I think that I can bear your tomb,' I said. 'It can't be worse than fog for getting lost in.' I said this only to let him know that he was quite forgiven. But as I said the word *lost*, heard it in my ears, I thought of losing, as I wished to, all our secrets. Sebastian loved this tomb; I feared it, or I had, until this moment when I felt that, in the fog, it might be suddenly a kind of sanctuary. Perhaps here I could help Bastian to unlock the things he'd locked so deep inside him. And so I added, 'But you know, if I can bear to go inside, then you can bear to tell me something of yourself when we are there.'

'You bargain, right at the entrance to my tomb?' he said.

'I bargain, yes. You know I'm claustrophobic. You're

something else. I don't know what the word for it would be. The tomb will be like Truth. Each time I go inside, I get to ask you something.'

'Anything at all? And I must answer it?' said Bastian.

'Yes, anything at all,' I said.

'How will you know that I speak truth?'

'I'll know.'

'Well, all right, then. If it will make you love my tomb. So will you lead the way there?'

'You first,' I said. He smiled, and took his time in rearranging the bedroll and the lantern, then got down on his knees, and ducked into the place where all the flat and squared stones ended. He ducked, and ducked away. I saw the light preceding him, then got down on my own knees and crawled after him. I thought of how, in London, I had asked him if the entrances to these tombs, these chambered tombs, were tight. 'Why should you care?' he'd said. 'That's my department, surely.' And as I crawled, I smiled, as Sebastian had. The light fell out behind him, and I could clearly see the perfect flatness of the stones that made this passage; the stones were huge, and from another island. As I emerged into the tomb, Sebastian was waiting, and he'd set the lantern right in the middle of the central chamber.

This chamber soared above us; the roof was clean and white, and corbeled, set with neat, dressed stones, set inward. The walls were clean and white as well, a different kind of crofter's cottage, built with blocks that were like great stone books set in a pile. The air within the tomb was just as clean and fresh as if the wind had blown it there. But this was a still wind, a great long stillness held within the air; it spoke in dialect as timeless as the rock the tomb

158

was made of. My gaze went upwards, then went down, went up, and then it turned to the four chambers that were set, as side-cells, off the main one. I looked at each in turn. One, closest to the east, was also largest, and although you could not stand in it, you could, I thought, stretch out almost completely. The northern one was smallest, and its floor was all one stone. One, to the south, was not yet excavated. I saw that it was there that Bastian worked, since he had left some tools, quite neatly stacked, before that door sill.

I looked into each cell. It was so strange, how right this seemed, that those who'd built this tomb had lived in villages like Skara Brae. They'd mixed up life and death, made houses for the dead that were like houses for the living, all dry stone chambers. The private sleeping chamber I'd crawled into at Skara Brae had been a good deal like these side-cells, although the rocks that made their walls were smaller; still, it seemed that in that age which was now gone you sometimes climbed into your room, your stone room, quite alive, and slept till morning, then climbed out again. But sometimes your bones were placed in a stone room by someone else, and then you slept forever. The rooms the dead were given were quite large, as well as clean and dry; their boundaries had been set and then had lasted fifty centuries.

'This is so lovely. So secure,' I said. 'Who could believe they did this in that age, without iron or steel or bronze, without the wheel, without a ruler?'

'They saw it in their minds,' said Bastian. 'They felt it in their bones. And then they built it for their bones and minds to live in.'

'They brought just big bones in?'

'Well, mostly. Skulls and thigh bones, arm bones, cla-
vicles. It's rare to find a small bone in these tombs.'

'And did they burn the bodies?'

'I think they did. Some think they let the bodies first
decay. I think they burned them, waited for the bones to
cool, then brought them in.'

'How did they carry them?'

'In baskets, I imagine. Because of weight. Sit down.' He
spread one quilt out in the chamber that was largest, to the
east, and let the end of it drape down across the door sill
there. Then he patted the quilt, his hand as gentle as I'd
ever seen it be; I sat where it had patted. He put his hand
upon my leg, and let it rest there, just as warm and soft as all
the stones were cool and hard around us. He let it rest
there, while he looked at me, and then up at the corbeled
roof. He smiled almost shyly, as if he wanted me to sit and
think about the bones that had once sat where we now sat.
And so I did. I thought of someone, a woman, who had
lived five thousand years before; she'd crawled into this
tomb not to love a man she loved, but, rather, to bury him.
He'd died quite young, much younger than Sebastian and I
were; it would have been a wonder if in that age *he'd* lived
in he'd lived until the age of forty.

So he'd died young, and when he'd died, the woman who
had loved him had felt as if she'd died as well, because he
had been woven into her as stones are woven into land-
scapes. Yes, she had lost him, lost him, and now that she
must live within a world where he was not, she felt as if the
world itself was fog. She'd stood beside him as he burned,
and watched the smoke that was the man pour up into the
sky which arched above her. She had done more; she'd
stood beside the smoke, and let it seep into her skin, her

hair, the deer skins she had worn the day they burned him. She'd breathed as deep as she could breathe to let the last of what was him enter her lungs, just slide inside her. And then, as others left the place where bodies burned, she stayed and waited until his ashes cooled enough so that she could embrace them. Indeed, she'd flung herself upon the pile of ash, and rubbed the ash into her skin till it was blackened. Then, with the help of others, who returned when she was done, she'd picked the bones that still remained from out of the ashes.

I saw this, in my mind. It was so clear. I heard the wind that blew; the noise it made within my mind was like a voice that spoke there. As she was gathering his bones, the wind rose, and began to blow away what still remained, as ash, upon the ground the man had walked on. At first, she moved to catch it, all the ash that curled away like water smoked from off the surface of the sea; then she just let it blow away, and watched him curling in the sky. Her man was gone. His bones remained, though. But when she sifted what was left, she found the small bones had all burned; the finger bones, the knuckle bones, the toes, were gone. And all the sweet integuments that had articulated his joints, those, too, were gone, along with ashes, blowing. His skull, though; that was left. His thigh bones and his clavicle, the great bones that had been his arms. His pelvis, too; she lifted it, and cradled it to hers for just a moment. And then she took the basket that she'd made to carry these bones into where she would set them; the stone that closed the tomb was pushed aside, and someone went before her with an oil lamp, which smoked, and smelled, and threw a strange and shadowed light here.

But she had followed, with her bones, until she got right

here, right to this inner chamber. And she had risen to her feet, and felt the corbeled roof, the arch soaring above her. Somehow it eased her pain to know that he, her man, would lie within this dry strong arch for five millennia. The stones would not grow tired, not fall asleep, not die, as men died, as she too would die someday. The stones would simply stay, let time run off them like water, and yet keep all rains quite outside of them. There was no water seepage in the tomb, no moss, no damp at all; it was still quite as dry inside as it had been when she had been here. And as I sat there beside Bastian, I couldn't think, in all the world, of any place I'd rather be, if I were bones. I'd lie here, safe, quite safe, just bones, look up and see the roof, look out and see the sea, as the fog cleared away, right through the entry passage. I said this to Sebastian, said I thought it would be nice, if I were bones, to lie and see this.

'But bones do not have eyes,' Sebastian said, and laughed.

'My bones would.'

'Yes, your bones would. You see things well,' he said. 'Would you feel safe here?'

'Yes, quite safe. Of course, the passage would be closed. That might make things a little different.'

'A little. But if your bones had eyes, they could see right through the stone; they'd know the bay was there, the firth beyond it.' And then we both were silent; in the silence, I could hear Sebastian's words again. *You see things well*, he'd said, as if he wished me to. But though I saw the woman, saw myself, as bones, and even saw my daughter, framed by birds – *Can I come in?* she'd said – when I looked at Sebastian, there was much I couldn't see, a dark place that no light illuminated. And I thought of our pact. I'd come

162

into the tomb, and he would tell me something of himself. What should I ask, then?

'Truth, now,' I said, taking his hand and holding it in mine, so that he would not feel as scared as I had felt when I had lost him in the fog. 'The picture that you have of you when you were young and blond. You looked so happy. What went wrong? What changed that?'

'That is your question? What went wrong? I'm happy now, with you. Happy that you are happy in my tomb. I, too, wish I could lie here someday.'

'You said that once. In London.'

'I remember. You'd told me your husband had made you make a promise. And I said, ''Well, all right, then. What promise shall *I* take? Something quite hard, I think, if you like fairness.'' '

'Yes. Then you said, ''Perhaps I'll ask you to make sure I'm buried in my tomb. Or that my thigh bones go there.'' '

'And did you promise?'

'No. How could I? If I had, I couldn't keep that promise.'

'No, you could not. But I can. Keep mine, until you free me from it. It wasn't matches I'd forgotten in the cottage. Do you think you'd be cold? If we took off your clothes, here in the tomb, do you think I could warm you?' He moved his hand, which had been lying, this whole time, upon my knee, just slightly down onto the inside of my thigh, and asked a question with it. And if I said, *Of course*, it was not with my mouth; my mouth said, 'You can be the kiln for me.'

And then we moved together, backwards across the door sill that we sat upon, into the largest cell, the eastern one. Sebastian was as tender as he'd ever been with me, as he took off my jacket, woolen sweater, vest, my shirt. He put all these things down, and then his clothes, as well, upon

163

the stone that we were lying on; he pulled the second quilt that he had brought right over us. We still had pants on, but he seemed in no rush to proceed. He said, 'Shall we turn off the light?' to which I said, 'Of course,' and this time with my mouth. He drew his chest away from mine, leaned over, shut the lantern down, let darkness fall within the tomb, and let me see that there was still a light that entered it. This fell down the long passage. Sebastian said, 'Look. The fog has cleared. The sun is shining there. It will be waiting for us.' And he was right, the light fell in, as if through a long window. But light or not, it was still darker in the tomb than it had been at any time when we made love, since we had come to Orkney. I liked the darkness, then. He put his arms around my back, and now our chests touched in the dark, my breasts were pressed against him. He slid his hand down to my buttocks, inside the pants I still had on, and held them as if he would hold them always.

I let him hold them. Didn't speak. I knew that if I spoke what I would say would be, 'Sebastian, I free you from your promise.' I wanted to, as much as I had ever wanted to say a word aloud – with spoken words to seed a silence. I wanted to in part because when I'd been lost within the fog, Sebastian, as it turned out, had been loving me. But I thought of our daughter – she who'd dreamed for me to come here to this island, where the gateway would be opened – and thought that if she came, it should not be within a tomb where bones had lain, no matter how completely that place fit Sebastian and me together. I loved him, oh so much, and I would have a child with him, but when the time was right; she should not be conceived here. And so, I held my silence, as Sebastian held me, then disattached the clothes that still remained on us.

And he was silent, too, said nothing with his mouth; only his hands, only his lips, only his thighs spoke. When time had passed, he took my hips, lifted me up, and let me down until I rested, oh so lightly, on him. I didn't move, not right away, but put my palms down to my sides, then took his hips between my hands, and felt the bone there. I knew my hands were on the part of him that would last five thousand years and still be, always, Bastian. They were dear bones, such dear, dear bones I felt beneath my hands. Sebastian's skeleton was revealed, it was a strong and pure thing, him forever. And on it, like a garment, the soft flesh that was so swift, so fleeting, it was like a flash of light in darkness.

Soft time. Hard time. No time. Then time again, and I lay down beside Sebastian, while he pulled me to him. 'That was so dear,' he murmured. 'Thank you.' And then he fell asleep, or almost so, his body twitching. The game of Truth had not gone far, I realized suddenly. Sebastian had just turned my words away, had turned them back upon themselves, as good at that as he was good at loving. But as I lay and felt him sleep against me warm and dry, I thought that I had language which would, in time, draw forth his secrets from him. Indeed, I felt, then, quite convinced that it would not be long before he let me see right to the heart of him. And I, who'd found – against all expectation – a tomb which made me feel protected, felt I'd somehow stay forever in this place where things were safe and where light always found its way into the darkest dark, just as the sun thrust through the cunning cunt which now lay waiting for it.

10

I WAS NOT SAD, though, when we'd left the tomb behind and gone back to the cottage. Sebastian heated water on the stove so we could bathe. There was a hand-pump by the sink. I'd never used one, and I loved the way it felt to pump and feel the air just pushing on itself until the water burst out suddenly. The stove got hot, I found; it heated water quickly. Sebastian's tub could hold just one of us at a time. He put it on the floor beside the stove, then filled it up with bucket after bucket of hot water. When I climbed in it first, at his insistence, he poured another bucketful over my knees, so that the water steamed around me. He washed my back with olive-oil soap, and let his hands remain upon my back the way he'd let them linger on my buttocks when we'd been in the tomb. I'd never seen soap made from olive oil before; it was quite brown, and seemed to have been carved off a larger block. When I had climbed out of the tub, and Bastian took my place, I washed him with the soap, too, not just upon his back but also on his chest and arms and shoulders. He closed his eyes as I was washing him, and seemed totally relaxed – that he was home, that I was there, that we were bathing.

'This soap is wonderful,' I said. 'Just olive oil in it?'

'And ash,' he said. 'All things that clean you must have ash in them.'

And we then had good days, I think eight in a row. I slept with Bastian again that night when we were clean, the cottage clean as well. The bed was hard, the quilts were warm, and I found that this thing I long had made so difficult was easy. I woke at times, but then I slept again; each time I woke, I saw the sea, which rolled and rolled beyond the western windows. I slept quite late next morning, and when I woke, I found that Bastian was up, and had made coffee and some toast; he sat at his desk, reading. He came to bed, though, when I called him, and we made love, a morning kind of love, at which I found that I once more had changed my mind. I wanted, now, not merely to give Sebastian the gift he'd sought – and give it to myself as well – but to discuss it first. I thought that maybe this was how we could pick up the game of Truth which we had turned off with the Coleman lantern.

For now, we had good days. No fog, no fights, no sense that we were riding something like a time-falls, slipping. We slept, and slept together. Sometimes I moved away, and slept alone, but when I woke during the night I moved back in and held Sebastian. We woke, made love, or didn't, went out, after we ate, into the cold and wind and sea and sunshine. Sebastian did his work, some every day, and it was as if the age we really lived in had just faded. We rose, and smelled the ocean, watched the waves, the birds, the sheep; the sheep were everywhere, no walls on Long Holm. Within the cottage, there was warmth from peat which, when it burned, left masses of ash behind the burning. Sebastian took this from the stove and, as we didn't need it to make soap, he dumped it on the grass outside the cottage. Once when the wind was blowing even harder than was usual, it caught the ash and made it curl off in the sky. It looked quite like my vision, except that Bastian stood beside the ash, and then leaped back, so that it would not blow into his face.

We washed, we drank, we ate, we thought – I thought, at least – that surely this was the beginning of something different. That this was just the time before the time-to-come, when we could talk in spoken language. For now, our bodies spoke; I waited for the time each day when we would go to bed again, together. Sometimes when Bastian went to work within his tomb, I'd take a book and go and sit outside the entrance. Corbin waited beside me, his paws crossed, his nose intent. He smelled the rabbits Bastian had told me of. When Bastian came back out, he said one day, quite grinning, 'You *both* want something yummy now, I think. Well, let's go and get it,' and so we walked down to the cottage where Corbin got a lamb bone, which he took onto the grass. I stayed inside and got Sebastian.

So we had eight good days. For now, I was contented to let things be, to just get up each day, and walk down to the sea with Bastian and Corbin. We took a walk each morning before Sebastian got to work; he liked to watch the seals climb out upon the rocks beside the cock-boat. They wriggled out, using their flippers, their bodies rippling, wave-like. They inched along as if they feared to shed their fur, as if they hoped it would not wrinkle off, snagged on the rock behind them. But when they'd reached the place where they were going, they stretched out in that wind as if it were the warmest sunshine. They bathed in air as Bastian and I bathed each night in water, and seemed to find the same deep sensual pleasure in changing elements. But I preferred to watch the birds upon these walks. They hunted fish, those birds, incessantly. They never seemed to find enough, always had room for more, and when one found a fish – dropped down and grabbed it in its beak or talons – it seemed, as it flew off, as if it wished to find a place where it could pin it, own it, keep it, not merely gulp it down and swallow it.

Upon these morning walks, if there were no seals on the rocks, Sebastian would throw a stick into the sea for Corbin. He'd walk right to the edge of rock, then throw the stick as far as it would go, not letting Corbin plunge immediately after it. 'No, wait,' he'd say. 'Don't move. Just wait until I say that you can go,' and Corbin, agonized and quivering, would do what he'd been told, although he clearly feared the stick would vanish in the deeps if he did not go right away to claim it. He'd strain and strain, waiting for Bastian to say, 'All right. Now go and get it, boy,' and then he'd leap from a high rock, his paws all braced before him on the wind, as if he pushed against the air, as if he almost flew in it. He'd land hard in the water, sink down and disappear, then come back up, his black head bobbing like a seal's. With powerful strokes of all four paws, he'd thrash the water until it churned; he seemed to lift himself half out of it. Then, when he'd approached the place he'd seen the stick go down, he'd start to weave his body back and forth as if he really wove the water. And when he got it in his mouth, he held it high and swam straight back toward Bastian, proud, as if he were an arrow.

'Good boy,' said Bastian. 'Good boy,' and then we'd walk back to the cottage, Corbin dripping, but holding, still, the stick that he had won like this.

Was it just eight days, then, that passed? I think it was. Upon the eighth night, I had another dream about the child. She once again had hair the shade of wheat, and wore a green silk dress, but this time it was sunset which I saw behind her head, sunset and in deep winter. I knew this, since the grass was black – as I'd been told it turned when winter storms were fierce in Orkney – and just as it had been the day we crossed the Pentland Firth, the sea beyond the shore was smoking. Midwinter sunset. It was the winter equinox. The sun was falling down the stone passage. The girl, though, in my arms, was dressed just in that silk, and as I held her, I felt that she was shivering. What kind of mother was I? What was I thinking? thought my dream. I found a lambskin, cured, and wrapped the child in it. At this, she smiled, a subtle smile, that seemed just like her father's and said, 'That's nice. I think maybe it's time that I came in now.'

I woke. I turned in bed to find Sebastian was not there; he'd thrown the covers back, had let some cold in. I touched the place where he had been; it, too, was cold, although outside there was a very early light. Where was Sebastian? He'd gone outside without lighting the stove, the fire, without putting the kettle on. I thought this strange, and could not guess where he could be. Corbin lay on the floor beside the bed. As I stirred, he did too, looked up and panted slightly. Then both of us heard Bastian outside upon the stoop. He came in, flinging the door before him. I saw that he was furious; his face, his walk – the way he threw his hands up – all revealed this. But I could not imagine what had taken him from where he was, in bed beside me, to this anger. He saw me, wide awake now, the quilt pulled to my chin as I looked back at him, concerned, astonished. He tried to calm himself, but seemed to pinch my neck between his fingers as he said to me:

'Where did you put my knuckle bone?'

I said, 'What do you mean? What knuckle bone?'

'My knuckle bone. The only knuckle bone there is on Long Holm save for the ones we have inside us.'

'You found a knuckle bone? I thought they didn't bury bones that small.'

'That's why this bone is so important. Where is it?'

'How should I know?' I said. 'You think I took your knuckle bone, Sebastian?'

'The bone is missing. So is the case I keep it in. I keep it here, right here, within this box upon the desk. Last night I took it out, and it was on the table when I cooked. You set the table. You must have moved it.'

'I didn't see it. Why should I lie? What's really wrong?'

'*That's* really wrong. Should it take more? Don't try and tell me what I'm feeling, Emrys.'

'Why not? Why is this *my* fault? For someone who's so smart about people who've been dead for five millennia, you're not that bright about the living ones. If you've misplaced a knuckle bone, why not just ask for help in finding it?'

'There's nothing I've misplaced but my good sense,' he said. 'To bring you here. To take you in the tomb. To let you see her photographs.' And when he said that, though I said aloud, 'I knew it!' with a kind of triumph, I hadn't known it, not till then, that moment. But now, I knew it wholly, and knew I should have known it ever since I'd seen the pictures on the walls around me. I'd seen the blurring at their edges, the resonance that they set off, the way that

171

right behind the thing that you could see in each, you could see all the things you could not see there. I'd seen that they were great, had seen, too, that they mattered so much to Sebastian that he would dress the walls of his white house in them. And I felt, in my heart, that this, this moment we were in, was like the moment when the tide begins to ebb again, when, having reached with its long hands as high as it can reach, it just gives up, and turns away. I thought, too, that, if Sebastian did not answer what I now asked, we would never learn a language in which to speak together.

And he did not.

'Who was she, Bastian? Who is she?'

'Who?' he said, as if this were a thing that you could say and get away with it. 'I don't know what you mean.'

'The photographs. What woman took them?'

'That's not the point. It wasn't she who took them, Emrys.' But he said this so bitterly, so sullenly, that he was clearly lying. He let his hands fall to his sides, and said, 'I can't believe it. I left it here, right here, upon the desk, in its black case. Well, quite a birthday present, to lose the bone the day that I turn forty.'

It turned out that day was his birthday. He'd never told me when this was, just that it was sometime during August. All day, he scarcely talked to me, so I could hardly make him feel that this day he was in was one to celebrate. And when I tried to help him search, he wouldn't let me, went outside and worked all day alone, and in the evening, got quite drunk. That night, he mixed his liquors. First whiskey, then some lager, then whiskey again, poured straight into a thick glass tumbler. I fed the stove, he fed the fire, and then sat before it drinking, staring into the flames, which turned to coals, which he made flames again. He wouldn't meet my eyes, and every time I spoke, just said, 'Leave it alone. I don't wish to discuss it.'

I had some beer myself. I had to, in that cottage which was so small Sebastian's anger filled it. Or maybe it was not anger – hatred, grief and rage, all mixed together, radiating outwards. The longer this went on, and it went on for hours, the more I longed to be just anywhere but Long Holm. I wanted to leave it all – to leave the island, leave the man, even to leave the child we might have had together. This was what I'd feared. The coal that he'd interred was clearly much much hotter than the peat he stared at. I wanted now to leave, go home, take up my life, the life that I had loved before I felt I'd lost it. I thought, then, it was possible to cross the sea again; I thought that countries could not vanish quite that quickly.

He drank. He drank and drank. He got so drunk that he could scarcely walk to bed; I had to help him as he reeled, quite surly. The walls were far too close, the tables, chairs, as well – all surfaces, he seemed to think, had been mis-placed like knuckle bones. I helped him into bed. I had to. He could not, himself, have climbed the bed and then climbed in it. I took off both his shoes but left the rest of what he wore right where it was. He fell asleep at once. It was as if the liquor he had drunk had taken him to some-where where there truly was no dreaming. And as I looked at him, I thought: *Who is this man? I do not know this man.* And now, not even twitching. In the time we'd been together, I'd grown used to this, had seen it as a thing which made Sebastian open, vulnerable, a man who even when he slept was not quite all asleep, but still half in the world of waking. But now he was just pole-axed, a thing inside a boat which had been tossed right to its bottom.

That night, I didn't sleep with him. I made a bed up on the floor. This, Corbin shared quite happily. I touched his head and curly back and paws, and felt a little comforted. I also found myself remembering the man I'd left for the first time since I had left him. I found myself remembering the way he'd say, 'Our world went wrong when we gave in to punishment. There was a time, before the wound, when that was not how people fixed things. There is no law, has never been a law, that can repair the world. Only love can do that.' Why had I left him? He, at least, had known me, known that I would never lose a knuckle bone, then lie about it. He'd known that I believed – believed back then, when he had known me – that words were what could knit two things together.

And he had loved me, too, not merely known me, since he'd known the things that made me who I was. If he were here, what would he say? That love itself was making something new – a better thing – out of two joints which otherwise stayed separate. That love, in fact, was like the thing that made the finger on a hand bend to the task of every making. Why did I love Sebastian if he couldn't see this truth? Or did I love him? Maybe I'd just needed him. I had been stranded, half-alive, half-dead upon the vast and silent Waters of Death or in the House of Ashes, and Bastian had been a wind that blew into my life and set me loose – a pair of new eyes I could see the world through. But did I love him? What was love but understanding which embraced? Sebastian had been right. He was a perfect stranger.

Next morning, I woke up, and saw that, in the night, a mist had once more rolled in, covering Long Holm. I lay and watched it through the windows, saw that it had closed the world off, and I would not, as I'd thought to, leave that day. I'd planned, before I slept, to tell Sebastian that it seemed time for me to leave the island; I'd planned to ask him, quite politely, if he would take me in his boat, since the ferry had already come and gone once. I'd planned, in fact, to pack before he woke, but now as I looked out, I knew that it was useless to start packing. I hated fog, just hated it, and not just when I was as lost in it as I had been the night we'd gotten here. I hated it from where I lay inside the cottage, looking out, and seeing nothing but fog itself there. It was as if the windows had each been boarded up, or papered over, as if we who were inside the cottage now – Corbin, as well – had all been placed into a kind of quarantine.

This fog was what we walked in; the exit from the cottage was here, but on the other side of it was nothing. I got up, lit the fire, made some coffee, looked at fog while Bastian slept, the liquor in his blood still holding him. I drank some coffee, looked at fog, and hurt, hurt through each part of me. I'd thought Sebastian loved me, thought of me as something light and lovely, treasured, wanted. I'd thought I loved Sebastian, that he was dark and powerful, a ley line I could walk along. And more than that, I'd thought that he and I together were one thing, that what was broken could be mended; I'd thought that, if I came here, set my feet upon this land, we could know the world as it had been before the Flood had taken it. Instead, we had just this. Sebastian loved another woman. He dreamed of her, the Axis Mundi of the earth to him. She might be dead and buried, or alive and well, but still, it was her bones he wished to hold to him.

And when he dreamed, half-drowning and scrabbling on the deck of consciousness, he dreamed of that lost instant she'd awakened him. Made him, perhaps. Yes, *made him*, as we'd said when I was young, and there was talk of someone who had – young – been taken. *Well, did he make her*, we had asked? Yes, he had made her, lucky him or lucky her; she had been made now. Sebastian had been made by someone, an artist whom he'd lost and now would never find again, for all his hunting. The Stonehenge bluestones had been carried all the way from Wales where they were found; in that way had the neolithic people spent their energies. But while Sebastian might admire them, might treasure every bone he found in tombs those people had built, he was not *of* them, he was of the dark time when things had flown apart, and would be neither filled again nor mended.

But so was I. If I had not been, I would long ago have given myself to Sebastian, wholly. I would have long ago torn down the last thin barrier I had placed between myself and what might enter me. It was a barrier that seemed thin as air that held the surface of the sea in place, until it cut it right in half, until it smoked it; it was a barrier that seemed pale as mist that blew outside, but covered over all the windows you might see through. Seeming aside, it was, as I was certainly aware, as real as any stone which blocked the entrance to a passage tomb. If it were not removed in time, that stone would keep the sunset of midwinter from falling deep into the central chamber. When I had met Sebastian I'd felt my heart and body had just been set upon a course toward a lost island. I should have gone with that, and all the way, and yet it seemed to me that, as the Greeks would have it, I'd been a plaything of the gods. Been forced to make a choice between two right things, two right lives. Whichever life I didn't choose would punish me.

But still, that morning, in the fog, until Sebastian woke, I really thought I wanted to go home again. And then he woke. He saw the mist, he saw I was awake, and said, 'Good morning,' in a voice as cool as stone. And now I wanted, as I heard his voice, not drunk, but far away, as far as if he spoke to me across the ocean, to stay and *make* him love me, stay and take him until, whoever she had been, I had replaced her. But when I felt this, it was as it had been that night in Scrabster when Sebastian had preferred the drinking of liquor in the pub to loving me. I'd hated how this made me feel, just desperate, just savage. My throat had hurt when I had felt him slipping from me. And now, when he awoke and said, 'Good morning,' cool as stone, I felt the same again. My throat ached. My whole body ached.

But still, I said, 'Good morning,' in as calm a tone as I could manage. 'There's fog again.'

'I see that.'

'Did you sleep well?'

'No. Did you?'

'Not very.'

'No dreams?'

'A few.'

'Not I,' he said. 'Well, so, a foggy day. I'll go and work. And you?'

'I think I'll write a bit,' I said.

And so he ate, and drank some coffee, and then left. Corbin left with him. I stayed and watched the mist paper the windows. Got up and tried to write, put on a coat, and went outside. Was panicked by the fog there. So went back in, to read, but that day, when I read, the words just stayed upon the page, they did not rise up to my mind and speak to it. When Bastian returned, quite late, and not for lunch, he said, 'I haven't found the knuckle bone.' This time, he said it sadly, as if he felt that he had lost not just the bone, but something in me which he had, against all reason, trusted.

I was so pleased to see him back, though, to hear his voice at all, that I said, stupidly enough, 'Well, maybe Corbin buried it.'

'No, Corbin did not bury it,' said Bastian. 'He doesn't bury bones which are in small black cases. Have you had tea?'

'No.'

'I'll cook then.' He did, but drank as well, and once again stared at the flames which rose from the peat fire. Each time I tried to talk with him, he answered, but shortly, as if he clipped his words, cut them on purpose. He bathed that night, not in the tub, but merely heating water on the stove, then stripping down and washing what was bared by this. And I, watching him do this, remembered how I'd felt the first time that we met, when I had wanted to strip his clothes from him. To free him, I had thought, from shirt and shoes, from pants and belt, and then to touch the body that I found beneath them; to take a careful inventory of all I had discovered, knowing that touching Bastian's body was what my hands were made for. Now, I'd had his body, had stripped it time and time again of every piece of cloth that covered it, and yet I wanted still to disattach this thing that wrapped him like a shroud; his silence was the silence of a tomb I did not love, which did not want me anywhere inside it.

The next day, there was fog again. I looked out, thought: *God help me, I just can't take another day of this*. I'd slept upon the floor again, but now I got in bed, and lay beside Sebastian, naked, wanting him. But he did not want me. When he woke up he didn't move at all, just looked at me.

I said, 'Sebastian, there's a dream I want to tell you. I had it twice, once here, once back on Mainland.'

'A dream?' he said. 'You still believe I can untie your dreams?'

'This dream was not just about me. It was about, well, us, I guess.'

'What us?' he said. 'There is no us. You are still married, Emrys. You have done nothing to divorce your husband. And you still think of him, I know, although you never mention it.'

'That isn't true.'

'No, no,' he said. 'I'm sick of it. Sick of your being married. Sick of the careful distance that you place between us.'

At this, I was enraged beyond enraged; I'd been about to tell him everything.

'I'm sick of *you*,' I said.

'So leave.'

'I can't just leave. I'm stuck here, on this island, until the mist clears. Then you can take me back to where I came from, and forget the whole thing ever happened. *She was and she was not, once*, you can tell yourself.'

'I knew you wouldn't stay,' he said. 'I knew you'd never do it.'

'You think you've made it easy for me, Bastian?'

'What's easy? Nothing in life is easy.'

'Oh, that's original,' I said. 'I see you've moved from silence straight to platitudes.'

He looked at me.

'I'll stick to silence, then, if you prefer. And I'll be glad to take you off the island when the mist clears. You should know, though, that could be days still.'

And it was, days still. Days of silence, sullenness, and lust. The more time passed, the more I wanted him. I thought that, if we could make love just one more time, somehow that would be how I would make Sebastian love me. But really, that was not the heart of what I wanted – nor was she, the daughter who I'd thought to have with him. I merely wanted Bastian, his body and his speech, the way his voice caressed, a deep thing that slid within me. But he, as if he sensed this, spoke little, in short words, short sentences, withholding everything that he could from me. The third day of the mist, I was so desperate I said, 'I'll take the boat myself, if you won't take me out of here.'

'You'll have to wait. It's far too dangerous.'

'Then talk to me, at least,' I said. 'What's happened to your speech? You used to use words so they almost burned me.'

He looked at me appraisingly, and did a strange thing, then. A thing so strange that, when I write of it, it still seems strange to me. I was upon the bed. I wore a long white shirt, a linen shirt, and wooly socks, and that was all. The cottage was quite warm, with all the peat we burned, as if to make up for what did not burn there. And so I wore just shirt, and wooly socks, and longing, and lay upon the bed, watching the mist roll by. When I said, 'Talk to me, at least,' Sebastian, who was reading a great blue book, looked up appraisingly. And then, as if he knew that when I said, 'I'll take the boat myself, if you won't take me out of here,' I meant, *If you won't take me*, he came and sat beside me, the book still in his hands. As if he looked for something that was lost, he flicked the pages, riffled through them. Upon the book's blue spine, in gold, the title read, *The Cairns of Orkney*. I saw this as he held the book above me. Again, he flicked its pages, but this time so that the paper as it passed flicked at my left nipple. And this aroused me, made me weak and wet, as if the thing that touched me was a bird's wing, soft and bent – an airborne feather.

'Yes, words arouse you, don't they, Emrys?' said Sebastian. 'You like this? These pages on your breast? I think you do.' But I said nothing, stared at him, my eyes quite hard and cold; he need not know my body traveled on the road he'd sent it.

'I want to leave,' I said. 'I think that's clear enough. As long as I am here, though, we might talk sometimes.'

'You act as if I've done this purposely.'

'Haven't you?' I said.

'Can I control the mist? The weather comes at my command, then?'

'You think that everything must come at your command. You lose a knuckle bone, and when it won't come back, you think that someone must have stolen it.'

'I found the knuckle bone,' he said. 'It fell behind the table.'

'Well, thanks so much for telling me,' I said. 'Why bother, though? You think you have me at your mercy, don't you?'

He looked again, appraisingly, then less so, almost kindly, and said, 'I don't think that. No, not at all.'

'Just get away, in any case. Just take your book and go.'

'But that's not what you want. Not really, is it?' said Sebastian.

And he was oh so right. By then it had been days, three days, since we had had each other. And he was hungry for me, too. I saw that in his eyes, until I turned away from them and stared out of the window. For just an instant, while I stared, the fog cleared, and in the clear space I could see the sea still rolling. There was a wall of white, which went between Long Holm and Haverskerry, half a mile beyond it. It went from land to land, with inlet in between, then smashed against the skerry, the wave attempting entry. But as it was refused, it curled sideways, reaching out as if it were a brush, white paint upon it. The fog then closed again, as thick as it had been before it cleared. The window was closed up, and I within it.

I turned back, met Sebastian's eyes again. He put his hand out, slipped it underneath my shirt. It rested on my hip. He let it stay there.

'I think that I could love you dearly, if you'd let me,' he said then. 'I think you want this to be over.'

'Want what?'

'This battle. Struggle. War. Whatever you would call it.'

'How over? So that you have won it?'

But that he did not answer. He just let his hand drift up across my waist, my ribs, the breast that waited. He touched my nipple very lightly with one finger – just the tip – and with each touch, I felt that where I had been moored, I was now drifting. Soon, soon, now, it would happen. I'd be lost. I could not hold my breath within me for much longer. And he, I knew, now knew this, since he took his hand and slid it toward my clavicle, to where the hollow in my throat was.

'It hurts you there, I think,' he said. 'The wanting me so much. Right there, within your throat, I think,' he said. But I said nothing, only felt his soft touch on my throat, and thought: *Oh god, yes, set me free again.* He then drew his hand out from underneath the shirt, reached up to touch my mouth, my hair, my cheeks, and then to hold his hand upon my eyelids. And as he did, I raised my arms above my head, stretching them out, still clothed, as far as they would reach there. There was no cunning in this, as there had been that time before, when I had thought: *I'll take the hurt on me*. Then, I had wished to punish him for all the time that we had been apart; then, I had known that he, if he knew hurt was in the air, would fly from it unless his hand inscribed it. This time was different. This time I felt no wish to punish him for all the time we'd been apart; this time, I just wished that time over. So as I reached my arms above my head, I was no starfish, splayed and happy; this time, I just felt instinct, pure and unadorned, that I must look like something chance had offered Bastian. I must look like a bone that lay within the earth, and that there was no other soul to claim now. I must look like a vessel that had washed against the shore, and bobbed there, now, without another master. I must, in fact, look helpless to resist whatever thing this man wished, so that he would wish to take me. Yes, take me, take me, that was how it felt, but this time I saw *taking* as a thing that might be done by Viking warriors, breaking into tombs to look for treasure.

So I raised up my arms above my head, and stretched them out, still clothed, as far as they would reach there. And he regarded this, as if some memory nudged him when he saw it. He seemed, at first, quite distant, quite abstracted. He placed his hands on mine, and held them on the bed; his palms were on my palms, so I could feel the heat there bake them. Then he let my hands go, slipped his hands across my forearms, touched elbows, upper arms, and shoulders. He touched my clavicle again, putting two

183

fingers there, within the hollow of my throat, as if to feel it pulsing; he then undid one button, right below the place it pulsed, touched there, removed his hand, and seemed to say that he was finished now. At that, I moaned aloud. I couldn't help myself. And he, his face quite gentle, reached up, took one of my wrists and pinched it, held it up above my head as if he, that way, helped me. But though he held it there, and even tugged a bit, I still felt that I was about to drown in him.

He knew this. Knew it well. He moved both my wrists so that they touched, then lightly pressed them there, while, with the other hand, he slowly opened up the shirt that covered me. Each white button on the shirt seemed, as he tugged, a separate circle he must rub away, erase, and he had just one hand with which to do this rubbing, as with the other hand he held my wrists above my head. Each button made me weaker. Each circle was a thing that, till it came apart, took up the air I breathed. At last the thing was done, the shirt was drawn apart, half to each side, so that it seemed a curtain that bared me to him. And when the curtain bared me, Sebastian, still with that one hand on my wrists, quite roughly ran the other hand across my breasts, my stomach, then down between my legs; with that one hand he roughly spread them. When he could not, with one hand, move them quite as far as he could wish, he said, 'Spread your legs wide now, Emrys. Do it.'

And I did. Spread them wide. As wide as they would spread. At which he took one finger, like the hand, now, of a clock, and placed it at the mouth of time, which fled from us. He pushed it in, just lightly, nothing hard, and then withdrew it, so that it seemed that I must scream from waiting. It was as it had been upon the plane to London,

184

when I felt I knew what it had been to sit on the Edain, and watch Uruk where it had risen from the grass up toward the sky, and then had grown and aged, and fallen. I felt: *Oh please, please hurry*. But Sebastian did not hurry. He looked at me, appraisingly, again. He wore his soft brown shirt with snaps, his old worn jeans, the dark-brown webbing belt with two gold rings through which the belt was looped, then looped back on itself again. He now released my wrists, but said, 'Don't move.' Then, sitting on the bed beside me, he reached down to his waist and slid the loose end of the belt first one way, then the other, so that the two gold rings that wed the belt unwed it. He pulled the belt through all the belt loops with a wisping sound, and had it in his hands, unlooped now.

'I think I'll tie you up,' he said then. 'Would you like that, Emrys?'

I said, 'Of course,' although I muttered it, my eyes half closed, my breath so short that I could not speak as clearly. And then, feeling afraid he had not heard me, thought I'd said another thing, I said, 'Of course,' again, and looked Sebastian in the eyes, at which he smiled that same old secret smile.

'I knew you would,' he said. 'Don't move, then.'

I didn't move. I felt as if I couldn't move, as if the weight of time itself was pressing on me. Sebastian took the belt, and let it trail, then took my wrists again, and wrapped the belt around each wrist in turn. And then – as carefully as someone laying radiating spokes of twisted string in harvest hills – he wrapped them one more time; and then secured them with the circles. He said, 'Try to get free. Try hard,' at which I tried – not hard – and found I couldn't do it. He then said, 'Good,' and reaching down, pulled one long

185

leather lace from one white canvas shoe, letting the shoe fall. He took the lace and looped it through the belt, and then secured it to the crank of the big mullioned window, so that, when he was done, I was not tied just to myself, but also to the dwelling I had thought to flee from.

And I was tied indeed. My hands above my head, my wrists together there, and in my heart a kind of ease, a great relief. It had been three long days since we'd been joined, and though I'd been, the whole time, held within the cottage, I'd been drifting there. Now the belt that tied my wrists was like the rope that moored a boat to land that it had sailed so far to find. And that rope went both ways. A rope, if it is tied, is tied to not just one, but two things. Sebastian let me lie there, not touching me while he unsnapped his shirt and took it off and let it fall beside him. He then took off the shoes that he still wore, his socks and pants, and lay beside me, naked. He danced around my body with his hands as if his hands were things that danced together. He sucked my nipples, too, quite hard, so that the tug might, at some other time, have hurt them, but now, it did not hurt, it just felt that his tongue was something else that I was moored by. And I, through all of this, just moaned and moaned, as if the breath that filled my lungs had now filled more than lungs, as if the breath was everywhere. At last, I begged aloud, 'Please get inside me now, Sebastian. Please, please, don't torture me.'

He smiled sleepily. He said, 'Oh ho, don't torture you. You think I torture you? You said before I thought I had you at my mercy. Do I? It seems you like it?'

'Of course I do,' I said. 'Of course. But please, please, come.' And here I whimpered, or made whatever sound you like to call the sound you make when all words vanish.

At that, Sebastian kissed me. Placed his whole body over mine, and kissed me, letting his hands drift down until they held my breasts in place. And then he poised above me, nudged just in, and stopped, a rock blocking the entrance to the passage. He let it go no further, but held it while his tongue touched at my mouth, a small bright fish that seemed to wander there. I let him kiss me, for a moment, then took away my mouth, feeling I could not breathe, feeling that if he did not push inside me now, the thing would kill me. I was a vortex that now needed to be filled, and if I was not filled, I would just die of it. My legs were still spread wide, and so I raised my knees, and pushed my body up to meet Sebastian's. But he, so cunning, pulled away as I pushed up, and then he said:

'But what is this? You have not got protection. I think you said that you had promised something, what? But now, this does not matter any longer?'

'Oh, please,' I said. 'I'll die.'

'Perhaps,' he said. 'All do,' and then he reached above my head, to take the leather lace and to untie it. He left me tied, but now just wrist to wrist, unleashed. He said, 'There now. You're free. Do what you will. You have to want this, Emrys. Let there be no talk afterwards that I have forced you.'

And I did want it, oh so much that, even though my wrists encumbered me, when I saw Bastian fall away from me and lie upon his back like something that was floating, I felt that he was now a raft and I, a sea-borne swimmer, had no choice but to take refuge on him. And this I did. I climbed upon him, my hands so tightly bound they made my two hands just one hand, which I could lean on; I climbed upon him, pushed my body down on his, and felt

187

Sebastian parting me, as if he pushed myself aside, like curtains. Then I just fell upon Sebastian where he lay. He was a rock. My body was a shaft that pinned him. But I was not a rock, because as all things fell – as I fell, he fell, and we fell together – I felt, as no rock could, that this swift passage that I made onto Sebastian's bare self was the journey I had sought since I had first perceived him. Yes, this was him, himself, his own self, very self; he slid within me like a fish, my own dark fish, I owned him. We both came right away, and now Sebastian raised his hips, and groaned, then let his hips fall down, away, and toward the deeps again.

11

FIVE DAYS NOW PASSED, before things changed again, and I have never been so happy as I was then with Bastian. He hadn't lied when he had said that he could love me dearly, if I'd let him. He loved me dearly. It makes me hurt to think of it. He called me 'darling' now, without an edge to it. His deep, rich, life-filled voice said, 'Sit. Come set your bones upon my lap. Then I'll make dinner, darling.' He washed not just my back, but all of me, each night, as if he felt my skin was finally unencumbered. One night when it was colder than it had been up to then, and I put on pile clothes to sleep, he didn't protest, but said, 'Well, all right. You can be seal as well, as long as you are mostly human woman.' And sometimes when we walked now, to see the sheep or birds or waves – the fog had blown away – he did not take my hand, but put his arm around my shoulder. He pulled me close to him, and had me walk that way.

Once, when we walked, he said, 'But you must start to write again. You now have something new to write about.' And once, as we sat on the rocks and watched the sun sink toward the west, he said, 'Did you not know this, truly,

Emrys? That risking love is risking death? All things that matter first require surrender.'

And he made love to me as well. In those five days, as I cannot forget, he loved me in each way we could imagine. He tied me up again two times, once fastening my wrists and ankles to the posts of the four legs that held the bed. I was a starfish in the ocean, spread again, but this time I was not just of the ocean, but the four directions, also; I felt, as Bastian secured me, that I was now the space that was created earth the moment that the mound had first been pinned to water. Another time, he tied me to the wall, my hands above my head, but so that I must stand – a standing stone again, but this time pointing to the heavens. But other times were other things; we tumbled like the tides of earth, like anything the tides might tumble in them. And I knew then that this surrender was nothing else but trust – trust that the present moment would contain the future in it.

Once, we lay together on the floor, where we had slid, as, while we lay in bed, Sebastian had found his hands upon my ankle bones. He took the ankles in his hands, then pushed them to the floor – the rest of me went down there after them – and then he kept on sliding until his lips were at my feet, my feet the things he loved as if they were the earth his feet might walk on. Another time, he told me, laughing low, that he would make me come until I could not speak and could not move, and this he had no trouble in accomplishing. It seemed that with his entry into me at last, his flesh within my flesh all unimpeded, that he had seeded me with something more than seed – that he had seeded me with something which could stop all fruitless longing.

Indeed, within those days, I saw for the first time that if you were just bright alive, this was quest enough for anyone. And though Sebastian had said that I had something new to write about, I felt no need at all to write it. Why write it? Life was better than any writing, as the circle folk had known; they had not even bothered to invent the letter. I was now in a place where silence, laughter, singing, touch said all the things one had to say that might be written. It seemed quite clear, as well, that since I'd found the spot where just to dance in place was to be strong as anything the earth was built on, I did not need to act, or even question what would come of this new love Sebastian and I had come to. And as for who the woman was, her pictures all around us, I felt quite sure that I had now replaced her within Sebastian's heart – that I'd become her, taken on her mantle. She had known first who Bastian was, and now would understand, I thought, who I was, what I felt, and what I saw in both myself and in her photographs. I saw that – as Sebastian had known before I had – love was not simply understanding. I saw that – as I'd known before he had – it was not anything that looked like wisdom, either.

In fact, love wasn't anything that could be built from pieces, brick on brick. It was much more a single slab of stone that first lay flat, and then was tilted up into the air and pointed toward the sky. It pointed toward the sky from that first moment of the tilt, for all the rest of time that poured around it. It leaned on air, and if you leaned on air – as she had done when she had done her work – then what you leaned on brought forth not just part, but all of you. Not just the part that wished to live, the part that wished to die, the part that wanted to submit, the part that was victorious. There was no separation, no *this* and *that*, now joined, but *this/that*, never even parted. You lived and died, surrendered, triumphed, all of them at once, if you could find a moment when you knew why you had come into the world – and then you came there. You looked at megalith or man, and found that love was what it was, the thing that made you whole, because it was the thing you'd die for. How could I envy her? We had done work that was the same, that sought to see the thing behind the thing that's seen. And I had Bastian now, his hands upon my body.

Days passed. The fog did not come back. The clouds blew off, and there was startling light about, the light of August, late, in Orkney. The world was clear, as clear as bright-blue cups, or bright-blue bowls, with sparkling water poured right up to their blue rims and trembling there. Each time Sebastian loved me, I felt so rich with seed, that I felt almost bathed in it. Who knew what things might come from all this seeding? The spring would show us what we'd planted. I'd dreamed the child again, which made three times in all; as Bastian had said of when I'd learned to sleep with him, three times makes it true, at least in fairy tales. And while this was not quite a fairy tale, this third dream had the feel of something magical about it. In this third dream, my daughter and I were in the circle of the Stenness Stones in that lost age when they were all still standing. My daughter wore the green silk dress again, but this time on her neck there was a necklace made of bone, and carved all round with cup and ring marks – mostly rings, as small as wedding rings. She grasped this necklace in her hand and when I picked her up, she held the necklace still, with all its rings clutched in her fingers.

192

And with us in the circle of the Stones were other women – who spoke a language which I knew, although it wasn't English, nor any Indo-European language I'd ever heard – and in this tongue a woman spoke to me and said, 'So this is our new daughter. Sebastian will be pleased. She looks just as I thought she would when I imagined her this morning.' The woman was quite lovely, and in the dream I knew that she was – as I was – Sebastian's woman. I wasn't jealous, though; I liked her very much, and she confirmed the reasons why when she now said, 'But is this wise? That the child should wear as thin a skin as this one? It may make her believe that she is different from the other animals. Why don't we go and find some dear skins for her?' The language of my dream, although not English, still had a sound that had two meanings, just as English did. And when I heard this woman – Bastian's woman – say the word, I knew that it meant *dear*, not *deer*. I smiled at the woman, said, 'Let's find some dear skins, then.' And then my daughter spoke; she said, 'Is it all right if we come in now?'

I woke. I thought about the dream. I felt that it had been the best of all. The other two had merely been a preparation for it. I realized that I'd known within the dream that Bastian's other woman was thought to be the wisest woman of our tribe – the one who could be counted on to guide things rightly. I'd been a kind of acolyte to her, and now I smiled to think that she was really me, since that was how dreams worked, I thought. But I smiled more to think that if Sebastian and I had a child – a child of flesh and blood – the day would come when she would suddenly learn language. That was what made our children, human children, human – that the day came when they would pin a name to things.

How are we different from the other animals? Sebastian had asked, then said, *I've always thought that it must be because we, men and women, have principles*. And now I saw that although *principle* was just a word – some sounds – without the word, the thing itself was quite inchoate, formless. And while our daughter would have principles, I hoped, she first would have the language with which they could be framed, constructed.

Indeed, I felt a faith in language that morning as I woke that I'd not felt for quite a while. I thought that, when our daughter learned to speak, she would converse with us, and not just of the world she saw there, right around her. No, she would wonder of the past, as well – of all the moments which had led up to the time when she herself had come into the world she saw. My past, and Bastian's, would be a thing she'd yearn to know about, a thing that she would read, when she grew old enough; she'd read us backwards, as if she had seen us in a glass and in the glass had learned the way that one untied all dreams. I would soon tell Sebastian about this; when I had tried to tell him of my first two dreams, he'd merely said, *There is no us*. Well, now there was an us, I thought.

And that *us* was so happy, for five short days, that it appeared to me, as I looked forward into days to come, that this sheer joy we felt could never end, or stop. I tried to think of ways to make Sebastian feel the same, and on the fifth night, as he cooked, I put on the silk dress that he had bought me. We both had bathed, and after bathing I felt clean as a seal, or cleaner – just brand-new again – and as we had no thought of going out into the cold again that day, I thought I would put on the dress and wear it to the table. I knew that Bastian would like this quite a lot, and so he did. I put it on while he was cooking, and when he looked up, saw me wearing it, he smiled, and then he walked away from what he did, and came to me and took me by the hips. He pulled my hips to his. He held me gently, saying, 'Dear bones. We'll take this dress,' and then he reached down, lifted the silk skirt up. He pushed it lightly, like a wave, with one hand, up my shins and knees, across my thighs, and right there to my hips. He did not hang it on my hips this time, but ran his palm over my stomach, and said, 'No knickers, Emrys. Take your knickers off, be bare beneath,' at which I smiled, and did, while he went back to cooking, and I felt more like a seal, fresh come from firth, than ever.

We ate. I loved to eat Sebastian's food; he was a good cook, and his presentations were elegant and simple. He had four dark-blue plates, with a high glaze on them. After the meal, we drank good tea, which he steeped in a brown pot that had been thrown upon a wheel, but looked a bit like Unstan ware. I poured the tea out. He insisted. He said he liked to see me pour the tea, because it took him back to that first day in London.

'So fortunate you wore no gloves,' he said that evening as I poured, and handed him his cup, which had a small handle.

He took the handle, sipped, then watched me sip my own tea; his eyes there, on my hands, made my eyes fall on them as well. And as I looked, I had a passing thought as I saw how my fingers bent around the handle. It really wasn't much, a moment when I thought that these – the knuckle bones – were more important to my life than any other bones I had within my body. If I had not had hands, and knuckle bones within those hands, I could not easily have written *Gilgamesh and Enkidu*; I could not easily have written to Sebastian. Nor could I, easily, have loved his body. I loved him with my hands more than with any other part; all other bones just faded in importance next to these. These bones, in fact, were what made everyone a maker of made things – of pots like the brown teapot, of plates like the blue plates, of tombs, of cottages, of books and boats, even of photographs. Those pictures which looked down on us from all the walls around could never have been taken without hands to take them.

'That knuckle bone you have,' I said, but idly. 'Why do you think it didn't burn with all the rest of the small bones and ligaments?'

Sebastian looked quite startled, set his cup down. And then, though just a little, his eyes grew hooded, as he seemed to search within his mind for what to say to me.

'My knuckle bone?' he asked, as if to gain some time.

'The one you lost,' I said. 'Then found again. Why do you think it didn't burn? I never saw it. Could I see it, do you think?'

Sebastian looked at me, still hooded. He seemed to think much harder than I would have thought he'd need to think about this question. He set his own two hands before him on the table, flat, and stared at them. Then suddenly he nodded, just once, an up and down, and got up from the table, walked to his desk. He opened the wooden box that held his pens and pencils, and pulled from it a thing he closed his hand around. Then he returned and sat, his hand still closed around this thing which, with an effort, he set upon the surface of the table between us. It was a velvet ring case, with gold around the rims which closed the two halves of the case together. He snapped it open now, and left it open, but he said:

'I'd rather you just looked. I'd rather you didn't touch it, Emrys.'

I looked. I had to look, I was so hurt by what he'd said, and wanted so to keep him from seeing how the words had hurt me. I had been idle, clean, a silkie, wearing a dress for him, and happier than I had ever been in life before. I was just open, wide, wide open, and now these words which came, it seemed, from nowhere, cut me to the quick; my eyes welled up with tears. He didn't trust me, still, with this damn bone of his. I was so hurt by that I couldn't seem to hold it. I surreptitiously wiped my eyes, and since Sebastian just stared down into the velvet case, lined with white satin, he didn't see me do this.

When I could see the knuckle bone at last, it looked like something that a child might toss while playing games of chance. It seemed a little scorched; of course, five thousand years before, it had been part of what did not burn on a pyre. The rest had burned away to ash, but this had somehow made it through the fire, and been set in the tomb with all the other bones. And then Sebastian had found it and brushed the soil off, and took it to himself, for reasons I could not imagine. I should have said, then, 'Why, Sebastian? Why can't I touch this bone?' But I did not. I was so hurt, and trying so hard not to show it.

So I just said, 'I see. An ordinary knuckle bone, I guess.' At that, he took it back again. Snapped the velvet case and put it back into the box from which he'd taken it. But as he did this, I could see that his whole mood had changed in just two minutes. I wiped my eyes again when he was not observing this, began to clear the table, and tried to clear my head. And as I did, there came into my head a picture of the child, who had been wearing, I saw suddenly, this dress.

This dress, the one I wore, no knickers underneath; it was so obvious, although I had not seen it. How are we different from the other animals? Because we try, hard, to forgive – because forgiveness is a thing that we have in us. And I would try hard now; it was *my* fault, perhaps, that Bastian still mistrusted me. What should I tell him first? That no divorce was needed, and that the ring I'd worn when we had met had merely been a symbol of the word, wed to the world? Or that I hoped, perhaps, we'd need a ring like that again, if we should choose to let a child – our child – enter the world, and someday tell the tale of all the lands our feet had walked upon.

I don't know why I chose the latter course. I don't know, really, why I spoke at all. It was unwise, to speak into this mood that Bastian was in, a mood of sudden silence. And not good silence, like the kind of silence I had felt these last five days, a silence rich with hope for what might follow it. No, this was now the other kind again, the silence of a tomb that does not love you, does not want your bones inside it. I wished to speak, but knew I shouldn't, and not because the words I'd wished to say had fled. They were still there inside me, waiting. No, it was more because, if words are seed which fall upon the air and seek for ground in which they can feel safe, they seek to fly until they find it. And I could sense that Bastian had turned away from any words I might say, that he would not allow them ground to grow in.

But still I spoke. I said:

'You know, Sebastian, I think we're going to have a child. A girl. I've dreamed her three times now. Each time, she says the same. "Can I come in?" What do you think? You think we'll have a daughter?'

And this I see, in my mind's eye, that Bastian turned to

me, and laughed. Laughed long and hard, and with an edge to it that was the edge of steel. Then he sat down upon the chair and crossed his legs, lifting his right leg, setting it across his left one. He laughed, but did not laugh with pleasure, although the laugh was not a cruel one; it seemed to leave me out of it entirely. I'd been aroused, before, when I had bathed, put on the dress and eaten, and even when the tears had welled within my eyes. Indeed, that's why I'd spoken – because I didn't want to lose that feeling I had had, that I was bound to Bastian with my body. But now, I just closed down. What was this laugh? It was not mirth. Sebastian looked at me, his eyes unwinking. It was that old look, *OK, prove it*, and as he held my eyes with his, he said:

'You think you're pregnant, Emrys? Well, you're not. Don't think it.'

'I didn't say that, Bastian,' I said. 'I tried to tell you of a dream I'd had.'

'Well, good,' he said. 'It will remain a dream, though. I'm fixed. I can't have children. My tube was cut, a long, long time ago. The thing can't be reversed. The doctor mangled it.'

And now he laughed more lightly, as if having told me, he was relieved of something he had carried like a weight within him. I didn't speak. I looked away. I felt an anger start to well within this place that I had made so open. It was not what he had said, it was the tone in which he spoke. It was the way he told me that this hope was ruined. Once, when we'd stopped at Orphir, looked out at Scapa Flow, and seen the place where Gunther Prime had blown a thousand men to death, we'd both been pleased by seeing that flat open sea we looked at as a symbol of vain hopes,

199

the hopes of history. But to laugh at *my* hopes, when they had started at that moment when I had thought: *I'm going to trust you, Bastian. Trust you to hold me in this world I've blown to.* My anger welled within me as if it were the boat that Gunther Prime had taken in that night through Holm Sound. It drew so deep, it seemed to draw so deep, that there was nothing left beneath it.

'I see. The doctor mangled it,' I said. 'I see you've had that checked. Well, good to know. But I would like to know, as well – why did you lie to me?'

'I didn't lie.'

'Oh yes, you did. You said that day at Stenness that women taken at the stones would bring forth children.'

'I said that? Well, it's true. That is the legend of the standing stones.'

'But when you said it, then, it was a lie, Sebastian.'

'No, not a lie. Just poetry,' he said. 'I thought you liked good poems. I thought you thought the truths they told were better than the truths we really have to live with. In fact' – and here his voice grew harder, colder, than I'd heard it since that same day when we'd fought within the Ring of Brodgar – 'I thought you thought that bearing words was what made us truly human.'

'Words lie,' I said. 'You lie. You're lying to yourself right now. You know you lied to me that day; you know you thought that if you told me of that legend I would let you take me there, beneath the stone. I almost did. You pushed your finger deep inside me, then you took it out and said, "So, Emrys? Shall we seed you?"'

He looked at me. He looked away. 'I don't remember saying that,' he said, but I saw that he lied again. 'And anyway, you think that I don't want it? I do want it, but

200

what's done is done. It can't be undone now. The thing is finished.'

'Yes, it is. Quite finished,' I said, as hard and cold as he had been when he had said I thought that bearing words would make us human. 'This whole charade. This lie you've lived and that I fell for when I fell for you. I think it's time for me to leave this island after all.' I was so filled with rage I would have said whatever words came spilling from my brain.

In fact, I did. I said, 'And by the way, these pictures that you love so much that you have clothed yourself in them? They're not as good as you imagine, Bastian.' At that, I turned away, as he had, though I was blind with rage, and he had been closed in by sorrow. I saw my socks and boots upon the floor, laced up the boots and then stormed out the cottage door and onto Long Holm. I still wore the silk dress, no jacket, coat, or sweater. My rage, though, made me hot; I didn't feel the cold cold wind that blew across the island from the ocean. I didn't feel the way it grabbed my shoulders, but I did feel the way the dress, around my legs, entangled them as I strode up the hill in the direction of the tomb.

I grabbed the skirt and hiked it up, then kept on climbing. The door banged open and then shut behind me. Sebastian's voice said, 'Corbin, stay!' and when I heard his voice, I felt like running. I felt just trapped upon this island. It was so small, it kept me trapped and choked with rage; it seemed to me the whole of what I'd felt for Bastian had been based on a falsehood. This was not true. Feelings can also lie, if they are like a chasm you can't cross, a wall you can't climb over. But still, I ran, although my running was quite hampered by the dress; my steps took me on up the hill and toward the tomb.

201

Below me, I heard Sebastian calling. 'Don't run. Come, Emrys, wait. I want to tell you something.'

I stopped and turned to call, 'More lies? Just leave me. You can keep your sterile seed, your knuckle bone. You took me with your hand. That's how you seed things best, I guess. I should have known, then, what the truth was.'

Sebastian stood a moment just as still as any standing stone. Had I not been so angry, I would have cried for him. Because I saw that what I'd said, so adamant, so cruel, had hit him just as hard as if I'd slapped him. He'd loved me then, that morning, back in London and I knew it; indeed, I knew that when he'd laid me back across the bed that he had known me as no other man had ever known me. And with his hands, he'd asked a question that I'd answered, without words. I'd let myself come back to life under his hands, I'd let him write my life upon my body.

In fact, I'd said that *yes*, I'd take him, since he owned me, he was mine, and I was like a sail which would have blown into the sky had Bastian not secured me. But he just heard my words now. Saw my hard face held hard against the sky, against the looming tumulus of the tomb behind me.

'Oh, that's it, is it, Emrys? You think that now you'll leave, now that I cannot give you what you wanted? Well, fine. You leave. That's fine.' His voice, like mine, was hard, as hard as hardened tablets, close to breaking.

'I'm sure it's fine,' I said. 'Fuck you,' I said, as well. 'Just stay away from me, Sebastian.' There was no fog around us, the fog was all inside this time; I started to move, to brush on past him, to go down and get my things. I'd take the boat, I thought, would strand him here upon his precious island. As I walked by he tried just one more time to reach me.

He said, 'No, stop. I don't think either of us wants this, Emrys. We'll both regret it if we make things worse.'

'Regrets?' I said. 'Do you know what one is? You think regrets are for the things you've lost. They're not,' I said. 'They're for the things you haven't done, and wish you had, or have done, and you wish you hadn't.'

'Oh, back to words,' he said. '*Regrets. Truth. Lies.* They carry quite a lot of freight for you. And yet you don't see how they don't mean just one thing. And as for loss, what do you know of it? What have you ever lost?'

'I've lost you, now,' I said. 'I can't stand anything about you, suddenly.'

'Well, what a shame. You picked me, didn't you? After we met, you wrote a letter first.' This was quite true, but it just made me more enraged. I didn't even speak, just hiked my dress up with one hand, and tried, again, to move down past him. This time, perhaps because I had not spoken, he reached out and grabbed my arm, quite hard, with one hard hand.

'You just don't understand,' he said.

'I understand you lied.'

'I had to lie. Would you have loved me, otherwise?'

'Of course I would,' I said. 'Of course I would,' and knew that it was he who did not understand, if he did not believe that. Just then, I did not think of how I'd lied as well, about the man I'd left, who was not husband, and for the same sad reason. Just as Sebastian seemed to think that I would not have let him take me if he could not also fill me, I'd thought that he, Sebastian, might not want me if he did not have to steal me.

But when I said, *Of course*, he did not, could not, hear it, but said, as if he thought this true:

'You never loved me for myself. Not for an instant.'

'Oh, and *she* did, I know,' I said, spitting the words out as if they were bitter seeds.

'Don't speak of her like that,' he said, and yanked me once again; I then yanked back, and just as hard as I could manage it.

And as I yanked, I fell, my legs entangled with the dress. I fell quite hard, and Bastian went down with me. We landed on the grass, half on a rock which hurt us both, and cut Sebastian's arm, the one he held me with. It was a bad cut, and it hurt him; his face was drawn up with the sudden shock and pain of it. I could have said then, 'Oh, Sebastian, are you hurt?' and soothed him, helped him, bound his arm up, taken him back down into the cottage. And had I said that, just five words, or even two – 'Oh Bastian' – I would not now be writing down the tale of it.

But I did not. I said, instead:

'Well, there's your blood. You're spilling it the way you spilled your seed in me. I thought you said your blood went to the women whom you loved. You'd better let me go now, or you'll bleed to death.'

He did not let me go. He was in pain, still, I could see, but now the rage *he* felt was strong enough to shroud the pain for him. He was then half on top of me, and now he said, 'We'll see. I think that I have something left, still, Emrys. Why don't I take you here, right here, before the tomb? A kind of parting we would both enjoy, I think.' And then, as he had done that night I took him in my mouth, he took my dress and lifted it from where it wrapped around my knees, and drew it right up to my hips. Once more, he tucked it in, tucked silk within the silk, so that my hip bones were the hook he hung it on. This time, there was no need to pull my pants off, since I had already bared myself. And this time, we were not standing, but lying upon the ground, the cold cold ground where baskets full of bones had once been carried.

'You can't be serious,' I said, as I attempted to free my hands.

'Oh yes, I am,' he said. 'Why not? A new thing for us both, I think.'

'I doubt that,' I said, struggling with the silk.

'It won't take long,' he said. 'Then you can take the boat and leave. Why not? Then it will be quite finished.'

'Get off me,' I said. 'I hate you. Let me go.' And I did hate him, oh so much, just then, I tried to kick him. I missed and hit him glancingly, a blow that struck his knee; he wrenched my leg back to the ground and held it there. He pinned it with his leg, and then he took my hands, and held them right above my head, while he unzipped his pants, to take me.

And he did take me. He was much stronger than I'd guessed or noticed when his strength was not an issue for us. I had the dress to cope with, and the ground was slick and wet, and I was still wet from before, which made it easy. Indeed, had I not been – not wet and ready, then – I don't believe he would have followed through with it. I know it didn't hurt, that when he pushed inside, there was no pain. I tried to spit into his face, although I missed my aim again. And after, he was quiet, as quiet as I'd ever seen him. He would not meet my eyes, as he climbed off me. He held out both his hands, to try to help me to my feet, and he said, tried to say, 'Oh Emrys . . .'

But I said, 'Just don't talk to me.'

'But I must talk. I didn't mean to do that.'

'I'm sure of that. But as you said, what's done is done. Now step aside. This is another country that has vanished.' And while I knew that Bastian had no idea what that might mean – I'd never told him of the night that I had left the man I'd left him for – I felt like that, felt that our love had been a land that had, just briefly, held us safe within its boundaries. But now, if there were walls, as there had been in Uruk-Haven, they'd fallen back into the sand they'd come from, and they would never be, could never be rebuilt, because such walls, once gone, took all the laws of building with them. I wanted, not to hurt Sebastian, not to punish him, as you might punish intruders, a child, or anyone you loved or hated – yourself, perhaps – but rather, just to let him fall behind me, as if he were a book that I had read and was now quite, quite finished with. Indeed, I wanted more; I wanted that book to fall into a fire and burn there. I wanted there to be, in the ashes left behind, no trace of what had once been written in its pages.

12

YES, THAT WAS HOW I felt. I do not feel that now. I feel that no books should be burned, all books are sacred. That they are made, and that they make us – make us who we are and who we will be, far into the future. They are like moments which stretch long, where there is *here* and *there* and *there*, but where the line of here and there becomes a circle; and this one, which is mine, is like the moment when I first came, bare, upon Sebastian's body. That moment, I now see, was like the center of the wheel that is the time I have on earth, the crucial core that all the spokes go out from. It seemed, when it had happened, that each thing I'd thought and felt and seen before that instant, as well as each thing I would think and feel and see that followed after, had all been caused by that, as if *cause* were a thing that could be found in either past or future. As if all that it takes to make a life is one brief moment, when what is locked is unlocked, and all time is freed by that.

But what that means is that all time is tied together, so when I look back to see that moment that I loved, I must see all the other moments also. They are quite inextricable: they are all threads which make up one great garment that I wear, which is my life, and which still robes me. Or they are words which, read together, make up what lies within my mind, which is the story of Emrys and Sebastian. And when I look into my mind, I see Sebastian looking back, from *here* and *there* and *there*, a hundred different places. Sometimes, he doesn't see me. He looks too hard at his own past to see me waiting for him in the passage. His eyes go past me, even now, as he looks one way, then the other, seeking a place to moor his mind or soul. But as for me, he is the place I moored myself, his hope and grief the spike I threw my soul on. And there is now no single instant of the time I shared with him which I would throw back to the place it came from.

That day – that last day – though, I walked down to the cottage. I did not run. And while I walked, I pulled the green silk dress above my head, and dropped it on the ground as I would drop the book I did not have within my hands, but wished to burn, then. Then, naked, just in socks and boots, I walked into the cottage and got my warmest clothes from where they had been stored. I put on first my pile tights, and then my pile shirt, and then my pile vest and jacket. My socks as well, grey socks that were quite thick and came up to my knees. I followed these with pants that were like wind-pants, black and made of nylon. I didn't stop with that, but put on hat and gloves; when I got to the boat, I'd put on the oilskins. All that would keep me warm until I got to Shapinsay. I walked out of the cottage then, not looking for Sebastian. In any case, I didn't see him and thought he must have gone into the tomb, which was just fine with me. I walked the well-worn path down to the geo where we'd left the cock-boat.

I noticed when I reached it that the tide was rising. So

what? That was just good, I thought. It helped me push the boat into the water, then jump in; once in, I donned the oilskins. I then turned to the engine; I had never tried to start an outboard engine before, but it could not be all that hard, I thought. You pulled the cord, I knew, until the engine caught. I pulled the cord. The engine did not catch. Some seals watched from the water as I pulled and pulled again, and smelled the smell of gas now climbing toward me. But I kept pulling; as I did, the boat drifted away from where it was to fifty feet from shore. There was a pole that I could, if I wished, pole back to Long Holm with. But I wished, more than ever now, to get away, and though the boat, as it moved past the still, safe waters of the noost, had started to roll, this did not, just then, bother me. What should I do? There was the sail. It was secured around the mast, but I supposed that it could be untied, and, as I noticed that the wind was picking up, I thought perhaps I could forget the engine and sail to Shapinsay.

I'd started to untie the rope that held the sail in place, still with that feeling which was now no longer anger. That feeling that all this was merely a thing I wished to leave behind – this island and the man who walked upon it. But now I heard him call me. Sebastian was down upon the shore, with Corbin at his side. He wore the long oiled coat that he had worn when we had sailed here. He was just buttoning it, I saw, but as he struggled with the buttons, I with the cord which held the sail, he called:

'Are you quite mad? You don't know boats. I'll take you off the island if you really want to go. Come back. Pole back if you can't get the engine started. Leave the damn sail alone, at least. You can't think – even you – that you will *sail* to Shapinsay.'

'Come back? No, I don't think so,' I said, still tugging at the knots that held the sail wrapped to the mast.

'A storm is blowing in,' Sebastian called. 'You must be blind. Look at the western sky. Come back now, Emrys.'

But this, those words, that voice, just made me more determined to get off as soon as possible. I'd noticed that the wind *was* picking up, and now I saw the western sky was darker than it should be at this time of day. The waves, too, seemed to grow; the boat quite rocked beneath me, and not because I rocked it while I moved. So what? I seemed to have no thought still left inside me but the thought that I must get away at once. The sail was hard to figure out, however, so I turned back to the engine, and tried once more to get it started. When Bastian saw what I was doing, he cursed, and said, so I could hear it, 'Stay, Corbin. I must rescue this fool woman.'

He then plunged in the sea, quite fully dressed, his oiled coat wrapped all around him, tugging at him as he pushed the waves aside; the waters here were not that deep, so he could walk all the way out to where the boat was, still just fifty feet from shore – though moving briskly westwards now. But before he reached the boat, the water was to his waist, then his chest. I hardly could believe that he was doing this. I yelled, 'Just keep away. You think I need your help? I don't. I'll leave the boat for you at Shapinsay.'

But he yelled nothing back. Just kept on pushing through the waves until he reached the boat and grabbed the gunwales, pushed himself across them. He landed on the floorboards, and brought a lot of water with him. I could not see how wet he was, because he wore that oiled coat of his. I did see that the water poured out of his boots as if it gushed straight from the bottom of the ocean. I watched, both furious and amazed, while Sebastian lay a moment, then said, as he got up and sat upon the bench I wasn't sitting on:

'Emrys. This is insane. Look at the sky. Feel how the wind picks up. You *must* come back now to the island.' He did not move to touch me, just put one hand up in the wind as if to show that, if his hand were sail, it would be blown by this.

'Don't tell me what to do,' I said. 'Not any more. You think I'm scared. I'm not scared.'

'Well, you should be, this time. You still don't know these seas. You've never sailed a boat of any kind. On top of that, you're terrified of water.'

'Not terrified,' I said. 'I'm just a little scared.'

'Well, scared, then. And you should be.' And as we said these things – *you're terrified, no, scared* – I heard an echo of another time we'd said them. Then it was gone, the echo, because Sebastian – although he still was careful not to touch me – picked up the pole from where it sat within its brackets. As he began to pole back to the island, I felt hot rage again, and moved around him to the engine. I'd failed to start it twenty times, but now, I pulled it once as hard as I could pull it, and the engine caught. So now I had the engine.

'Get out,' I said, quite loudly, since the engine was a roar, although it was still set on idle. 'I'm leaving. Get back in the sea, if you don't want to come.' I revved the engine, just to test it.

'My god, I think I'm cursed,' Sebastian said. 'You really are quite mad. Another stubborn woman, mad and bossy.'

'You picked me,' I then said. 'You must like us like that. Get out now, Bastian, or I'll take you with me.' And when I

211

saw that – far from getting out – he was now moving back to where I sat, and where I had my hand upon the tiller, I screamed at him, 'Don't touch me,' at which he stopped, though any other day or hour he wouldn't have. Above us, birds were wheeling, in that heightened way they wheel, and call, before a big change in the weather.

And then, to make things more complex, I saw that Corbin had now plunged into the sea, off the rock from which he jumped most mornings. He swam hard toward the boat. His big black head was gleaming as the water flew around him from the movement of his paws. He reached us quickly, and when Bastian saw that Corbin, too, had now arrived, he groaned, as if the whole thing was too much for him. He reached over the side, and lifted Corbin in, and said, 'Well, all right then. I'll drive the boat, if you insist on leaving.'

I moved. I went up to the bow, and sat there, Corbin next to me. I could see Haverskerry from where I sat and so could see it was half under the water. When Corbin moved and leaned against my leg, as if to say he liked this boat, all boats, I put my gloved hands on his back and patted it, at which he shook his body so that water flew from it. It somehow calmed me, seeing this – a thing a dog does always when it's wet – and now I looked at Bastian as he sat in front of where the engine, running, idled. He moved to use his left hand on the tiller, and it seemed to me he held his right hand rather awkwardly; I didn't realize then, this might be from the wound that he had gotten. I saw him settle, awkwardly, the oiled coat so that it covered both his legs. And then he pushed the engine into gear. The boat began to bounce as we moved forward toward the larger ocean. It seemed to leap upon the waves in such a way that it would have been playing had the boat known how to play.

But it did not. It lifted up, and came down hard, so that we thudded, time and again, upon the surface of the water, and when Sebastian went quite wide around the edge of land, I looked beneath me, saw that there were rocks submerged by tide there. I looked down, saw them, felt the thud as we moved out beyond protected bay into the open ocean, and almost said, then, 'Bastian. You're right. This crossing is too dangerous. We should go back to Long Holm.' But when I looked at him, and saw the way that he was now intent on doing this successfully, I didn't speak. He knew the sea, and now that he had said that he would drive the boat, he drove it as he always drove, with great great concentration. In fact, he seemed to take a kind of satisfaction in this task. It was a clear task, after all, as clear as any tomb that needed excavation. It was, as well, a thing that he could give to me right now – when he could not take back the thing he'd give a lot to have returned to where it came from.

And where is that, that place? The place where thoughts are still unthought, and sights unseen, and actions not yet taken? I cannot find it, any more than Bastian could that day; it lies across a sea that flows one way. And although *cause* may be a thing that can lie either in the past or in the future, the *end* is always something that is found in just one place – a place that lies unreachable behind you. I know that, now, as well as Bastian ever did, just as I know at last what he was really hunting when he hunted me. I wish that I could reach it, that end that lies behind; if I could, I would set forth upon a journey as hard and long as any passage made by Gilgamesh. I would let nothing stop me till I found the place I sought, and, if it were a tablet, write on it quite differently. But it is not a tablet one can scratch upon, erase; no dwelling one can reach by changing course for it; and it is not an island floating formless on the sea, which one need only find to pin to earth again.

No, it is not. The place cannot be reached, and Bastian knew it then, just as I know it now, and as I also know, now, Bastian. And so he set his hand at the one thing that he could do to take back the last way in which he'd taken me. He pushed us past the rocks and out to sea, and turned toward Haverskerry; we could see Shapinsay beyond it. But more, we could now see, quite clearly, just what kind of sea this was. From where we were, we saw the cliffs of Gairsay. Saw a tremendous breaker crash against the cliffs and send salt spray a hundred feet into the air. I might not know the sea, but this I knew, that in the time I'd been on Long Holm, I had never seen a wave like that before. Another roller came and crashed and sent its spray so high, this time, it fell above the cliff and poured down off it.

As for the boat, it seemed to reach into the sky before it fell upon the sea so hard it shuddered through its floorboards. At this, I did speak. Yelled. I had to yell, the wind had picked up, was so loud now.

'All right,' I shouted. 'Let's turn back. You win. I'm not as crazy as you think.'

Sebastian nodded, shouted something I couldn't hear, and turned the boat. We then discovered that the sea, which had seemed merely waves, gigantic waves, was running to the south like something blown there. Not blown by wind; blown by a bomb, exploded somewhere north, in the North Sea's Atlantic passage. The cock-boat's little engine could hardly breast the waves alone. With this hard sea beneath, it could, we saw, make little progress. We were a quarter of a mile, no more, beyond the rocks – less than half a mile from shore – but as Sebastian turned the bow right toward the shore and took the engine to full throttle, we were going nowhere. The sea was running not just fast, but, as I was to find out later on, as fast as it had run since the last storm of winter – knots on knots on knots again. By now, just five minutes, no more, from when we had set out, a full Atlantic gale was blowing. How could the sea become like this this fast, as if it, too, had anger that could surge within it? How could it be that we could make no progress toward the land, although we could see land right there, and waiting right before us?

It was as if we were becalmed. The engine pushed at things it could not push against. The small boat scrabbled on the deck of waves that tilted up as if it sought a hand that would come from the waves to save it. And then the rain began. There was no fog, not then, but water lifted in the air, just as it came down from the sky; they mixed and mingled. And then when I could not, in truth, see anything at all but sea, I seemed to see what we were in for very clearly. I saw Sebastian, standing now, holding the tiller with his leg; he stood, and rocked from side to side, just balancing. He tried to see. I saw the way his oiled coat was blown around his knees, and caught around his legs, re-vealing them. It was not like a sail; it wrapped him up, as the wind pushed, so that I saw his bones, his sinews, as if nothing lay to wrap them in. And though he drove now more than ever like someone fleeing from a war-torn country – not looking back, just looking forward – I saw that there were wars which were so wide, so deep, so high, the best drivers on the earth could not escape from them.

Sebastian saw this, too. He saw that we would never make it back to Long Holm. He struggled with the sea, and then, with one quick twist, he changed his mind, deciding he would run before it. He thought we had one chance, and one chance only, so he turned and aimed the bow toward Haverskerry. It could be seen, just then, though dimly, through the mist and rain, the slashing knives of water that cut our vision. And it lay *with* the sea. The waves were crashing on its northern shore. If we could make it there, we would be safe enough, Sebastian thought; at least we would be off the sea, which was still rising.

Seas, yes, and getting higher. Salt, salt, so in the air it was as if salt was the only thing that could be breathed now. Birds calling somewhere out of sight, not as they'd called within my dream – not happy, shrieking dire warnings. One moment. I was holding Corbin, my arms wrapped around his chest, as if his chest might be an anchor. Another moment. Fog appeared and tore across the bow, real fog, a shroud of it which clutched the mast, then let it go again. I now was sitting down upon the floorboards watching Bastian at the tiller. As I had moved down to the floor, he'd moved back to the bench, and sat there struggling with the engine. He yelled at me, 'Put up the sail. Just let it out. The engine's going to die at any moment.' And then, a thing that is not shredded, torn – the way the rope that held the sail felt as I unwrapped it, let it go, and saw it fall into the sky and vanish there. It ripped out of my hands, at which the sail dropped down, unfurled, and somehow caught against the ropes that had been meant to hold it. It blew out, right before the mast, a square sail filled with air so that it seemed it must explode with it. It looked as if all of the air of earth had now been gathered in a single piece of sailcloth.

'That's good,' yelled Bastian. 'Leave it. It goes our way. The engine's fading.' And when he said this, I could hear a kind of choking as if the engine was beginning to drown. It gurgled, choked, and died, but Bastian kept his hand upon the tiller; without a rudder, or a way to really sail the sail, we would have lost, and all at once, all four directions. So he stayed at the back. I did not hold the ropes the sail was caught on. They were caught on the boat itself. I crawled on hands and knees to where Sebastian sat, and threw my arms around his legs. I didn't speak. I huddled at his knees, just holding on. His coat had blown right back, and holding to his knees, I felt how wet he was. He wore just blue jeans, a thin shirt, a sweater, underneath his coat, and all were soaked, just as his boots and socks were. He was not shivering, though. Not yet. He peered ahead, looking for rock, aiming for rock, as if he knew that rock was at the bottom of everything. I saw just water, water in the sky, water upon the sea. It had no form, there was just water everywhere. The boat tossed less, now that it ran before the sea, but it rolled more, and as it did, it felt as if the whole earth was unmoored, both outside and within me. I felt as if I floated freely, in a place that had no laws, no rules, never had had them, never could have them. The thing we called direction had just vanished from the world, had been a dream the world had had that it had woken up from. And then, and just ahead of us, forty or fifty feet, I saw a rock, dry land, a mound just rising.

It was the rock. Out of the sea it rose, dark rock, covered with slime, with seaweed, but there, and right ahead of us. Sebastian wrenched the tiller, pushed it as hard as he could push and turned the boat enough to east so that we'd hit the skerry. Then he said, 'Hold this, Emrys. Exactly where it is. Don't move at all,' and grabbed my hand to put it on the place he took his hand from. He then leapt past me, toward the bow, fell to his knees, and loosed one side of the square sail that held the winds of earth inside it. He hoped, I think, to take the boat in less hard than it would go as long as that square sail was driving it, but although he loosed it – loosed one half of it, at least – the other half still held the wind, and still behind us, wind and waves were pushing us. I had a moment, just a moment, to try and guess how hard the boat would hit upon the rock, and then it landed there. The wave that lifted us just pushed us up into the sky as if the cock-boat had become as light as sailcloth. And then it fell again, and fell upon the rock; it fell quite like a tree, quite as the trees had fallen once to make the boat for us. The boat uplifted, up and up, and then it crashed as hundreds, thousands, of boats within these seas had done before it.

I felt a splintering, shuddering, jarring, deep vibration under us, and, as I clung still to the tiller, I saw the floorboards had been breached by water. They'd sprung into the air, had tilted upwards, when, from deep beneath them, the rock we'd landed on just pinned them. It pinned us, too. The boat caught on the rock as if upon a knife, and though it pulled to get away, it could not do it. It had been caught and where it caught, the water rushed in; I watched it flood into the boat, around my ankles, then my legs. For just a minute, half a minute, not so long, perhaps, I felt that I, as well, had just been pinned there – that there was no way I could move from where I was to somewhere else, that I would die within the boat, would drown on dry land, somehow. I felt, in fact, that this great rent that had been made right in the midst of all the boards that made the boat

I rode in was like the rent which I had known would one day tear the world, and which would never again be mended. I stared, quite sickened, at the tides that roiled around my ankles, my legs, and then I saw Sebastian lurch toward me. He shouted, 'Come! We must get out!' and when I didn't move, reached down and put his arms beneath my armpits. He hauled me to my feet as if I were a sack of grain; he helped me fling my legs over the gunwales. And then he tried to steady me until I found my feet, but as he did the boat was sucked back, rammed onto the rocks again, and splintered.

'Jump, jump!' he shouted now, then, 'Corbin, come!' at which I saw that Corbin clambered to the gunwales right beside me. He slid onto the rocks, scrabbling, as I did, and skidding, since the rocks were slick with seaweed. And they were sharp. I fell down on my knees and scraped one. But this was dry land, not a dream; the world was steady underneath. I had just time to notice that there were still seals upon the skerry, three seals who looked at us, their eyes surprised, before they slid into the sea and vanished there, and then Sebastian landed next to me upon the rock, much harder than I had. He fell hard on his knees, and slid a little backwards. I grabbed him, though, by just one arm, and though he cried out as I did this, I didn't realize he was in pain and just grabbed harder. He slid no more, but put his other arm around my shoulder, held me hard, and so we lay as if we had been caught not just upon the skerry but on the reef of one another's bodies. And I thought then, right then, that it would not be bad, perhaps, to die, as long as Bastian held me to him. As long as we would not be torn apart, ever again, by anything on earth – by words or deeds or thoughts or wounds, by any of the deep abysses.

I held him. Clung to him, as he held me. I noticed that he smelled of salt, and that his face, which pressed on my face, seemed quite cold. Then he said gently, 'We must move now. We have a lot to do before the boat sinks,' and let me go, and rolled away from me. The boat was ramming on the rocks about ten feet behind us; he went to it, leaned in and somehow got the sail off. This he brought back to me, and thrust into my arms, said, 'Take the sail and Corbin and climb up to the top and wait there till I call you.'

'No. I want to help.'

'This will be help. The boat is dangerous to work around. I need to try to get some boards loose.' So I climbed right up to the top of Haverskerry, and found the place the spike was driven; this marked where rock would be still, when the tide was highest. I shoved the sail down in the rocks, held Corbin with one arm, and watched while Bastian pulled the gas tank from the cock-boat. He shoved it back behind him, and then began, not wearing gloves – he had no gloves – to pull the boat apart, as much as he could do this. He still seemed hampered by one arm, the arm that he had cut, and as I saw the way he favored it, at last I realized why he did this. He got the benches loose, the pole, the mast, some floorboards; all were tossed to the rock in an untidy pile. The wind was blowing hard, and waves were rolling in and in, which made the hard work Bastian did now that much harder. He tugged at boards, the boards tugged back, and right below him were the waves that tugged the seaweed; this seemed now more like the rock's long hair than ever, and as I looked, I thought the waves were pulling as if to say they would not stop until they had their way with it. With hair, with rock, and also us. I watched and thought: *This is my fault.* It was my fault, just as the rock was my rock

– this rock a foolish man who had my name had thought to claim once. The threaded spike he'd sunk in it was right beside me, spiraled with rust, spiraled with iron, and reaching just three short feet up into the sky above us.

Just then, I saw Sebastian leap back, and when he did, I sprang to my feet and started half to walk and half to slide down to him. 'Corbin, you stay!' I said. 'Don't move,' at which although he strained with every nerve to disobey, Corbin braced his paws, and stayed, though agonized and quivering.

When I reached Bastian's side, he said, 'It's going now. Don't get too near.'

We watched and saw the boat, or what was left of it, just plundered by the waves that pushed it up before they took it; it was upended, and then filled with water until it sank and slid into the deeps, seeming to pull the water right around it down with it. That water fell into the center where the boat had gone, as if the boat had made a hole within the sea, which must be filled back up again. The sinking was not smooth, because the sea was moving and the waves were rolling, but it was smooth enough to sicken me. My eyes were tied to it, the boat, the place the boat had gone. I almost felt the water close above me. And I remembered what it felt, to look and see the world become a perfect mirrored thing which closed around you; how it felt to see the air you held within you passing out, a hundred perfect spheres, just like the spheres of memory.

Then Bastian pulled me back. Said, 'Help me get the wood up to the top. We'll light a signal fire. Perhaps someone will see it. If not, we can keep warm until the tide turns and the storm dies. Come, you take the gas can.' He pushed it in my arms, then grabbed some planks, led the way right to the top of Haverskerry, where Corbin waited. He found a place within the rocks where rock sank down to make a place the fire could be set, a little sheltered from the wind. We went back down and got more boards and then the mast and then the seat; the boat's pole had slid down into the sea and floated off by then. When all the wood was up, Sebastian said, 'Stand back,' then poured the contents of the gas can on the boat's remains. He lit one splinter with his lighter, then threw the splinter down; the gasoline caught and flared quite brightly. It almost died before the wood caught, but at last it did, and as it burned, it threw real heat. We all three sat and faced the fire.

And as we did, I felt, for just a little, safe. We had still twenty feet of rock, or maybe twenty-five, below us. We were all safe, the fire burned; I was not really wet, and felt quite warm with all the clothing I had on, and with the oilskins. I knew Sebastian must be colder, as he had been soaked through, but I believed, then, he was quite invincible. I took my gloves off, held my hands out to the fire, and let them feel the heat that poured out of the flames just bake them. Sebastian held his hands out, too. We sat in silence, while the waves rolled to the south, and though there was no lull in wind or wave, there was a lull in us, and in that lull, which was a stillness of the heart and mind, I said:

'I'm sorry, Bastian.'

'I'm sorry, too,' he said. And when he said this, it was not as it had been the other time he'd said this, in the fog outside his tomb, when I'd been lost in fog and blamed him for it. It was as if his voice had grown much younger, gone right back to when he was the boy that he had been when he had smiled at she who held the camera. And I, on hearing this, this voice, still deep, still filled with life, but with a kind of youth that was the way his eyes were when they did not challenge me, thought that if there ever was a time when he would tell me, dare to tell me, that time was now, our boots and buttocks on the rock, our four hands stretched together toward the fire.

'Who was she, Bastian? What happened?' I said. Sparks flew into the sky, fretted the air, and then were snuffed out by the wind, turning to ash in it. Sebastian stayed still, looked at me, then at the fire, then at the place the boat had splintered, sunk, and vanished. And when he spoke, his voice was like the voice I knew again – though filled with sorrow, now, so deep I could have drowned in it.

'She was my wife,' he said. 'She was an artist. You know how good she was. I married her when I was still a boy, just twenty. But she was not a girl. She was a decade older – beautiful, and wise, and strong, and bossy. I loved the fact that she was bossy; she would tackle any task the way she tackled what she did with her box camera. She knew that she could do it, as she knew that she could take a picture that would show you more than you had ever seen before. She saw things in her mind. So when, the second year we lived in Shetland, she found out that she was pregnant, she must see the scene of it.'

'What scene?'

'The scene where she did not go into hospital for the birth. The scene where she would be a pregnant goddess. The scene, in fact, where she would have the baby in the small cottage that we lived in, and I would help deliver it. She was Orcadian. She'd been born on Mainland, in Birsay, near the brough; there is a stone house there, near Marwick Head. Her mother had had a home birth; so would she, and that was that. She hated interference of any kind, from anyone.'

I didn't speak. My mouth felt dry. I stared into the flames, while Bastian paused a long, long time before he spoke again. The flames were long and thin, because the wind was sucking them toward the south.

'She was so stubborn, maybe that was it. Not bossy, stubborn. And so lovely; when she was pregnant, she did look like a goddess. Her hair was dark and curly, and she wore dresses all the time, tight dresses, shin length, which blew around her legs as if they loved her just as much as I did. And she wore rings, a lot of rings, all gold. Some thick, some thin; the one I gave her the day that we were married in St Magnus was quite thick, and it was beaded on the edge. It looked as if small drops of water clung to it. Because it weighed a lot, she kept this ring, our wedding ring, in a black velvet case when she was working with her camera. But there was one thin ring, as thin as wire, which she wore upon her forefinger. That picture that you asked about; she took it just as she had told me we would have a baby. And I remember this so clearly – the way that when she pushed the button on her camera in the sun, the gold ring on her finger glittered.'

Another pause. I still said nothing. I feared to move, although the wind, when it picked up to gust, shoved hard at me.

'I loved her, Emrys. God, so much. She was my life. And she was older than I was. I thought that she must know what she was doing in this. She studied books, and took me through them, page by page, to show me how it all would go so smoothly, if I only helped. She put her finger *there*, then *there*, upon the page we read together, like someone who would make the world dance as she wished it. I think of that, more than the rest. Of how her hands were art themselves, of how they were the essence of all things human. But when the time came, and she lay inside that cottage on the bed, with only me beside her, nothing there was dancing.'

This pause, the one that followed, went on so long that finally I spoke:

'What happened? Tell me, Bastian.'

'She died. Not in the cottage. When I at last saw how things were, I carried her to the car and laid her in the back and drove to hospital. I drove as if I thought that I could drive the car right off the earth and into air, could make it fly for me. Before, I had been young, a boy, with all the time there was on earth. But now, that was all gone. One moment, and it changed completely. My wife lay in the back, not even groaning any more, or screaming, as she'd screamed within the cottage. She lay like something that had been tossed into a boat, quite pole-axed, huddled at the bottom. And she was wet, wet through, with sweat and blood and all the fluids that had gushed forth out of her body. The only thing that had not come from where it was, inside, was the one thing that most needed to, the baby. I drove like someone mad, almost crashed through the door where they received their patients. But she was dead. She'd died alone, behind me, in the car. The baby was dead, too; he'd strangled on the cord which led to him.'

What could I say? The words had fled. There were no words for this. There was no comfort to be found in sound, I thought. Our hands had come back from the fire as Bastian talked and now I put one hand out and took his hand in mine; my hands were warm enough, but his was freezing. I put one hand below it, one above, and held it there between my own as if I somehow, thus, could truly warm it. He shook my top hand lightly loose, though, and took the one that was the nearest to search it with his own, as if he would now memorize each bone in it. He took one finger, then the next, felt them from tip to where they joined the hand; he stopped when he got to my forefinger. This, he stroked, until he stopped upon the knuckle where it hinged and bent in two, bent down upon itself.

'This is the knuckle,' he said. 'I think this is the one, the one she used to stop the world with, taking pictures. I took it from the ashes when they burned her and the baby. It seemed a miracle to me that it had made it through the fire. Her wedding ring burned with her, but not the knuckle, so I took it. Later, I had myself fixed. What's done is done, and I'd already failed her. But I believed I needed punishment for what I'd done, or not done. Would not do again, this way, at least.'

We sat. The fire died. Sebastian held my hand a long long time and then he said, 'But you must put your gloves back on. You will get cold. You must stay warm, until the tide turns.' And as he said this, my mind went back to when he'd said, *I knew this, from your hands. You should have worn gloves, if you wished to hide from me*. It had been he, though, who had hidden, and yet in plain, plain sight. How could I not have seen where he was standing? How had I been so blind to what was there, behind the thing that I could see, to what was blurred about its edges? Indeed, how could I not have known the place he hunted was a place where thoughts were still unthought, actions not taken? How could it be that I'd not known that, when he slept and twitched as if he could not rest, he was hunting land where women could be wet, just wet, wet, wet, without all of the waters of earth then gushing forth from them? And how had I not known that, when he did not groan aloud in love, as I did, it was because he had been seeded long ago with silence?

The storm continued. Water rose. The rock we sat on seemed to shrink, although it was the tide that rose to claim it. The fire was quite dead, and Sebastian was not warm. He was soaked through, beneath that oiled coat of his. And now he told me that he thought that he was cold, in part, because he'd lost a lot of blood when he had cut his arm upon the rock. It had cut deeper than he'd thought. It almost went down to the bone, he said. I tried to see it, tried to feel it, but he just took my hand, and curled it on his other arm, and held it there.

'Too late to staunch it. It has stopped,' he said. 'There is no blood coming out now. It is just stiffer than I wish it were. But you are warm, at least. That is amazing, that you should be warm the one time you have reason to be cold. You wore the proper garments for the day, I think. It seems that no one saw the fire, nor smelled the smoke. We must get through the tide now. We have just two more hours before it turns, I think.'

But it was less than that. The water rose and rose. When we had just ten feet of rock left, Sebastian found the sail where I had thrust it in the rock, and with some struggle, tied it to the spike beside us.

'Why are you doing that?' I asked.

'In case someone comes by.'

'But we will be here. They will see us, surely.'

'Yes, probably. I take back everything I said about that

man, that Havers, though; a foot of ground can be a world, if it has this, this metal spike, for us to cling to.'

'For us to cling to? Why?'

'The waves drive hard. I think today they will roll over what is usually exposed here. We must hang on, if that should happen. But Corbin cannot hang on. He has to swim.' At that, Sebastian bent down, and put his arms around the black and curly hair and hugged it hard and tight and long. Then he stood up, with Corbin cradled in his arms, and threw him out as far as he could throw him in the sea. This time, no stick for him to find; he was the stick himself. 'Go, Corbin,' said Sebastian. 'Do what you were named for.' And Corbin, who I would have thought would just have turned around, and come back to the rock, instead began to swim, and straight toward Long Holm, straight away from us. His head bobbed on the waves. Once, as we watched, a wave hit him so hard it covered him, but then his head emerged again.

'Oh Bastian,' I said. 'He'll drown.'

'Perhaps,' he said. 'But maybe not. That I sent him to the sea, he was not washed there – that will help him. He has no thought of drowning in his body.' Sebastian put his arm around me as he said this, pulled me to him, as if he knew that I must think of how it felt to drown, of how the world had told me that it owned me, and how I feared that Corbin, who had thought the world was just a great round shining pot of light and smells and tastes, might soon find something not so pleasing in it.

But then, a wave hit. Hit us both, and hit us hard, a great rough wave, a good deal higher than the other waves that rolled on by us. It knocked me down, the whole world tilting, as I was taken by surprise, as it just lifted up my body from the rock it rested on. I think it might have washed me off, had not Sebastian, who had fallen as well, caught me with his hand and shouted, 'Grab the spike! You have to grab it, Emrys!' at which I reached for it, as he did, but not before some of the wave had gotten in my mouth, making me taste the salt in it. I grabbed the spike, although the wave which just went on and on, felt strong enough to rip each finger loose, to rip each finger right in half. My fingers ached, I ached all over, as I clung, hard, to the cold spike, and felt my body lift and pull against my fingers. Sebastian felt this, too. Our hands were all upon the spike, our four hands clinging to the iron. The sail flew out above us, and tangled round itself, just as we did; we tangled round ourselves, and one another, as well. And it was then, when I felt sick, sick from the motion, sick from the salt, sick from the cold, and how each finger ached, that words came to my mind, two words, the words I'd seen the other time the firth had tripped and sickened me. Bring Deeps, I thought, Bring Deeps. Ten bubbles which I'd exhaled, two pennons which had caught upon the reef of me. Was this what that had meant? Our four hands on the spike that was the only thing that held us safe were like the hands enlaced on someone's sepulcher.

'Sebastian,' I said. 'Don't let me drown. Please, please, don't let me drown. I can't hang on. I'm never going to make it.'

'Calm down,' he said, beside me. 'We have to ride the wave out. Then I'll take care of you. Don't worry, Emrys. Just calm down for now.' And so I did calm down, although our bodies floated on the tide that rushed from north to south, and west to east. But with Sebastian asking me for calm, I felt that this was something I could at least attempt to give him. Our bodies hit, then came apart, then hit again, and hard, together. We were like scraps of cloth, perhaps, that had they not been snagged upon this tiny metal menhir would just have blown away upon the wind that blew us. Indeed, there was a moment when my right hand came quite loose; a second wave had followed fast upon the first one.

But Bastian grabbed my wrist and gripped it while he pushed me down, pushed me against the rock, then threw himself on top of me. The wave washed by. The rock was bare again, though small pockets of foam were lodged around us in the places where the rock was ragged. We both lay there, exhausted, and freezing cold – I was cold, too, now – and soaked through to the skin, the bones, the marrow. Our feet were almost in the sea, because by then the tide had come up to the place where it would turn and ebb again. After a moment's rest, Sebastian struggled with his clothes; he took his oiled coat off, let it lie beside him. Now for the first time I could see where his arm was cut; despite the soaking in the sea, his sweater still had blood in it. Another rest, and then he wrestled with the belt he wore, brown webbing with two golden metal rings which cinched it to itself. It was both wet and salty, half-frozen, and it stuck to all the belt loops that he'd looped it through that morning. But when he tore it loose, he slapped it on the patch of rock that was beside us where we lay – the rock's new garment.

'I'll have to tie you to the mast,' he said. 'An old, old custom, I believe, when storms get bad. We like old customs, Emrys.'

I think I nodded. I didn't speak. I couldn't speak. The last word I had said was *drown* and that word seemed the end of language. But I hope that I smiled, at least a little, as Sebastian held me down with both his legs and struggled with the webbing. Then, when it was ready, as untangled as it could be, he tugged my wrists and lifted them above my head and tied them. I was so cold my hands were almost numb, but with my gloves on, still had feeling, because I felt the way the belt went first around one wrist and then the other. Sebastian drew it tight, not too tight, tight enough, then laced it back and back again, the belt forming two circles. One circle was the warp, the other was the weft, and I was like the loom on which he struggled hard to weave them. Then, with a tug, he fastened the belt down upon the spike, and looped its end back through the metal circles. He pulled against it, made it just as fast as it could be. The rusted spirals of the iron spike helped to secure it.

'There now,' he said. 'You're safe. It won't be long. And you are warm, or warm enough, in all that pile. You must just keep your mouth above the water when it comes again. You need your mouth, immortal babbler.' And when he said this, though I felt convinced that I *was* safe, that what Sebastian had done for me would save me, I felt a stillness grow within me, a great long stillness in my heart, as if it were a place where, though the wind was blowing, waves were crashing, wind and waves had both been suddenly suspended.

I said, 'What do you mean?'

To which Sebastian answered, 'You can't imagine I would let it happen twice, I think.'

And now the stillness grew, although the wind still shrieked and moaned around us, sounding like the cry of voices. The waves still broke so hard they seemed like stones that fell; my heart and mind, though, saw and heard only Sebastian. From that first moment that we'd met, our bodies had conversed, had spoken the same language, the same dialect, but only now, too late, this moment when our bodies were about to come apart forever, could I decode just what the words emerging from his mouth meant.

I said a thing I can't remember. For once, just purely babble, a rush of language that was mostly sound. 'Oh god, oh no, you must hang on, Sebastian. You're strong, you must hang on. The tide will turn, you said yourself.' To which Sebastian, still beside me, made a movement with his arm; it was the arm that had been wounded. He moved it now as if he wished to toss away the wound, to let it fall upon the rock. This was a fragment of himself that he would lose, and happily, if he could. But though he tried to shake it loose, pinching it in his hand, his hand closed in upon itself in pain, in effort. He looked at me and smiled, a sad sad smile, then said:

'I'll try. Of course I'll try. But if I can't, then you must take the rock. I've said before, I can sleep anywhere.'

And then, before I had a chance to do a thing – to moan or cry or scream or tell Sebastian to untie me – a giant wave rolled in again and hit us, and although Sebastian grasped the spike and tried his best to hold it, he just couldn't. He was then half on top of me, and I could feel the way his body moved down, then up, then down again. I saw his eyes close tight, as if he willed himself to do the thing he couldn't do, to make his hands work as hands worked, to hold the world down. His coat, which had been tossed beside him on the rock, was caught first by a wave, and then the air; it blew away without him in it. I saw the coat, and though I needed, then, no further portents of the thing that was to come, I cried, 'Your coat! Your coat is gone,

Sebastian!' And if Sebastian heard this, perhaps he knew *my* words now well enough to know that what I had within my mind, though not as words, was when we'd met for the first time. Then, too, like any silkie, he had shed his cloak, and seeded me, not with a child but with a dream of happiness. That dream I'd bear alone, if he would not stay with me now, if he would soon be, as his cloak was, quite, quite gone.

But it was I who was quite gone. All thought, all words, all of the things that we think make us human had deserted me. I could not help him, I was tied, but I now struggled with the bonds as savagely as any captured animal. At last, I screamed aloud, 'Sebastian, no! If you are leaving, then you must free me, take me with you. This is no choice that you can make for me. It's mine to make,' but at that moment, I felt the tide just heave him up and rip him loose and tear him off the rock I was still tied to. He was a scrap of cloth, a feather in the wind. He fought for one last moment, then he threw himself upon the breasting tide that took him. It was as if he said if he must go, he would go well; he'd make himself into a sail for all the winds of earth to blow to some new island. I raised my body up as far as it would go and tried with all my might to get my hands loose, but Sebastian had tied them so I could not do this. As I collapsed, I hit my head upon the rock below the spike and everything went black as I was thrown right out of consciousness.

And when I woke, or when I came back from the place where I had been, a place about which I remembered nothing, I found that I was still alive and that the storm

233

was dying now around me; although the wind still blew across the sea, still cut the waves, it did not cut them now in half, did not make sea-smoke. The waves were calmer, calm enough so I could see far out across them, east and south and north and west, in all the four directions. I could see Shapinsay, and Long Holm, and beyond Long Holm, Wyre and Rousay, Egilsay off in the distance. The tide had turned and was now down below where I was tied by thirty feet or more; the skerry was exposed to air again. Some seals were on the rock, and as I woke and moved and made some sounds, they raised their large round eyes and looked at me. One of them wriggled closer, then stopped and yawned and showed me each bright tooth before she closed her eyes and lay at ease again. I ached all over, and my head hurt, where I'd smashed it on the rock. My wrists were cut and rubbed with salt. I knew, and did not know, what had happened, right away; I saw, and did not see, what life would be now.

Because, although it was not long before a boat came by, and seeing the square sail that fluttered raggedly above me, came closer to investigate, then sent some men onto the skerry to untie me, lift me up, and carry me to their boat, I still thought it was possible that Sebastian had swum to shore – that he had found dry land as Corbin had. Yes, Corbin had. He'd made it back to Long Holm, where the same boat that found me had found him first; he was upon the boat when I was carried there. He'd stood upon the rock that he had leapt from when Sebastian threw him sticks, and barked and barked at the small boat as it went by him. So it had stopped and picked him up and searched the island, found no boat, and no one there, but things in disarray within the cottage. In Orkney, everyone knew Sebastian, knew where he lived and what he did. He was admired and liked, and now a search was mounted for him. But this search found, not Bastian, but me instead; the men who found me said that it was lucky Sebastian had tied the sail upon the spike above my head, because when they first saw me on the rock they thought I was a fur seal tangled in a net. A dead fur seal. I was quite motionless. And even when, with their binoculars, they saw that I was human, they thought it was too late to help me – thought they went to get a body. But now they took me off to Mainland, to a hospital, where I remained in bed for seven days, like something planted there. I had concussion. Deep wounds in my wrists. I was dehydrated, had swallowed sea water. But they all said, the doctors, nurses, that I would be fine soon. 'You're going to be just fine,' they said, while I stared at the ceiling, and if I spoke, spoke only to inquire about the sea-search.

But when I was released, the search was over. They had looked, I was informed, for three whole days for Bastian. If he had been alive, they said, they would have found him; it was strange that they had not, in any case, found his body. But that could happen sometimes, I was told. The seas of Orkney were so wild that there were deeps so deep the dead never came back from them. People were kind, although they didn't know me. With help from Bastian's friends on Shapinsay, I was returned to Long Holm for a time. And only when I got there to the island, walked into the cottage where no fire burned, was I at last convinced that Bastian had not been back there. If he had come back from the sea he never would have left her pictures on the walls, and they were still upon the walls, I saw. If he had come back from the dead, he would have with him, where he was, the small black velvet ring-case that contained her knuckle bone. I held it in my hand, the ring-case, opened it again, and touched my finger to the satin that lined it. The wedding ring had burned; it had been gold. And Bastian had known, I think, that he would never wear another one. *When I can hold you in my arms*, he'd said, *I want to feel no other arms around you. If you should come to me, and I to you, then we must come to one another unencumbered.* That was his dream, a vain one. As for mine, I'd thought that he and I together would make the world quite new, would build, together, a tower to heaven.

But we did not. There's nothing new upon the earth; the same old truths are always true, and never new again. Whatever language we may speak in, it still remains the same – that love is sighting a wild shore that seems like home to us. And then, when we have landed, finding that though we've crossed great seas to reach it, we've somehow dragged our old life there behind us. Yes, dragged it, like rope, like chain, like a great anchor made of stone which cannot be dissolved or lost in water. All of the boats that take us over those wild seas must carry to the new, far shore a little too much freight with them. Each boat is like a word – it may be *time* or *sight* or *knowing*, even *sex* or *death* – but all of them are dragged back by the things they drag behind, so that when they deliver us to land – the land that Gilgamesh called Faraway – it does not seem quite like the place we had envisaged. No, that place had new frames; a brand-new frame lay round that world, and that place had new things contained within it. We wanted it so much, to land upon a brand-new shore, our wanting was a kind of wind that blew us there. Indeed, our wanting was a great hard exhalation of desire, a breath that was the air of earth all gathered in a single valley. But when it left that valley, storm, and hit the sails of all those boats, we saw at last the world was not a place that you could have through wanting it. You could try, if you wished, to pin words to the world, as if you wrote with sticks upon clay tablets, but all that you would do would be to mark the hopes you'd lost, making for each new hope a gravestone. *Remember Death*, you'd write upon the stone. *Death waits us all. The hour none knows. The sleeping and the dead are brothers.* You could attempt to write a new thing, but you'd find that you had written, once again, *Memento Mori*. And you would find that each word that you wrote was like a bird which flew, a black scrap on the sun, to somewhere where you could not follow it. When Gilgamesh set out upon the road which would ensnare him, his mother raised her arms above her head, entreating Shamash. *Why have you inflicted a restless heart upon my son? Why have you touched him in the soul's dark chambers?* Enkidu spoke to Gilgamesh as well, saying, *My friend, my love, turn back. The road* . . . The rest is missing.

But not in my translation. No, I filled it in, that place where the clay tablet had been broken. *The road is dangerous*, I wrote. *And on that road lies death for one of us. I cannot see which one will die, though. If it were I, Enkidu, I would not care. It is the fact it may be you, my Gilgamesh, which torments me. How would I live without you? Where would I go, what would I do? What road would then be left for me to travel?* I filled that in, because I saw the words so clearly in my mind, or heard them in my ears, a deep deep thing that slid within me. But I did not put in, at all, the final tablet, Twelve, which I did not believe had been engraved upon the clay when all the rest had. It is a dark dark tablet, in which Enkidu comes to life again, and has dark things to say

237

about the life he's left. If I wrote *Gilgamesh and Enkidu* today, I would include that tablet in my book, as it would seem a lie to leave it out now. One column reads: *Know that the man with seven sons will live forever.* Another reads: *The man who has no sons, I have encountered him within the house of death. He wanders there unburied. He fell from a high mast onto the earth, as trees or stones fall, and his hands were badly torn. Have you, too, seen him?*

Yes, I'd include that now. Because the true truths never change. For all the good that does us, we who are the hunters. For all the good that does us, when we see, right there before us – standing at the place where two paths cross – a man we are amazed to somehow recognize. We see him there, that man, and feel we know him, know him as we know ourselves, forgetting that we rarely know ourselves until it is too late to help us. But though he is not ours, that man, as we believe, he nonetheless will make us come to him, because he owns us suddenly and wholly. There is no need for him to steal us; he need just reach out with his hand and take us, and then make us, in the taking. He is the gateway or the door we walk through to discover the rest of all the time we have on earth, which seems to stretch so high and wide and deep that it will never leave us with no place to stand on. But once we've passed quite through the gate, and been transformed by it, we find that time is still a thing that will betray us, leave us stranded.

That's how I feel, at least. Perhaps I'll feel again the way a boat feels when, becalmed for years, the wind arises, fills its sails and drives it onwards. Perhaps I'll feel again that I have been translated or transformed, made whole, by something in the world outside me. Perhaps I'll even feel again that that world can be fixed – rifts can be healed, abysses can be crossed and things can be filled up which are now empty. Perhaps the rocks of Orkney, made, not made, and drowned beneath the deeps may not seem always just a loom upon which Bastian let his fate be woven. But now, time merely feels like something that has tied me to the place I am, and will not let me leave it. *Oh set me free again*, I think. *Please set me free again. This hurts me in the hollow where my throat is. I cannot bear the wanting him.* Nor can I bear the child I lost. My only child went down with Bastian; she lived upon the other side of what he'd tied in him.

Before I left Long Holm, I cleaned the cottage. Took her pictures down from the white walls where Sebastian had hung them. I have them now at home, back where I live alone and where I see them when I sleep and when I wake and when I get back from my classes. I see them always, but I also stand and study them at times, when time is like a vessel I cannot drink from. Corbin lives with me too. *Alone, well, with my dog. Some seals, at times, for company.* No seals, but Corbin wakes when I wake, puts his paw out, and looks at me with his black eyes, which saw the flood, and then saw dry land after it. As for the knuckle bone, her knuckle bone, I took it from the velvet case and buried it inside Sebastian's tomb on Long Holm. I knew, although he'd never told me, this must be what he had planned to do. Indeed, I thought that he had cleared the tomb, in part, so that the tomb would let him do this. I lit the lantern, called to Corbin, then had him wait outside, at the small entrance to the tomb's long passage. I got down on my knees and crawled, the lantern in one hand, up the flat passage of dry stones which had been laid there, the passage where a woman, five millennia before, had crawled once, carrying a great round basket. Within the basket, bones, the skull and clavicle and pelvis, the thigh bones, too, of her lost man, who'd died quite young, and then had burned to ashes. Before he'd died, though, he'd been woven into her body, heart, and soul, the way that stones are woven into land-scapes.

I had no bones. Just the one bone, which I had slipped into a pocket on my breast, and so the passage in was swift for me. I set the lantern on the clean white floor which had survived so long, and sought a place between the stones where I could push the bone so that it would not be discovered by the archeologists who would now come here. This was not easy, since the stones were set so tight, so neat, so all together, and finally I moved out of the central chamber to the stoop where Bastian and I had once played Truth as if it were a game, and not just everything that you could be quite blind to. Here, on this stoop which was before the eastern cell, I'd asked Sebastian why he'd been so happy in that photograph. He hadn't answered, but instead had asked if I believed I could stay warm within the tomb if he should warm me there. So here I moved back in, inside this cell, and found a place where there was one small crack just big enough for me to push my finger in. And not just mine, but hers. I took the knuckle which had once been what had made an artist's finger work and set it upon mine, then pushed it deep back in the stone, where it would stay, well, half forever. Here, I had felt his flesh, his soft flesh, sweet and fleeting, as fleeting as a flash of light in darkness. *What promise shall I take? Something quite hard, I think. Perhaps I'll ask you to make sure I'm buried in my tomb, or that my thigh bones go there.* Soft time. Hard time. No time. Then time again, as I took up the lantern, got down upon my hands and knees, crawled out into the day, found Corbin waiting.

And then I flew away. I still believed, or half believed, that Bastian must be alive, that he'd been washed up on the shore of some far island; I still believed, or half believed, that I would one day hear the phone ring and pick it up and hear his voice from somewhere far across the sea say, *Emrys*. I still believed, and not just half, that one day he must come back, be tossed back from the deeps that he had drowned in, and that, when that day came, I would come back to Long Holm, and be there when his body burned to ashes. I wouldn't care what people thought. I would stand right beside the smoke and let it seep into my skin, my hair, the clothes that I would wear the day I burned him. I'd breathe as deep as I could breathe to let the last of what was Bastian enter my lungs, just slide inside me, and then I'd stay and wait until his ashes cooled so that I could embrace them. Or, if a wind rose, I would stand where Bastian curled off in the sky, and catch him in my hands, a stream of something, smoked like water. Indeed, if I had not believed that this would happen, I could not have flown away, across the Pentland Firth, deserting Long Holm; I never could have come back to the far place I had come from.

It was not there, of course. The place I'd left was gone, quite gone, just as Sebastian was. No flesh to burn, no bones to bury. But unlike that lost place, which seems like fog to me – my life before I met him – I can remember Bastian so clearly. I look into my mind and see him there. The whole world fades, and only Bastian is real to me. I am not always real to him; I sometimes catch him looking almost through me, as if he sought to see what stands behind me. I wait where two paths cross, and he comes out from where he was, and walks into the passage where I wait for him. And there he hunts me, hunts me, though, as you might hunt not prey, but something that you know you'll never find again. I move to meet him, hold him tight against my body, say, *Please take me, Bastian. I've sought you all my life, a ley line I could walk along.* But then he speaks, the real Sebastian speaks, and in his deep, rich, life-filled voice, quite unadorned by any of the things with which our kind has clothed the world to try to make it safer, he says, *So, did you like St Magnus, Emrys Havers?* He says, *Oh yes, they let you out today from hospital, my girl?* He says, *Oh ho, don't torture you. You think I torture you?* and smiles sleepily. He says, *You take the rock, I can sleep anywhere,* and then he says, as he falls off into the storm, *Remember me.*

And oh, I do. He did not say, *Remember me* or, if he did, I didn't hear him as I struggled to get free so I could follow him, nor did he say, *I will come back to you,* but he comes back, it all comes back, each word he spoke, each movement that he made, each moment that he put his hands upon me. His voice slid deep within me. His gestures fell on me like rain. His hands upon my skin made me the world around me. I can still feel the way I felt when he first pinned me to the bed with one hot hand as if I were so light I'd float into the sky if he did not secure me. I can still feel the way I felt when I felt that I could not breathe, that if he did not push inside he'd kill me. And I can feel the way his fingers, two without and two within, were like the pulse of time upon my body, made me immortal. The way he took me with his hand, the way he came within my mouth, the way he slid his tongue between my legs as if he marked the birth of language. He had no dread disease that was not life itself, and when I came upon him it was the moment that made me. He placed his body over mine, drew down his hands and parted me like curtains, and when I said, 'Oh please, I'll die,' he said, 'Perhaps. All do,' but then he rolled upon his back like some sweet raft for me to climb on. And when, a sea-borne swimmer, I fell upon him and he slid within me like a fish, my own dark fish, I knew that it was I who owned him. He still asks me a question: *This choice, will Emrys make it now? And if she does, what will I do to her?* I make it *now*, and *now*, and *now*, and now I say, and now I say:

I cannot put you in your tomb, Sebastian. You lie inside me.

A NOTE ON THE AUTHOR

Elizabeth Arthur was born in New York City to a
Hungarian mother and an Irish-American father. She
was educated at the University of Victoria in British
Columbia, Canada. She is the author of two memoirs,
Island Sojourn and *Looking for the Klondike Stone*, and
four previous novels, *Beyond The Mountain*, *Bad
Guys*, *Binding Spell* and *Antarctic Navigation*. Her
work has twice been recognized with fellowships
from the American National Endowment for the Arts,
and in 1990, she was the first novelist selected for
participation in the Antarctic Artists and Writers
Program. *Bring Deeps* is her first book to be published
as a UK original.

A NOTE ON THE TYPE

The text of this book is set in Berling roman. A modern face designed by K. E. Forsberg between 1951 and 1958. In spite of its youth it does carry the characteristics of an old face. The serifs are inclined and blunt, and the g has a straight ear.

ANTARCTIC NAVIGATION Elizabeth Arthur
£12.99   0 7475 7167 8

Morgan Lamont is a young, ardent American woman who is inspired to lead an expedition to the South Pole; an expedition haunted by the same tragic journey, eighty years before, of the British explorer Robert Falcon Scott. For Morgan, Scott's life, his dream, his death and the very concept of Antarctic navigation are obsessive emblems of a search for integrity. Freed by her mother's quixotic and frightening sacrifice and the generosity of a hitherto estranged grandfather, she sets out to fulfil her own dream – to vindicate Scott by recreating his historic polar expedition, taking her through the dazzling white Antarctic vastness known as the Ice. Both extravagant and austere, and pulsing with colour and detail against the stark Antarctic ice, this is a novel as singular as the continent it reveals, immersing us in the adventure of Antarctic exploration and the power of the human spirit to navigate the new and the unknown.

'A vast and beautifully written book about a modern woman who sets out to re-create Scott's fatal 1912 Antarctic journey reads like a wonderful Victorian novel, weaving historical and contemporary dramas with rich sub-plots and vivid descriptions of the harsh landscape' *Vogue*

'An awesomely written yet understood novel, taking in relationships, politics, love, ecology and metaphysics … *Antarctic Navigation* is a strange and wonderful novel, reminiscent of Kim Stanley Robinson and J.G. Ballard in its haunting and poetic style' *Ink*

'One almost feels that the author wrote it under the influence of Scott … So convincing that for several chapters I was deluded into thinking that she was telling her own story and that she had actually been to the pole' Beryl Bainbridge

To order from Bookpost PO Box 29 Douglas Isle of Man IM99 1BQ www.bookpost.co.uk
email: bookshop@enterprise.net fax: 01624 837033 tel: 01624 836000

bloomsburypbks

www.bloomsbury.com/elizabetharthur